The Butchered Writers Present:

Caught in the web

A Dark Web Horror Anthology

Table of Contents

Caught in the Web

A Dark Web Horror Anthology

The Butchered Writers present stories from the darkest corners of the World Wide Web. Places that are so extreme, vile, and disgusting that you won't find them on the normal internet. When curiosity about the dark web comes calling, you'd be better off to ignore it. It could be the last link you ever click on.

*TRIGGER WARNING: Some stories contain extreme horror, SA, and graphic violence.

Introduction

Fear is real. You can't taste it, touch it, see it, or hear it. But you can feel it, and feeling is what makes us human. A small fear-seedling can sprout into paranoia, anxieties, and phobias that permeate every aspect of our lives. There's no running or hiding from fear. It stays with you until you come face to face with your apprehensions and put an end to them—no matter how enormously harrowing the fears have become. Fear can teach you about yourself. Are you strong enough to take on these horrors head-on? Or are they going to send you cowering with your tail between your legs? Of course, reading about horrors that are birthed from fears stimulates our minds by inquiring thoughts about our own person. What we believe about ourselves and our character to be true, and what is true, are poetically intertwined in the best written horror. Would I go back into the creature's lair to try and save my wife? Would I stab someone in the leg if it meant being closer to obtaining the money needed for a life-or-death operation? Could I survive on a raft in the middle of the ocean with shark fins circling? You may be intimately familiar with your fears, but you can't know how you'd react until put in a certain situation. We'd all like to believe ourselves capable of emerging victorious when presented with circumstances of our ultimate fears. The horror stories that stay with you, tucked away in your mind years after reading, pique the curiosity of your own character. They make you think about how you'd react—in situations hopefully you never find yourself in—when coming face to face with the horrors that your fears have sprouted.

Terror Monthly is written and designed to play out your fear-driven horror fantasies. Stories written by The Butchered Writers arise from questions presented from our own fears and horrors. Hopefully our horrors can become some of your very own.

Room_404.exe
By Raven Tomes

"Finally found work," Nolan says, tossing his duffel into Ryan's car with a grin. "You can stop calling me your couch-surfing brother now."

Ryan laughs. "About time. What is it this time—another app startup?"

Nolan smirks, eyes on his phone. "Something like that. They're an indie tech group. Private invite, good money, and the benefits are nuts."

Ryan frowns. "Private invite? Sounds shady."

"It's not," Nolan says quickly. "They just don't post jobs publicly yet. It's new VR research—full sensory integration. They say it'll change gaming forever."

"VR, huh? That's your thing. Still, three months overseas, no contact—seems extreme."

Nolan shrugs. "That's how NDAs work. Don't worry so much, Row. You'll get a postcard or something."

Ryan sighs, pulling up to the terminal. "Just don't ghost me like last time."

"I won't," Nolan grins, opening the door. "Hey—maybe I'll send you something cool when they launch."

Ryan smirks. "Better be worth the wait."

They hug briefly, awkwardly. Then Nolan vanishes into the crowd, and Ryan drives off, unaware that this will be the last time he ever sees his brother alive.

Three months later, a package arrives. The label reads *N. Lang.* Ryan freezes as he unfolds a single printed slip inside, stamped with the company's logo:

CURIA ENTERTAINMENT STUDIOS.

Welcome Gamer, to the Final Escape from Reality — every decision a consequence, every action final. Choose wisely.

Disclaimer: Closed Reality Immersive Experience.

Disconnection invalid during Active Session.

Inside the box lies a black console and headset, slick and clinical. The paper smells metallic, like cold circuitry.

He plugs it in. The screen goes black. The sound hums low, like static breathing through walls.

BOOTING: Room_404.exe

NEURAL CONTACT REQUESTED. PLEASE FIT HEADSET.

Ryan fits the headset. The world cuts out.

At first there's nothing—just a flat black screen, humming softly, like waiting in the void. Then light crawls through pixels until a room bleeds into existence.

Concrete. Cold. A single bulb flickers above like a dying star. Shadows stretch unnaturally long. At the center, a chair. A body slumped in it, head covered by a filthy hood. Leather straps dig into skin at the wrists and ankles. The abductee twitches once, then stills.

Twelve faint silhouettes stand in a ring around the chair—masks, smooth and featureless, reflecting the bulb's glow. The floor glistens, and when the light buzzes overhead, the liquid catches red.

The sound of wheels. A stainless-steel tray rolls into view. An attendant in black latex gloves and apron pushes it slowly, methodically. The wheels squeal, echoing against concrete like teeth on metal. Tools rattle softly: clamps, cutters, a bone saw. Each instrument gleams like it remembers pain.

WELCOME, PARTY-404.

YOU ARE 12. HE IS 1.
THE ROOM CHOOSES WHO SUFFERS.
YOU CHOOSE HOW.

"Holy shit," someone whispers through the headset. Another voice laughs—a nervous, high-pitched sound. "Okay, that's... realistic."

A woman's voice chimes in, confident. "I'm Sun. Let's do this. It's just a game."

Ryan says, "Row." His brother's nickname for him. *Why did he say that?*

SESSION ONE: DIGITS.

The abductee jerks as if hearing the words. The attendant rolls the tray closer. The chat flares alive:

Sun: *this haptic feedback's insane*

Gremlin: *my fingers feel numb omg.*

FullStop: *is that smell... blood??*

The attendant hums softly, a mechanical tune out of time. It selects a pair of bone shears from the tray and grips the abductee's left hand. The abductee thrashes weakly, muffled sobs spilling beneath the hood.

When the shears close, the sound is both a crunch and a pop. The scream that follows is raw, serrated, endless. It fills every corner of the headset. The metallic scent of blood floods Ryan's nostrils. It's warm, heavy. Something wet splatters across his vision—a simulated droplet, red and glistening—and his hands burn as if dipped in boiling water.

The abductee's finger hits the floor with a soft meaty sound. The attendant sets the shears down neatly, wipes them with a white cloth that turns pink, and moves on.

COMPILE BEGINS IN 00:60. DO NOT POWER DOWN.

Ryan can still hear the abductee sobbing faintly as the light dims to black. The smell lingers—iron and sweat, layered over bleach. He rips the headset off, collapses against the sink, and vomits until his throat burns.

When he looks up, the hub glows faintly red, humming, as if still breathing.

The next morning, Ryan's alarm drags him out of a dream that feels wet and sticky. He sits on the edge of his bed for several seconds before realizing the faint scent of bleach is still in the air.

At work, he stands in line for coffee when he hears voices from the breakroom.

"Man, that thing was insane," says a voice he recognizes—Kyle from IT. "The way it feels real—like, you can *smell* stuff. They said it's part of the neural sync patch."

Ryan freezes mid-step.

Another coworker laughs. "You're talking about that game? The one your fiancée got you?"

Kyle grins. "Yeah, she said she was testing it from her new job. It's creepy, but kind of addictive. It's called Room_404.exe or something."

Ryan's stomach drops. The mug in his hand trembles. Kyle's fiancée—Ella—had also gone overseas recently for a "confidential contract."

When Kyle notices him standing there, he gives a small, awkward nod. "Hey, Hale. You game?"

Ryan forces a smile. "Sometimes."

Kyle shrugs. "You should try this one. Feels like hell but looks like heaven."

The words stick with him all day, festering in his brain like static.

⫷╫⊪ 🎙 👁

That night, the console powers on by itself. The hum builds until it rattles the glass of the picture frames on Ryan's wall. He tries to unplug it, but the cord feels hot, pulsing like a heartbeat.

SESSION TWO: CORRECTIONS.

The room fades in. The same bulb flickers overhead, but the concrete looks darker now, slicker. The abductee is still there, bandaged stumps where fingers used to be. They breathe in jagged, trembling gasps.

The attendant returns, pushing the tray. This time a branding iron glows orange in their grip. The heat shimmers in the air.

Sun: *no no no no way this is fake right*

Gremlin: *omg I can feel it I can FEEL it*

FullStop: *someone say stop please stop*

The attendant presses the iron to the abductee's chest. There's a hiss, and then the scream—high, ripping, animal. Smoke billows up, thick and greasy. The smell—burnt hair, charred skin, the ammonia tang of urine—hits Ryan's nostrils so hard he gags.

Orchid: *I can smell it, oh god, I can actually smell it.*

The abductee convulses, their chest blistering beneath the metal. Ryan claws at the headset, trying to tear it off, but the system won't let go. His body jerks as if the pain is bleeding through the neural link.

The attendant finally pulls the iron away, leaving a perfect black circle seared into flesh. The abductee wheezes, twitching.

COMPILE BEGINS IN 00:60. DO NOT POWER DOWN.

When the world fades, Ryan slams the headset onto the floor. His skin still feels hot. Smoke seems to hang in the air, even though there's nothing burning.

He spends the night on the bathroom floor, shaking, waiting for dawn.

Ryan doesn't remember falling asleep, but when he wakes, the sun is already setting. His body aches like he's been bruised from the inside. The console's red light is blinking again—steady, patient, waiting.

SESSION FOUR: CONSEQUENCE.

The room loads slower this time. The bulb stutters. The air feels heavier, filled with the taste of rust and old blood. The abductee sits motionless in the chair, breathing shallowly, chest blistered and glistening. The attendant's mask glows faintly in the dark, a single LED pulsing like a heartbeat.

VOTE COMMENCING.
OPTION 1: EXCRUCIATE.
OPTION 2: MERCY.
OPTION 3: REPLACEMENT.

Ryan's hand hovers over the screen. "No," he whispers. "I'm done." He tries to log out, but the menu doesn't respond. The other players' icons flicker as votes appear beside their names

Sun: I can't do this again
Gremlin: just end it
FullStop: please pick mercy please
Orchid: someone has to choose

Ryan refuses. The timer ticks down from thirty seconds. He stares at the abductee's limp head, the trembling shoulders, the way the hands twitch in the bindings.

00:10.

00:09.

00:08...

His hand shakes. "I won't."

VOTING CLOSED. COMPILING RESULTS.

The light dims. A final message flashes:

> OPTION SELECTED: EXCRUCIATE. RETURN IN 12 HOURS.

The headset powers down.

Each hour crawls past like a lifetime, his thoughts looping between guilt and denial. He can't eat. He can't sit. The console's faint hum seeps through the walls like a living pulse. When his shift starts, he goes to work anyway—anything to escape the waiting.

Time stretches, warps. Every clock ticks too slowly. His coworkers' voices sound far away, muffled by the sound of blood rushing in his ears. The world tastes of rust. His hands won't stop trembling.

At 5:00 p.m., he's already in his car. By 5:02, he's speeding through traffic, red lights blurring past like smeared fire. He bursts into his apartment, panting, and the headset's red light is already pulsing faster.

He sits. He doesn't breathe.

SESSION FOUR: RESULTS.

The screen flickers to life. The bulb overhead swings on its cord. For a moment, the chair is empty. Then the camera pans.

The room is red. Splattered. The walls drip. Something wet slides down the concrete like paint. The tray is overturned, its contents scattered—shears, clamps, a length of coiled wire slick with gore.

Pieces of the abductee are everywhere—fingers, flesh, the floor glistening beneath the bulb's dying light. Something wet drips from the ceiling. But the head—

The head is still intact.

The hood is gone. Eyes open. Lifeless. His brother's eyes. The same half-smile from the terminal, frozen mid-promise.

Nolan's face.

Ryan freezes. His brain refuses to translate what his eyes are seeing. For a heartbeat, he waits for the game to glitch—to undo itself—to tell him this is all simulation.

Then the system speaks.

COMPLETE. 11 PLAYERS REMAINING.

The scream that tears from Ryan's throat is animal. He rips the headset off, throws it across the room, and staggers backward, crashing into the wall. He can still taste it—hot copper and smoke. He dry heaves until there's nothing left to bring up, then sobs until he can't breathe.

He calls his brother's number anyway. Straight to voicemail. Again. Again. The recording is calm, normal, Nolan's voice warm and smiling. "Hey, it's me. Leave a message."

Ryan collapses against the wall, still dialing when his trembling hand slips and hits a different contact—Kyle.

No answer.

He grabs his keys and drives. The night feels wrong—too quiet, too still. The streetlights seem dimmer than they should be.

Kyle's apartment door is unlocked. Ryan pushes it open to find him sitting on the floor, slumped against the couch. The glow from the headset still paints his face red. The TV hums softly in the background, static crawling across the screen.

"Kyle?" Ryan whispers.

Kyle doesn't look up. He's crying, shaking violently. His voice comes out shredded. "It was her."

Ryan stares. "What?"

Kyle looks up at him, eyes hollow. "Ella. My team voted last night. When I logged in tonight—she was gone. They... they tore her apart." He buries his face in his hands. "I didn't know. I didn't know it was real."

Ryan kneels beside him, grabbing his shoulders. "It was my brother," he chokes out. "Nolan. They killed Nolan."

The two men cling to each other, shaking. Neither of them speak for a long time. The only sound is the faint hum of static from the TV.

Then, without warning, the screen flickers to life.

BREAKING NEWS: Authorities are investigating the disappearances of several individuals linked to a private VR development company, Curia Entertainment Studios.

Ryan and Kyle both turn toward it, frozen.

"Officials say dozens of missing persons cases may be connected to a closed beta test for an immersive VR experience known as 'Room_404.exe.' The company's headquarters in Singapore appear abandoned. Online domains and databases have been erased. Every digital trace returns the same message—"

The anchor pauses, pressing a finger to her earpiece.

"—404. File not found."

The words echo through the apartment like a death knell. Ryan stares at the screen, tears streaming down his face. Kyle makes a broken, animal sound that barely resembles a sob.

The TV flickers again, but this time the anchor doesn't move. The image freezes—her mouth half open, her eyes too wide. The sound cuts. Silence.

Ryan lowers his head into his hands. "They'll never find them," he whispers. "No one will."

Kyle doesn't answer. He just stares at the frozen image on the screen, breathing shallowly, like he's afraid to move.

Outside, a siren wails in the distance. The city keeps moving, oblivious.

Somewhere else.

A courier sets a small, black box on a doorstep in another city. The house is modern, glass and steel, the kind that swallows reflections whole. The address label reads a new name.

The box hums faintly.

Inside, the console glows red—its screen flashing to life on its own.

Welcome Gamer, to the Final Escape from Reality — every decision a consequence, every action final. Choose wisely.

Disclaimer: Closed Reality Immersive Experience — Disconnection invalid during Active Session.

The red light pulses once. Then again.

BOOTING: Room_404.exe

Highest Bidder
By Andy H

The trolley rolled down the dark, dank hallway. Its small wheels slowed their progress every time it hit a rut or a crack in the concrete. It was rusty and had not been used for its original purpose for some time. It squeaked and whined as it went along.

The boy, just a teenager, lay on the flat surface, trying to move and wriggle free from the straps holding him down, but they restrained even the slightest of his movements. He tried to yell, to scream for help, because surely there must be someone close who could save him. The dirty rag jammed into his mouth started to creep down his throat with his effort and bile attempted to rise up his gullet. He kept it down with sheer force of will. The strap across his forehead prevented him from even raising his head to see where they were taking him.

The boy had no idea how he'd gotten here.

The last thing he remembered was partying with friends at a club on the outskirts of the city. He'd stepped outside for some much-needed fresh air after having too much to drink in such a short amount of time. After that, everything went blank. His clothes, shoes, and wallet were gone. The only thing left were his boxers.

The trolley continued down the corridor.

Above him were the shapes of light globes. The ones intact gave off a dim light that strobed his vision as he passed beneath. A shadow wheeled him to wherever he was headed. He couldn't see the person clearly and in a way was glad for that.

Around him, the walls and ceiling were cracked with zig-zagging lines. It was obvious, even in his state, that this place wasn't on anyone's grid. Terrifyingly, this meant he had little to no chance of being found, let alone rescued.

The trolley crashed through a curtain of thick plastic strips, the type that might hang in a butcher's freezer. His heart hammered faster as the trolley came to a stop and the brakes on the wheels were engaged.

His eyes rolled to see the partly-visible figure move down a long hallway off the room he was in, and his eyes widened in horror. He would have screamed if he'd been able.

The man was shirtless, wearing a blood-stained apron over his stocky, muscular torso and had coarse black hair, like an ape, covering his arms. Huge, imposing, and intimidating, he looked like he was built for brutality.

There was a mask covering his face, and it was this, more than the man himself, that made the kid's blood run cold.

The mask's fleshy skin was like an old, tanned piece of leather. Only the man's eyes, black as the devil's, reflected the light within the blood-rimmed eyeholes. The lips of the face were stitched shut with a series of tight crosses, the ends of the thread dangling in knots at the corners. At each side were ragged edges where the ears had been cut away carelessly. The man's exposed head was bald, with a sheen of sweat upon his shorn dome.

He picked up a large bore IV needle and plunged it into a vein in the boy's arm just below the crook of his elbow. The tubing ran from the arm to a hanging glass bottle on a stand nearby.

Footsteps echoed from somewhere the teen couldn't see. He tried to prepare for who might be coming, but whoever it was wasn't ready to be seen. The sound drew closer, tapping against the tile.

"Is he ready?" said an authoritative voice.

There was a grunt from beside him. A man's smooth hand reached down and undid the clasp of the strap at his forehead. He didn't want to look, but knew he had to.

There was another person in the room with them. The man's back was turned, so he couldn't see a face. He put a pristine plastic apron over his dark blue suit, fastening it around his waist, then reached down and picked up a mask from side table and placed it over his face.

When he turned, the boy let out a moan of raw distress to see the face of his friend Steve looking back at him. Or rather the stitched-together face of his friend. The face had been sliced from Steve's head and stitched back together, a line of tight staples making it a patchwork of ruined skin. Fresh blood still seeped from around its edges.

Steve hadn't been dead long. He wasn't the only one who had been taken from the club.

The man slowly adjusted the flow of the boy's makeshift IV.

The boy felt a rush of ice hit his veins. His heart started to beat slower. His limbs became leaden and heavy. He was sure he wouldn't be able to move them even if he wasn't tied down. He struggled to keep his eyes open, breathing through his nose past the gag.

"There," the man's voice purred, "that's better. We wouldn't want you to miss the show."

Turning around once more, he reached for a camera set up on a tripod and pressed a button. A red light blinked in readiness. A laptop sat nearby, and he pushed the power button.

The man stepped back, spreading his arms wide.

"Ladies and gentlemen, welcome to tonight's auction."

Mac was late, he was going to miss it. He jumped out of the truck, the engine ticking as it cooled. He left his keys in the ignition and ran into the house. The front door swung shut at his back. He wondered what would be on offer tonight.

His mouth filled with saliva at the thought. It was getting harder to get fresh meat, at least the stuff he was used to, at a reasonable price these days. Hopefully, he could grab a bargain this evening.

He wouldn't be able to get the choicest cuts. They went for more than he could pay, but maybe there would be something. He put his wallet on the counter, making sure he could grab his credit card if needed, then opened his laptop.

Good. He hadn't missed much.

Dr. Stanforth sat back in the padded chair in his office. He watched the masked man prance about on the screen. He shook his head, but didn't turn off the computer.

He needed fresh organs for his experiments and donors were few and far between. The young man on the gurney looked healthy enough. He had cash to waste with the practice doing well and all. He was sure tonight would be his lucky night.

Reed Smith ushered his last customer out the door and flicked the latch. He spun the sign to *Closed* and pulled the blinds. Retreating back behind his desk, he lifted the tablet from underneath.

The boss didn't know he had it at work and wouldn't be pleased if he found out. He didn't use it often, but tonight was special.

He wasn't buying today, but it never hurt to look.

Brad always gave him a little extra if he was able to goose the prices a little.

All across the world, in homes and offices, people turned on their devices. From tablets to computers, they were there to watch...and to buy.

"So, I see we have our regular bidders here tonight, and some new names. To everyone, welcome."

The man masked in Steve's face turned and nodded to the monstrosity next to him, who lifted a meat cleaver in one of his beefy hands. He walked over to the boy and hovered over him.

"Let's start with an appetizer shall we? What am I bid for this juicy, meaty leg? The whole thing will be dressed and packaged, shipped straight to your door."

He waved his hand up and down the limb.

"Meat on the bone, sinew, and tendons. I know some of you like that. You know what you have to do. Let's start at the bottom and work our way to the tasty parts. As always, there is a time limit."

The stained blade lowered and stopped just above the boy's ankle.

The man in the suit looked back at the computer screen.

"No? Not enough flesh on this cut? You want more, do you?"

The steel edge moved up the boy's leg to just below his knee. That brought a response from whoever was online. Money started to come in thick and fast, the numbers on the screen ticking ever upwards. A bell sounded and the man checked the screen.

"Ah, one of my favorite discerning regulars. Congratulations ghoul130. This is for you." He nodded towards the butcher.

The cleaver rose, then fell. The razor edge bit into the meat just below the left knee. The metal sawed back and forth, scoring a deep line in the bone. It was pulled from the leg and then fell again, chopping through splintering bone. The butcher cut through the last strands of vein, muscle, flesh and fat.

The kid opened his mouth and screamed. The ruckus bounced around the tiled room as his gag fell to the floor.

The lower leg came free and thumped onto the top of the wheeled trolley. It was placed in a box filled with ice and the lid was closed carefully.

The boy's eyes streamed with tears, snot dribbling from his nose and over his lips. He wanted to plead, to beg, but the words stuck in his throat and would not come out. He watched with shock as the man tied off the leg, the cord biting into his skin. The bleeding slowed but didn't stop.

"Better fix that," the auctioneer said.

The butcher picked up a chef's torch and flicked it on. He passed the blue flame across the stump of the leg, searing the wound. The flesh started to crisp and small wisps of smoke drifted from the cooked meat.

The auctioneer went back to the camera again. "Now that things have gotten going, why don't we offer something bigger?"

The boy watched, horrified. He was still conscious as the big man put down the cleaver and picked up a bone saw. The butcher shifted towards the boy's shoulder. People knew what was about to happen and the bids rolled in.

Again the bell sounded. The auctioneer rubbed his hands together and nodded his head. "The left arm, if you would be so kind."

The toothed edge of the saw was lowered and pushed down into the meat between the boy's shoulder and neck.

It began to move.

The boy's head rocked from side to side as the blade cut through the skin and into the collarbone beneath. His screams were high-pitched and hoarse, filled with suffering. He was still conscious even though he should have been dead from shock at the very least. Yet, he continued to remain awake and aware.

The surgical saw made short work of the bones and tendons of the shoulder. One last push and the toothed edge cut into the blood-soaked surface he lay on. The smell of piss and shit hung in the air, the boy had soiled himself.

The auctioneer moved back, but the odor didn't seem to affect the monstrous butcher.

As before, the arm was put it into a cold case. The boy watched through tear-streaked, bulging eyes as the fingers of the severed limb twitched and spasmed. The auctioneer stepped closer, wafting a hand in front of his face. He scrutinized the boy's eyes and his pallor before looking up at the bottle connected to the tube in his arm.

"It looks like we have time for one more auction, folks. Unfortunately, they don't keep fresh for long." He uttered a mad little giggle. "So, I am going to submit the organs as a one-time offer. Start your bidding now."

Once more the numbers on the screen started to climb. They went slowly at first, but rapidly increased. Soon only two numbers were still rising. The bell rang and the counters stopped. The auctioneer clapped ecstatically.

The butcher went to work.

The boy on the trolley watched as the big man raised the knife to each side of the clavicle and made an inexpert Y-incision toward the sternum. A thin line of red appeared, growing thicker as the knife bit deep. With his huge hands, the butcher peeled the skin and flaps of muscle to the sides. He dropped the knife and lifted a pair of curved steel shears.

The boy's movements were weaker, his strength fading rapidly. A line of bright red blood slipped from the corner of his mouth and dripped onto the metal under his head.

One by one, the man snipped through the ribs then inserted a spreader. The butcher ratcheted the ribcage open until a popping sound caused him to stop. He released the tool and picked up a smaller pair of snips, which looked delicate in the big man's hands. The butcher went to work, cutting the organs free and placing them in small, travel-sized ice coolers. As he cut through the veins holding the kidneys in place, the boy lapsed into blessed unconsciousness. Even the concoction in the bottle failed to keep him alive any longer.

As the last of the fluid drained from his system, the boy's heart labored to beat. It slowed and slowed then stopped as the butcher pulled it from his chest and placed it into a box with the rest of his insides.

The auctioneer turned to the camera.

"I'm afraid that's all she wrote, folks." He gestured to the remains of the body. "The rest will, of course, be offered at a reduced rate. Not as fresh as when the blood is still flowing. But I am sure you all won't haggle over a bargain." He held up a finger. "However, the head and skin will not be included. Join us next week for another episode of Fresh Cuts."

He turned off the camera and pulled off the flesh mask covering his face. Taking a deep breath, he turned to the butcher. "Peel the head and send it with the organs, please. I'm sure the buyer will appreciate the gesture."

He knew that Stanforth, one of his longest running buyers, would love the head for his experiments. *He is one sick bastard that one*, the auctioneer thought, smiling to himself.

"Take the skin off what's left, then get rid of it."

The butcher grunted and nodded, then got to work. Taking off his apron, the auctioneer straightened his suit jacket and walked away, the whine of a bone saw powering up following him down the long hall.

The skin would be stretched, cured, and tanned like leather. It was amazing how some people didn't know what their goods were made of. The auctioneer made wallets, purses, and even re-bound old books in dermis. The shop he owned at the campsite was making good money. He made a mental note to give Reed a little extra for

jacking up the price at the end. The guy knew the doctor would be all over those organs.

Mac let out a sigh and smiled as he closed the laptop and leaned back. The meat in his freezer was getting low and he was glad he had managed to secure some more.

The site on the dark web had become the best place to satisfy his *desires*. Chopping up people was getting riskier these days. He knew that his purchase would be delivered to the same place at the same time within 24 hours. He had enough to last that long.

It had cost him an arm and a leg, but he was happy. He started to giggle, his shoulders shaking as he realized his own sick little joke.

Dr. Stanforth shut off his computer and poured himself a glass of ten-year old scotch. He'd paid more than he wanted to, but it would be worth it to have the organs.

People were willing to pay any amount for good black market replacements. He would make his money back threefold. All he had to do now was wait for the delivery to reach him.

Reed turned off the tablet and stashed it back under the counter. He grinned, knowing he would make some good bank from this. Brad would see him right.

He stood up and flipped the sign back to *Open*, unlocking the door at the same time.

A car pulled up to the pumps and a man got out. He ran through the rain towards the door. A woman was still sleeping in the passenger seat of their car.

The door opened and the man came inside, shaking his jacket off onto the floor.

"Evening," Reed said, his tone friendly and welcoming.

"Uh, hi...sorry about the floor."

Reed waved a hand. "No problem, I was about to sweep anyway. Can I help you with something?"

The man pulled a water-logged map from his pocket and started to unfold it.

"My sat-nav crapped out on me, don't know how the old folks managed to get around." He smiled and Reed returned it.

"There some cabins around here somewhere? Trying to get away from the world for a while."

Reed leaned over the map and jabbed a finger down.

"That's where you want to go, friend. Just keep going West, you'll see the turnoff, can't miss it."

The man put the mess of paper back in his pocket and held out a hand.

"Thank you, very kind."

He turned and lifted his collar against the rain as he stepped back outside. Reed watched as he went, his hand reaching into a pocket of his overalls to pull his cell out. Without looking, he dialed a number he knew by heart.

It rang once...twice, then a voice answered at the other end.

"Hey brother, what are you like for inventory? Have a couple more that you may want to take a look at." He listened to the response on the other end, nodding his head. "I sent them your way. You should be seeing them soon."

He hung up and put the phone back in his pocket.

The Devil's Foot Fetish
By John Clements

1. The Day It All Started

It happened such a long time ago, but I can still see him standing at the edge of the bed with the sweet metallic smell of my own blood in the air.

Malcolm and I were dating for about a year at the time, and we had just moved into this tiny studio apartment in that rustbelt town. We lived a hardworking life. I waited tables at the diner around the corner from our place and Malcolm was struggling to find a job. Money was tight, but I was making decent coin on tips from gawking men. Any extra money always went into savings. I was strict about that because Malcolm never had the discipline to save. Despite it all, we were comfortable. We were hardcore introverts and didn't go out much, unless it was to a movie or occasional gig.

I'd just finished my shift on a Friday evening and was booked off for the weekend.

I went home, hoping Malcolm had cooked something because my legs were killing me from the rush that day. But lo and behold, when I got home I didn't find ramen noodles or at least an egg, just a pile of dishes and the bed unmade. He was still asleep when I left for work, so I'd hoped he would pick up while I was gone.

After cleaning, I made food and sat at my *command centre* (just this wide desk I found on the street and refurbished). Three monitors and a decent PC, donated by my boss when he found out I wanted to be a writer, sat on my desk. I spent some time surfing Facebook, checking in on what my mom was up to, and listening to the latest music videos on YouTube. Another hour passed until the rush from the day caught up with me. It was seven pm, and Malcolm wasn't home yet, so I decided to take a shower and hit the hay.

After my relaxing shower, I found him by the computer. He was never a smiler, but the grin on his face was cute, if not a little creepy. He didn't stand to greet me, so I hugged him from behind and kissed him on the cheek; he leaned into it.

"How was your day?" I asked.

"Busy," he said. His eyes were glued to the screen. It was black with a single white cursor, blinking slowly.

"Find anything? I saw the bookstore had an opening," I said.

"Nope." He turned to face me. "Even better. Come on, sit down."

I sat next to him and the screen changed from black to what seemed like a dark Google landing page. He looked at me with wide, excited eyes.

"The dark web!" he exclaimed.

"Huh?" I had no idea what it was.

"Babe, this is the sickest thing you'll ever see," he said, jerking his head towards the monitor.

It was our idea of fun on a Friday. Searching the internet for the sickest and most vile shit we could find. Back in 2008, the internet was still relatively young. People were learning how to share Facebook posts and had to wait five minutes for a ten-minute YouTube video to buffer. It's funny that, for all the mundane things that were still in their infancy, *other* parts seemed to be maturing quite well.

I was always a fan of the macabre. Malcolm called me the Bride of Lucifer, but I think he just had a thing for goth girls. Or he had a thing for Marla from Fight Club, so it didn't help that my name is Marla. We scoured the internet for the gory and the insane. Kids today have it easy, there's a wannabe ghost hunter or serial killer expert on every corner of social media. Back in my day, we really had to search for it.

I couldn't help but shiver with excitement, despite feeling drained. Malcolm took us on a journey that night. At first, we didn't expect anything other than a bunch of edgy teenagers trying to be scary. We found a weed dealer and a 'cursed' movie prop guy, I still speak to both of them. We also found a site that sold *legally acquired* credit cards, driver's licenses, pay stubs and even email addresses of some top CEOs. Not by design, but by pure coincidence, as we went deeper and deeper down this rabbit hole, the shit we found got worse. Even for me.

Recipes surfaced. I loved cooking spaghetti and pies. I could also make a mean curry, but not newborn smoothies and dog burgers.

Our journey down the colon of the internet continued.

Morgue Viewer was another one we found pleasure in looking at. It was a couple of John and Jane Does, piled up in morgues around the state. You could request customized footage or pictures for a small fee. For an even bigger fee, you could view the manifest and pick someone named. You could also *buy* parts or *all* of the bodies. For a thousand bucks, you could even own your own John or Jane Doe. Legs, arms, and heads were up for grabs. *Delicate* parts too. It was like Rotten dot com dialed up to eleven. The Janes were selling like hotcakes according to the leaderboard on top of each page.

We got so caught up in the excitement, we couldn't just stop on one site.

HomeWatcher was another interesting one. For a fee, you could log into people's home CCTV systems. We watched couples fight, have sex, and eat dinner. It seemed normal, if not a little invasive. We drew a line at the feeds of rooms that had kids in them, although they had the highest views.

Malcolm seemed a little too excited for sites involving live models and sex dungeons, but he was always an edgy prick. He had a soft heart, but sometimes I think he liked to piss people off or creep them out just for the fun of it.

After a while, I was starting to lose my fight with fatigue and my head began dipping as I sat next to him. Before I fell out of my chair or slammed my head onto the desk, I decided to go to bed. I leaned over and kissed Malcolm on the cheek, his eyes never left the screen, but he grabbed my arm.

"Come on, stay. We're just getting started!" he said, still fixated.

"I'm beat, I need some rest. I'll take a look later on," I replied, pulling my arm away.

I walked away when he didn't stand up to kiss me back, but I heard him typing and gasping in awe at each site. My mother didn't approve of him, she found Malcolm to be a bad influence on her *precious* daughter. After washing my face and brushing my teeth, I got into bed and could still see the glare from the computer in the living room. I couldn't see exactly what he was looking at, but I heard women moaning and screaming. They weren't moaning in pleasure, but rather pain. A power drill whined loudly, but he turned the volume down before I could complain. He looked over at me and blew a kiss, I caught it, falling asleep to the red hue the screen threw across the apartment.

2. I Don't Judge

I was glad to be off on Saturday because it was a rare treat for me to sleep late. Which in my world meant nine am. I threw my arm over to Malcolm's side and found it empty. I sat up in bed and looked around the apartment, calling out to him, but there was no response. It was a little disappointing he didn't find a job, but I was hoping he'd gone out again to find something. With me having the day off and all, I decided to get some chores done. After a light breakfast of buttered toast and some strong coffee, I cleaned the kitchen, living room, and bathroom. Even though our place was small, it was so crammed full of useless shit it took forever for me to put it all back in place. We'd been avoiding the mountain of clothing piled up behind the bathroom door. I knew Malcolm wouldn't do it, so I tossed it all into a few trash bags and left the apartment. It was always relatively quiet on our floor, so when I heard the rattling of the chains on our neighbor's door, I stopped, almost dropping the bags, and reached for my pepper fog. The door didn't open all the way, just a peep, and I could see the old man leering at me. We didn't know much about him, but everyone on the floor avoided him. There was a story floating around that he'd killed his wife years before. I was neutral on it.

"You and your husband were extremely noisy again," he murmured.

"*Boyfriend,*" I corrected him. "I'm sorry, Al. I didn't think we were noisy."

"The music. That damn music," he said, grinding his teeth.

We didn't play music at all, at least not when I was awake. Malcolm did tend to do that though, even while I was sleeping. It wasn't our first complaint from Al, but at least we weren't the only ones being pestered by him.

"I'm sorry, Al. I'll tell Malcolm to keep it down. He's been struggling..."

The rude bastard closed the door before I could finish talking. Anyway, I decided to use the stairs because the light in the elevator wasn't working. Luckily, the laundromat was just around the block right next to the diner, and I was hoping it wouldn't be full. I just wanted to enjoy my time off.

Just my luck though, the laundromat was closed. Not without reason. A Chevy truck was being pulled out of it. Hundreds of shards of glass littered the ground, with some pieces floating in blood flowing from the body that was lying on the sidewalk. Paramedics were trying to get the driver's lifeless body from the front of the truck while police were pulling yellow tape around the building.

Before I could even get close enough to see, the crowd had grown so big it was as if a celebrity was doing their laundry there and I couldn't get any closer. It was too hard to see who was hurt through the shoulders of pedestrians and patrons from the diner, but I saw the shoes of the dead person on the ground. White Nike sneakers browned from age and dirt, now soaked in blood. The blood seemed to form a circle around the logo, almost as if the blood respected it and didn't want to ruin that part of the shoe. A cop began shouting at everyone and it quickly turned into a stampede, with some people rushing to get away and others taking that opportunity to get closer.

I decided it was better to just leave. I could easily view shit like that in our newly found rabbit hole.

Before going home, I popped into the diner and ordered some food for the day. I didn't feel like cooking, and I was in the mood for some of our signature greasy, bacon-fat infused eggs. Janet, my elderly colleague and work mother, twisted my arm to stay for lunch with her. She convinced me to go visit my mom, something she always nagged me about during work hours. When she went back to work, I took my food and dragged the heavy bags back home. I was no stranger to walking while carrying heavy things, so I got home quick and used the stairs again.

I was greeted by the sound of a woman screaming in my apartment. Dropping everything, I kicked the door open and aimed my pepper fog. Instead of finding an intruder with a hostage, I found Malcolm sitting at the computer. He didn't adjust the volume or even look at me, instead he just waved a hand as I brought everything in.

"Where were you today?" I asked.

"Job center. Had a garden maintenance job and a cashier opening at some convenience store," he said. "All shit. *Your* bookshop job was taken too."

Patiently, I put the bags in the bathroom and the food in the kitchen, then walked over to drink some water. I drank a few glasses, hoping it would drown my anger, but my cheeks were too hot and tense. "Malcolm, what was *so* shit about those jobs? They sound good."

"I'm too good for it. Come on, can you picture me in a garden? All sweaty and dirty? Or in a convenience store uniform? Fucking goofy shit."

"Well, I can picture us making more money!" I yelled. I didn't mean to, but I just couldn't fucking take it when he wouldn't look at me while I was trying to talk about something serious. It seemed only when I screamed or yelled, he would turn to look at me, as if I was the bad guy.

"Whoa, relax," he pleaded, waving his hands as if I was about to hit him. I wish I had.

"Seriously, you need to go back there and choose one of them."

"I don't," he smirked. It made me so angry, but it was cute. "Don't you like it when I'm sweaty and dirty?" he said.

"Malcolm, I'm serious"

"So am I, Princess," he said, winking and moving closer. He took his shirt off and undid his belt, I backed away until I bumped against the kitchen counter.

"Promise me you'll go," I said.

"I will," he whispered, moving to my ear, his hot breath sending a shiver down my back. "After this...Princess."

I'll save you the details. We had some of the best sex that afternoon in a long time. I felt like an entire week's worth of stress poured out of me. It's like time sped up, because by the time we were done, it was already dark out and we wolfed down our dinner. It was dark web time, and I poured us each a pint of wine, then we assumed our usual places in front of the computer.

We tread over a lot of old ground we did on Friday, seeing the same gross shit being recycled on different sites. As we soaked the wine in and the bottle got emptier, we opened another and scrolled endlessly on the computer. Images of body parts, humans and animals alike, flashed across the screen. It all started to blend in, but then something caught my eye. I placed my hand on Malcolm's to get him to stop. He clicked on the site and we were greeted by a childish drawing of a severed foot in a high heel.

'WELCOME TO THE DEVIL'S FOOT FETISH' flashed on the screen behind the logo.

We were then taken to a site that looked just like eBay, but with a red background instead of white. And instead of secondhand TVs and washing machines, the items for sale were shoes.

"This looks interesting," Malcolm said as he scrolled.

Pictures of trainers, high heels, sneakers and sandals were for sale. At first, it seemed like an ordinary shoe shop, or pre-owned at least, as most of them were scuffed and dirty. Then he clicked on a pair of shoes that had blood on them. It looked familiar. The shoes had patches of dry blood, and one had blood circling the logo just like the one I'd seen earlier that morning. Clicking on it enlarged the image and gave us a description:

Gender - Male
Age - 16
Type - sneaker
Features - blood, fresh
Time - 7 hours
Price - $2500

"Jesus Christ," I muttered. "I saw those..."

"Dead people," Malcolm interjected. "This is...something else."

We scrolled and clicked on a few more:

Gender - Female
Age - 38
Type - sandals
Features - none, funeral wear

Time - two months
Price - $500
Gender - Female
Age - 71
Type - heels
Features - none, funeral wear
Time - one week
Price - $250
Gender - Female
Age - 19
Type - sneakers
Features - blood, fresh
Time - 24 hours
Price - $3500

"What do they mean by *time*?" Malcolm asked.

"Time since the person wore it, maybe? Time since they were...killed? Could be all of the above," I replied.

"All dead, though?" he asked, then pointed to the screen. "Look."

He hovered the mouse over the top of the page and a bar appeared with different tabs with the following options:

DEAD
ALIVE
CUSTOM

He clicked on alive. There weren't as many as there were dead, but the results shocked us both.

Gender - Female
Age - 32
Type - whole foot encased in purple high heel
Features - red toenails, high arches

Time - fresh, on ice
Expiry - two days, preservation options available
Price - $10000

"That's gotta be fake," Malcolm said, rubbing his face. I wasn't sure if he was disgusted or uncomfortable. I was both, but I was also curious. We'd seen stuff worse than this, and I know people have some weird fetishes, but there was something about this that put me off. I wasn't sure if it was because of the Nikes I saw.

I told Malcolm to click on 'CUSTOM'.

There wasn't anything for sale, but it seemed to be a forum like Reddit, a thread where requests were made.

'Looking for male, preferably 18-25. Still fresh and athletic, no corns or athlete's foot. $5000'. There were many others for females, but a name stood out in particular.

'Female. Soft and clean. Fresh, NEEDS black toe polish. $15000 - contact Mr. Sleaze'.

'Female. Short toes. No polish. Can be severed. $2500 - contact Mr. Sleaze'.

'Any gender. Need big feet, no hair. Must be freshly cut. $1500 - contact Mr. Sleaze'.

I closed my eyes and rubbed them, hours of screen time finally catching up. I stood and went to wash my face. Every time I closed my eyes, all I could see was shoes and feet. I decided that was enough for the night and the wine was reminding me of its presence as I got dizzy, so I climbed into bed. My head was spinning, and I wanted to call Malcolm over for some action, but he was already climbing into bed next to me. He was breathing slowly, but loud. I knew what was coming. He kissed me on the neck, then followed all the way down to my belly and then went lower. He didn't take my pants off, but he went lower. I didn't know what to expect, but I was game for anything at that point. He went lower and stopped by my feet, peeling my socks off. He looked up at me from under the covers and smiled.

I went with the flow. It tickled and felt weird, but I let him do it, it was getting him off. I knew that once he was done, he would be rock hard for it. It really wasn't my cup of tea, and I always suspected he had a lot of kinks he never told me about, but I don't judge.

3. The Dinner

About a week passed after that night and work kicked my ass. I had been struggling to get a good night's sleep. I don't know how to explain it, but I was awake yet unable to move a muscle or even look around. Janet quit, as did two of the cooks, so there was a lot of slack to be picked up. Malcolm was still job *hunting*. He was distant and quiet since our night, although he did cook dinner every night and served it with this lovely wine he'd bought that week. I thought he was just shy, but something felt off. He knew all my weird kinks, and I didn't judge his or mock him, but he was cold and distant. I even wore my heels that I hated to get his attention. It didn't work.

I told my boss I needed some time off. He was very reluctant to give it to me, but accepted it, assuming he realized he couldn't afford another upset employee. So, with a week off ahead of me, I planned to use it wisely. It was Friday afternoon, and I'd just gotten off the phone with my mom who lived upstate and was struggling with housework after an operation on her hips. I packed for the two of us and had the money for logistics, but the hardest part wasn't over. Convincing Malcolm to go with. I knew they didn't get along, but I also knew how similar they were. They just needed to spend some time with each other!

Malcolm came in just after three pm, tired and distraught. He'd interviewed for his dream job, but didn't get it. So, I had to play my cards right. He blew me a kiss and went to the bathroom. He wasn't in there long, and when he came out he saw the bags on our bed. His face changed from tired to angry.

"What's going on?" he asked.

"Babe, I want to go see my mom. I thought we could take a bus and go enjoy the peace and quiet of the suburbs for a while. I got off work."

He shook his head then chuckled, walking over to me. "Your *mom*? Why would I do that? She hates my guts! Plus, I have something planned for us." He smiled and took my hands.

"Babe, I kinda want to go to my mom. She could use my help," I replied, trying my best not to sound stern.

He pulled his hands away and went to sit at the computer, but didn't turn it on. Instead, he swirled on the chair. "You can go, I'm not going."

"Babe, I already spoke to my mom. She's actually excited to spend time with us. And you as well."

"You just want to leave? You haven't even heard what I have planned for us. That's how it is here. I get shat on from you when I'm not *doing* anything but then when I find something, you still have something to cry about. Can't you make up your mind, Marla?"

I choked on the ball in my throat. "Malcolm, I..."

"Forget it!" he exclaimed. "I'll go at it alone. It's always been like that. No support from *anyone*."

I walked over and hugged him. There were tears coming out of his eyes, but no sniffles or any other indication of crying. He was a good actor, and I fell for it. I punch myself when I look back. To be twenty-one again.

"Can't she just come here for dinner? I'll cook," he said.

Surprised, I nodded and asked what he wanted to cook.

"Pasta, something nice. You'll see. Call her and tell her."

"Sure, I'll do that," I said as I moved to the kitchen to get my phone. I felt his eyes follow me, I turned to look at him. He was staring at my feet, almost drooling.

"Stay where you are," he whispered, unbuckling his pants.

I listened and didn't move until he was done. I didn't mind. I had my own kinks which he catered to, but something did feel off.

My mom came over later that day. Even though it was inconvenient, she wanted to make an effort. He cooked a nice seafood pasta and bought a nice bottle of champagne too. I was impressed and so was my mom. When she arrived, she looked around at our apartment and seemed disappointed, shrugging it off.

"It's something," she said. "My place wasn't much bigger when I was your age."

She looked over at Malcolm, who was standing in the kitchen and stirring the food.

"He find a job yet?" she asked, struggling to sit down. I helped her.

"Not yet," I said, looking over my shoulder. "But he's trying. He said he has a plan. He's a planner, a hustler. I have faith."

"Good, good," she said. I could see by the stoic look on her face that she forced herself to say something positive and not start something up.

We didn't have a dinner table, but the small oval-shaped coffee table in our living room made a good alternative. Malcolm hovered over to us with our food, looking like a waiter in a high-end restaurant.

"Think you might have a knack for that, I'm jealous of your plate handling," I said.

He didn't reply and instead gave an awkward grin.

Mom nodded in agreement. "You're a good-looking guy, Malcolm. You'll definitely get good tips," she said, fishing in her purse. She pulled out a note and whistled, then tucked it into the waist band of his jeans.

Malcolm couldn't help but smile. I was just happy they were interacting with without wanting to rip each other's throats out. My mom played music. I was surprised she knew some good classics. The

Who, Nazareth, and Jefferson Airplane. Dinner was so good we ate in silence. Our cutlery clanged on the plates to the sound of Love Hurts. Every time I looked over at Malcolm, I caught him glancing over at me before looking away.

After we finished, Malcolm brought some more wine and poured us each a glass.

My mom put her hand on her glass and shook her head. "None for me, thanks sweetie, I still have to get home."

"You sure?" he asked, his eyes sleepy. "I can fix you a cup of coffee."

"Sounds good. No cream, no sugar."

Malcolm nodded.

"How have you been sleeping, Marla? Did you go to the doctor?" she asked.

"It feels like sleep paralysis. Like I'm awake, but I can't see anything or move. At all. I don't know what a doctor is going to do…"

"You're overworking yourself at that damn diner." Mom had that maternal habit of cutting you off to scold you. "Waiting is a good way to make some money, but not in a scummy part of town like this."

"I agree," Malcolm said, walking over with the coffee. He handed it to my mom and she nodded gratefully. "There's so many nice ways for her to make money. I know a guy who is looking for some people. Great pay too."

"Why haven't you tried it?" I asked, regretting it when his face melted into a frown. My mom kicked me under the table. I was genuinely curious though; I don't know why he had to be so sensitive.

"Females. He, or *they*, are looking for women only. Must be because women have better smiles than men." He laughed.

My mom and I nodded in agreement.

"Well, Marla should take a look at it. She has a great smile," my mom said. "I can't stand the idea of her working in that place. I know the owner. A perverted asshole who was a caught being a peeping Tom back when I was in high school."

We all looked at the door when there was a loud bang against it. Malcolm was just about to open it but jumped back as a piece of paper slid under the door. He picked it up, unfolded it and read it out.

"Please keep the music down. Albert." Scoffing, Malcom tore it up.

"What? It's not even that loud." My mom laughed, then burped. "Fucking loser."

I don't know if it was Mom's sudden potty mouth, which was very rare, or the wine was starting to claw its way into my brain, but the room began spinning. I burst into a soft giggle. Soon, we all laughed. It was louder than the music.

"Well," my mom said, finishing her coffee, "it's getting late. I think it's time for me to hit the road."

"Really? Do you want us to walk you to the station?" Malcolm asked.

My mom shook her head as she stood up. I couldn't stand up straight. My arms and legs felt heavy and dragged down, like I was chained to cast iron balls. She leaned over and kissed me on the forehead, then chuckled.

"Too much wine, huh? Take after me. I know that feeling too well. You take care, sweetie. Go see a doctor about *sleep paralysis*. Or else I'll come back here and knock you out and you'll get some sleep then," she said, winking.

Malcolm walked with her to the door. She told him to make sure I go see the doctor or else. He agreed and gave her a hug. As soon as the door closed, the lights went off. I thought it was a power outage, but the computer was on. I managed to turn. Malcolm was by the light switch.

"What are you doing?" I asked. He seemed to be floating in the darkness, his face illuminated by the light on his phone.

"I told you," he said, then slipped his phone into his pocket, "I have something planned that will help us out."

My head suddenly felt like it would snap off and roll onto the floor. We all drank the same amount of alcohol, but in that moment I couldn't understand why I felt that way. I tried standing up again, but Malcolm raced over to me and grabbed my shoulders, easing me back down onto the couch.

"Couldn't help yourself with the wine tonight, huh? I wanted you to shower first at least," he said.

I muttered something to him. To be honest, I can't remember what. He laughed at me. There was a tap on my cheek, followed by his kiss on my neck. Like putting a child to bed, he laid me down on the couch then knelt down to face me. Wine was on his breath, and he kissed me again. I saw his shape in the darkness I knew it was Malcolm, but I felt like something else was in there with me.

He stood up and walked to the bathroom, then turned to me and said, "I'll be back. You're gonna love it, I promise." The door closed with a soft click and I heard the water switch on.

A few minutes passed as I lay in the darkness and started to feel better, but my arms were struggling to cooperate with me. My eyes adjusted to the pitch-black apartment and I could mostly make out where everything was. The inky blackness was interrupted by the computer screen turning on. A picture of us standing under the marquee for a Saw V viewing on our first date was now our lock screen. It went black, then powered on again. I wasn't expecting any emails at that time of night. I managed to push myself up, and using the couch as a guide, I moved to the desk and sat down. Jesus, I remember the headache I had when I unlocked the PC. I squinted as it felt like someone took two knitting needles and stuck them into my temples.

I didn't have to search far or check in any folder. Right there, on the home screen, he had his chat open. Malcolm usually used Facebook to chat with friends, but I knew immediately this chat was related to the dark web. There was a feeling I was being watched, so I looked over at the bathroom. The water was running and something was being scrubbed.

There were so many chats open, with different usernames. The same edgy shit we saw all over the dark web. Mr. Sleaze was there too. It was him that just messaged. I didn't want to look at the chats, but a voice inside me yelled, scratched, and clawed to open just one.

I chose the chat box with the user named Gore Master.

There wasn't any communication except from Malcolm. He asked, 'You like this? How much?'

It was followed by a picture of my feet. I was on our bed and over the covers with my feet posed differently.

Gore Master just replied with a smile emoji.

Mr. Sleaze had the biggest thread open with Malcolm. There were more pictures of my feet and some even had my face with make up on while I slept. Some pictures were with my feet covered in ketchup and others with heels on. Mr. Sleaze kept replying with smiley faces even when prompted for a price from Malcolm. Seeing all this sobered me up; my mind raced. My first instinct was to kick the bathroom door down and my second was to run away. I took a deep breath. Inhaled, then exhaled. *Okay*, I thought, *maybe he's just trying to make some money for us*. He didn't hurt me, he must've... drugged me? I don't know why. He could've just asked, I would've said yes...

But then I read what Mr. Sleaze just sent through.

'$20,000. Send one for now, you'll get half. If I'm impressed, you'll get the other half. Make sure it's cut above the ankle and her nails are black. I want it clean too.'

Another message said, 'I want it. Make it quick. She'll be a star.'

It must have been the adrenaline, because I shot up from the chair and almost fell over the couch as I rushed to find my phone. It wasn't anywhere to be found, and everything began to spin again. I fell onto the couch and the light from the bathroom splashed over me before his silhouette blocked it out like an eclipse. He must have noticed the open chats across the screen.

"Babe," he said with a hushed and soft voice, "you weren't supposed to see that."

"Is...this...your...plan?" I heaved, out of breath as my eyes closed then opened slowly.

He came closer and bent down to face me. His voice echoed until I couldn't hear him anymore. "You have the goods...just... let me..."

4. The Nightmare

I was awake and couldn't move. However, it wasn't like before. I could still turn my head. My senses remained aware, and I had the ability to control my eyes. I was in bed. My arms, especially my wrists, were riddled with pins and needles and tied above my head with rope looped around the bars on our steel headboard. My legs were open, with each foot tied to opposing bed posts at the end of the frame. My clothes were on, except for shoes and socks. Nothing budged as I pulled and shook my hands and legs. My limbs and joints were numb, like the blood was drained from them.

"Malcolm?" I called out. The bottom of the bed sunk in with his weight.

"Don't panic," he whispered. "I'm going to turn the lamp on, but don't panic, okay?"

Before I could respond, the red light illuminated just enough for me to see him walking to the end of the bed. He was naked except for a black ski mask pulled over his face. I struggled again, hoping the knots would loosen, but it didn't help. That's when I realized the plastic sheeting crackling under me.

"Sorry if it's cold. I didn't want to ruin our bedding."

"Malcolm, what the fuck are you doing? Let's just have sex, I can't do this kind of thing."

"See? There's that fucking poser behavior. What happened to being *real*? Is this too much for you?"

"Yes, yes it is. Please, Malcolm," I pleaded, remembering the messages.

As if he could read my mind, he cat-crawled up to my belly. His eyes seemed wild; he wasn't blinking. "Mr. Sleaze needs it. He's willing to pay."

"Malcolm, take all the pictures you want. Just please don't..."

He got off the bed and slapped my foot. "I will fucking do what I need to do! You always wanted me to start bringing something in. To contribute! But you! You have a problem with everything I do!" he yelled.

"Malcolm..."

"Shut up, Marla! Listen to me carefully. I've given you a high dose of morphine. I'm sorry for treading you on those waters again, but it's needed for what's coming."

"What's..."

"You *shouldn't* feel it. I am going to take the left foot for now. It's your...perfect one. Mr. Sleaze even gave me a contact for prosthetics. You'll be back on your *feet* in no time. After that, we'll figure it out together. I'll be with you every *step* of the way."

I screamed. I called out for help. It didn't do any good, no one came. My jaw nearly came off its hinges as he stuck a ball gag in my mouth and taped over it. I shook violently, a last-ditch attempt to get my hands loose, but it didn't make a difference. The headboard was loose and would often bang against the wall when we had sex, but there wasn't enough energy to slam it hard enough to be audible on the exposed brick wall.

"I'm going to miss it. *Really* going to miss it," he said as he disappeared into the darkness, away from the low light of the lamp next to me. I could hear feedback from the speakers by the computer, followed by *Love Hurts*. I heard him humming to it as he came back. He spread something out over the bed in between my legs. Even in the low light, I saw the glint of steel and a snaking rope he uncoiled. He tied it just above my left ankle. It was so tight I screamed, thinking he'd already started cutting. I kept gagging and the muffled sounds were not enough to alert anyone.

"Marla, just fucking be on my side with this, okay? For this one time."

I always wondered why he wore the mask that night and it's only now that I realized he must have been hiding from himself rather than me. He kept adjusting it as if he forgot he was wearing it. He grabbed the saw and ran his thumb over the blade. I shook again, but he punched me on the thigh.

"That's only going to make me cut more than I should. Marla, relax. Just let me do this. The money...oh, the money," he said. He looked over at my left foot and lowered himself over it.

"I'll miss it, but sometimes... I...oh God," he said as he kissed it. I tried kicking him, but my foot wouldn't listen to me. I couldn't feel the kiss, but I could feel the cold steel. He got it into position, yet didn't start cutting.

"Oh, I love this song," he said, running to the computer. It was loud, I couldn't even hear myself think as Nazareth echoed through our apartment, rattling our windows. "I love you, Marla, you're making a sacrifice for *us*, for *me*. Mr. Sleaze will be so happy with this beauty..."

My ears began ringing.

My face was wet from gushing tears and sweat.

I couldn't hear the music. I couldn't hear my screams. I must have been wailing. The bed was shaking violently as was I. He didn't stop. He didn't relent. That blade kept digging into my flesh and he struggled, using both arms to get it done. Suddenly he stopped, but

I could still feel the saw lodged into my bone. I was in a constant shiver. Something landed on my forehead. It was a piece of the rope that began to loosen itself. I looked around and saw Malcolm standing at the door, the bright light from the corridor outside stabbed into the apartment and landed directly on me.

Albert's eyes shot from Malcolm to me. I screamed again, but the music was so loud. All I wanted at that moment was for him to look again. My hands came loose with a strong tug, and I immediately ripped the tape off my mouth and spat the gag ball out.

Malcolm was still standing at the door and Albert was gone. He saw I got loose and walked over slowly.

"Marla," he said. "It's almost off."

I grabbed the saw and pulled. I still think the scream I let out must've burst my eardrums, or it was just the guitar solo of Love Hurts that pierced my ears. His hands were on mine. I closed my eyes and threw my hands up, waiting for his fists to come raining down. I opened them once more with anticipation. Our door was wide open, and Albert was standing behind Malcolm, his meaty arms snaked around his neck. Malcolm's face was turning purple, spit dripping from his mouth onto Albert's forearms. His hands were pathetically pawing at the big man's arms, but eventually fell limp. Albert released him to the floor.

I tried getting off the bed, but pain shot up my body—a reminder that my foot was hanging on by a thread. Albert caught me before I fell to the floor. He wiped my face with the bottom of his shirt and ran his hand through my hair.

"Help is on the way," he said. "You just relax, help is on the way."

"T-thank you..."

He chuckled. "Your loud music saved your life."

I laughed too. My eyes closed as I couldn't keep them open. I just wanted to dream and be somewhere else, away from the nightmare.

5. Now

That was seventeen years ago. A long time ago and at a place that's now far away.

I'm alive. I'm well. My son just finished high school and he's driving *me* around. My husband passed away last month and that brought up a lot of stuff I was bottling up, especially what happened back *then*. I may have kept it hidden, but it was always there. I still see that naked man in the ski mask at the end of my bed. I still picture my foot hanging by a thin tendon. It's not that I am scared, it's just that I am angry. I'm angry I have to live with this, I'm angry that I'm infected with... regret. I'm angry that I didn't see the warning signs all along.

Malcolm.

He got committed. He's been there since 2009, but was let go last month, right after Mark passed away. He emails me, begging to meet up or even send a *photo*. I haven't responded. They just sit in my inbox, waiting. My mom, who lives with me, barely remembers him and she never held it against me, despite her opinions.

I don't know if he'll ever stop reaching out and I don't know if I want him to. I know it's driving him crazy that he's pouring his heart out and begging for forgiveness, not getting anything in return. He doesn't know where I am, I hope. I can only hope. In one of his emails, he said I'm a star and I should catch up on the site we browsed all those years ago. *Magnificent Marla* is what I'm called, apparently. As I look down at *both* of my feet and despite my limp, I feel great.

I was on the train the other day and realized I was getting a lot of looks down there. A lot of nodding and sly grins from men and women with their phones out. I'm sure one of them was trying to take a photo. It seemed that Malcolm was right, I must be a star. I see it all the time now, the looks. They just won't stop. Even at work, people glance down at my shoes.

Or maybe they don't look at all. Maybe I'm just fucked up. I guess I'll never know for sure.

Cunt Hunt

By Melinda Pouncey, Sarah Moon, and Nora B. Peevy

Off in the distance, yards away, Page heard leaves crunching under heavy footsteps. What was out there she didn't know, nor was she anxious to find out.

Page steadied herself, her breathing shallow and too loud in the quiet forest. She knew instinctively not to give whatever was coming any sign of her presence. Having woken up naked, cold, and disoriented on the forest floor, she discovered a black hole where the memory of her abduction should be. She was having a few drinks with friends and called her boyfriend to pick her up when the group parted. Stepping out into the cool night made her inexplicably dizzy, and then she woke up here.

Holding a shaky breath, she tried to calm her nerves, digging her bare feet into the soft dirt, ensuring she wouldn't somehow stumble and fall.

A quiet, consistent beeping emanated from a bush as a bulky man moved in closer. The beeping wasn't coming from him. Her eyes frantically searched the moonlit trees, but he was still too far away to make out his face.

The beeping came closer. His footsteps grew louder. He wasn't coming for her as his steps skirted the top of a nearby hill. Page slowly crept deeper into the trees, creating distance between the hunter and prey. The rate of the high-pitched sound quickened like a racing heartbeat.

The sound of his tongue clicking gave her a chill, his words, like icy daggers, sent a surge of adrenaline running through her veins. Fight or flight gripped her, but her feet couldn't decide which to give action to.

"Here kitty kitty..." The man's voice was little more than a whisper. "I know you're here." The beeping quickened faster.

Page searched the dark trees for the source, her eyes flicking between the man and wherever the sound was coming from. She backed up behind a tree. His silhouette outlined by the glow of the moon, crept eerily over the hill.

"Ding, ding, ding! Gotcha!"

Page knew she was no longer alone as the silhouette of a naked, petite woman was dragged from behind a tree almost directly ahead of her. The woman screamed as the hunter grabbed a handful of the woman's long hair and dragged her across the forest floor like a rag doll. She didn't stand a chance. Page continued to watch in horror as the young woman struggled to break free. Her screams grew louder as her hands clawed at the paw gripping her.

"It's you or me, darlin'. And you are going to make me rich. It will be quick, I promise."

With a swift swipe of something sharp, the woman's neck exploded with a spray of her lifeblood. Her screams fell silent as she bled out right there in front of a man she never knew. The beeping of her tracker quieted with the final beat of her heart.

In that moment, Page knew she was being tracked. It was a matter of time before she would be slain the same way. She had to escape, she had to cut out her tracker. She had to survive.

Sticky fingers of one hand clicked the mouse while the other was shoved down his pants. The greasy, middle-aged asshole would have been the next Ted Bundy save for two things: he was too disgusting to attract any woman, and he spent every moment that he wasn't harassing women on dating apps on the dark web. He got off on watching young women being tortured/killed but was too cowardly and lazy to do it himself. It was lucky he'd stumbled upon this feed tonight. Somewhere in the world naked women were being hunted like game and he was loving it. When caught, they were killed in inventive and painful ways that made his mouth and his dick salivate. It was so... stimulating, it gave him fantasies to savor when forced back into the real world.

On the screen, number eight had just gotten her throat slit and Gary's hand moved faster. As the camera focused on the blood pouring from her throat, a banner plastered itself on the screen. IF YOU'RE ENJOYING TONIGHT'S GAME, PLEASE ENTER PAYMENT NOW. TIER 1: $100,000, TIER 2: $250,000, TIER 3: $500,000, ELITE TIER?

Gary gave a shout of frustration and slammed his fist on the table. Goddamned capitalism was ruining the dark web. Used to be a guy could see content like this for pennies on the dollar but now the prices were insane. He checked the latest cryptocurrency rates and gave a wistful sigh. Out of his league. Figured. Oh well... there was always that red room with a whore or two getting their just desserts. They were street skags. Not young and pretty like the girls here but he had a good imagination. He could pretend the bitch getting sliced and diced had that pretty brunette's face. With a final curse, he left the site.

Josh checked the livestream on his laptop. In one window was an open spreadsheet with code names and a score tally that changed in real time based on the input of the paying customers. AI was a godsend for keeping up with the live chat and assigning points based on keywords. Only two more to go and all the hunters would return to Grayson Lodge, an off-books resort in the wilds of the Pacific

Northwest. The company owned acres of land that were put to good use once a year hosting the biggest reality show on the dark web.

Josh was an organizer and game runner. He kept up with the hunters and prey through numerous cameras set up in various parts of the forest. Drones took aerial views of the action. For the past eleven hours, he frantically switched camera angles while watching the spreadsheet bloom with input. Now, the action had died down considerably, and he was able to take a breather. In the control cubicle he was alone, but the lodge had many such rooms and he was only one of the staff that kept this lucrative enterprise going.

Three years ago when he took the job, he didn't know the extent of what he was getting into. He was no stranger to cruising the dark web in his spare time, mainly to obtain cheap drugs to sell to classmates. Josh fancied himself a bit of an entrepreneur and had gotten into cryptocurrency at a young age. It all seemed innocent at the time, but his skills at navigating the web had been flagged by the Gamemaster, a shadowy figure he never met.

He was approached in a chat room by someone who called themself "Evan". Evan enticed him with both money and threats into the game. Now, thanks to this annual gig, he would be finishing college at the end of the semester with no student loans and a tidy sum to start his own business. It was tempting to set up something like the places he saw on his dark explorations: experimental drugs, organ harvesting, cannibalism, fetishes of every stripe, and, of course, murder. But, if there was one thing he had learned, it was that this game was as dangerous for the seller as the buyer of such services. One slip, and your whole life would go up in flames.

You had to be cautious, savvy, mega-connected, and more than a little foolhardy to risk it. He was none of these things. Once this hunt was over, he was planning on cashing out and disappearing. It wasn't easy to live off the grid these days, but Josh was sure he could manage. He wasn't greedy like some of these chumps. That was the key in his mind, don't be greedy and keep your mouth shut. No bragging to friends or flashing cash around—no drawing attention. Josh had seen with his own eyes what that could lead to.

Josh watched the cameras as "Cindy" aka Brooke and "Laura" aka Page ran at opposite ends of the forest, trying to stay one step ahead of their respective hunters, Carlos and Anton. Carlos was a middle-aged veteran who never even saw action in his life even though he lived and breathed a military aesthetic, unnecessarily dressing in camo most of the time and sporting a buzz cut. He would probably trip over his own feet before he found his prey. Josh knew he wouldn't last long in the second part of the hunt, the part no one talked about. The part that even the hunters themselves were unaware of. Josh smiled. He couldn't wait to see the look on Carlos' face when the man found out.

Then there was Anton. That guy was a true psychopath with skills that made Josh sweat. He had a hawk-like face with sharp blue eyes that relished the pain of others, even when no one was in pain. After one look at him, Josh wished the staff were allowed to bet on the participants like the top tier subscribers could. He was sure Anton would take it all this year.

Brooke stopped to brace herself against a tree, panting with exertion and desperation. When she awakened in the forest, she had no idea what was going on. Like Page, she witnessed the death of another girl and quickly determined that somewhere on her body was a tracker that would lead to her death. She ran her hands over every inch of her skin and through her hair, but nothing turned up. Her stomach tightened at the horrifying thought that the tracker wasn't on her but *in* her. Some sort of implant, maybe a chip like they did with pets. Only this thing beeped. Brooke didn't know why or how she was targeted for this sick game but had to play whether she wanted to or not. She was determined to keep moving. If there was an audible beep, she would take off in the opposite direction. A sucky plan, but the only one she could think of in her current state of fear and distress.

Just as she prepared to move, a beeping sounded off from her left. Torn between giving away her position and getting the hell out of there, she froze. The speed of the beeping picked up, matching the beat of her now pounding heart. That spurred her decision—she darted through the trees.

Rather than the calculated and controlled escape she imagined, she found herself dashing headlong through the trees, not knowing which direction she was going or what she might be running towards. The underbrush grew thicker and her foot caught on a tree root camouflaged by a fern. She flew forward, crashing into the trunk of a tree head-first with a loud crack. Stunned, she fell to the ground, her ears ringing so loudly she didn't hear the beeping until it was almost on her. She tried to push herself upright, but her limbs refused to obey. That's when she realized she'd broken her neck.

For a moment, the man stopped and looked around in confusion. Brooke gave a whine of pure terror, allowing the hunter to spot her. Like a gift given from mother nature on a silver platter, she was at his feet.

Watching the camera feed, Josh snorted. This guy was an idiot. He took a sip of his iced latte and chuckled at the comments from the subscribers.

"What's with this guy?"

"She should be hunting *him*."

"He's boring. Kill the cunt already, soyass bitch."

Carlos reached down and tried to pull Brooke to her feet. She cried out but was limp as a rag doll. Cursing, he pulled a ten-inch hunting knife from his boot. He shoved it in her belly and began to saw away, splitting her from her neck to her crotch. Trying to pull the flesh open, his hands slipped again and again in the blood. When he finally managed to tear enough flesh away to expose the torn peritoneum, he gave up with a growl of frustration. Panting, sweat dripped into his eyes.

Tears streamed down Brooke's cheeks, but due to her injury she felt none of it. Pitiful moans and whines issued from her lips, but she was giving him and the audience nothing. Her body gushing with gore, she breathed her last silently with an anticlimactic final exhale.

The subscriber chat exploded in rage as Josh watched the rapid scroll of words laced with curses and insults roll by. He could feel the heat of it to the point he was glad to be safe in his isolated control room. The display made a trickle of sweat run down his spine. It sometimes amazed him what people were capable of. He never wanted to be the target of some of these freaks' berserker wrath.

With a grimace of distaste, the Game Master punched in a code on his computer. At the Grayson Lodge, his recruitment manager picked up.

"Who found this dipshit?" he barked.

"Got him through the usual channels," someone on the other end answered grimly. "He met all the criteria, boss. The team thought he'd make good sport."

"Well, now we know better, don't we? Fuck it, he still might. Make sure he gets a middle position on the next round. Put him in the center of the board and let him try to fight his way out. With any luck, he'll provide at least a little satisfaction for our subscribers." His finger hovered over the "call end" button. "Oh, and Tony, tighten up the recruitment. I don't want this happening again. We have a reputation to maintain." He smashed the button without waiting for a reply.

Stupid fucker probably lost them some subscribers tonight. Unacceptable. They had to impress the high-rollers, or the game wasn't worth the candle. He rubbed his temples and sat back in his chair, watching the monitors with a jaundiced eye. The stats looked good, though. Only three had ditched the livestream after that pathetic performance. He would be reading the complaints for days. Their clientele was always quite vocal about their preferences, and he did his best to accommodate They had the right. After all, they paid enough.

Game Master checked the grid, zeroing in on the last contestant and her hunter. He had high hopes for this one. She was a Yale graduate, fit, 24 years old, single, an outdoorsy type. One of those cunts who thought they had it all. Those were the perfect prey. The ones who had the brains to elude a hunter just long enough to keep the customers interested, but not so long to bore them.

It should have been a certainty if Cindy's AKA Brooke's hunter proved to be as good as he looked on paper, they would have made an extra twenty million at least, just from the betting alone. Oh well, no use crying over spilled milk. They were making plenty from this little enterprise regardless of the ones who logged off.

He looked out his penthouse window overlooking the city. Lights twinkled like stars above the dark urban canyons below. The Game Master sat above it all like a god. The feeling of power that surged through him during the hunt was incomparable to the power he wielded daily in his corporate life. The hunt was driven by desire, not greed. He didn't need this, but he craved it with every fiber of his being. It wasn't just about the kills. It was the planning, organization, and execution of the hunt that fed him like water nourishes a flower, though the bloom it birthed was dark, sadistic and born of an obsession for complete control.

He returned his attention to the monitors. His slight weariness was gone, and he turned up the volume. It was quiet except for the rustle of wind through the trees. Then, he heard the beep. A wicked smile played over his face as he zoomed in to admire the deer-like litheness of "Laura".

Page crept through the woods, listening. Startled a little at every noise louder than the sound of her nearly silent footsteps and the rush of adrenaline-fueled blood in her ears. The back of her neck was a little bloody from the tracker she managed to locate and remove with a sharp rock. She had climbed a tree with a thick canopy of leaves and lodged the tracker in the bark about halfway up before dropping back down and setting off in search for a place to hide. There was a ridge just ahead where the trees thinned out and she hoped there might be a cave or rock cleft. Anything in which she could wedge herself so as to not be easily found.

Goosebumps pebbled her skin. She wished she had something to cover herself. Whatever crazy thing she'd fallen victim to was so grotesque and perverted as to be unimaginable. Knowing she wasn't the only one, made it all the more frightening. That poor girl...

She tried to put that image out of her mind to stay strong and focus on surviving. If she could find a road, any sign of civilization, she could get help or at least walk until she found it. Hampered by the unknown of where she was or what direction to go, only made her more determined to get out of this. She would be damned if she let these guys win.

Page made it to the ridge and used the wide trunk of a pine as cover, doing a sightline check with her back to the slope. She didn't see anyone but knew that wasn't a clear indicator of safety. He wouldn't be able to approach without being seen, though she was in a poor position to escape if he did. Still, she somehow felt safer this way, taking a moment to take a breather and make a plan. The minutes felt like hours, yet she wasn't going to hurry and end up making a mistake that would cost her life. If he was smart and had discovered her deception, he would be waiting for her to make her presence known.

Well, she wasn't going to give him that satisfaction. The other girl had been killed with a knife, but maybe this one had a gun. Considering that possibility made finding a place to hide even more urgent. Page kept to the trees as she climbed up the steep slope. A few yards up, she found what she was looking for. There was a depression filled with pine needles just behind a tree. She took another look around before pushing them aside and curling up into the depression. Then Page grabbed handfuls of the needles and covered herself as best she could. It was an uncomfortable position, and the pine-scented needles pricked at her exposed skin.

Her hope was that he would give up when he couldn't find her. Then on, it would only be a matter of getting out of the wilderness to find help. Yes, easy, just walk naked through miles of wilderness and die of exposure before she made it anywhere safe. She shivered and her stomach growled. Even if she didn't make it, dying of exposure or starvation had to be better than being gutted or shot by some psycho. At least she'd be going out on her own terms, denying the sick fuck his victory.

In her craziest imaginings, Page never thought anything like this could happen to anyone, let alone her. She knew nothing of the dark or deep web and had no idea her plight was being broadcast live to a loyal and rabid audience.

She didn't know how much time had passed when she heard the first unnatural scrape of a boot against the freezing ground. Page didn't anticipate how little the pine needles covering her would provide protection against the cold. She held her breath, trying not to shiver, and prayed the man would skirt the ridge and continue on.

Her prayers proved useless as the man seemed to zero in on her location. She could hear him climbing the ridge just as she had in almost the exact same spot. Unerringly, he came and stood over her hiding place.

A sharp stick thrusted suddenly into her thigh, causing her to give a shout of pain and surprise. The man wasted no time. He flung a handful of needles aside and grabbed her arm, pulling her to her feet. Page fought like the cornered animal she had become. She scratched at his face, aiming for his eyes, but he was wearing night vision goggles. Even then she didn't stop kicking and punching in an attempt to gain any sort of advantage, fighting for her life.

The man took little more note of her efforts than he might a rabbit he was removing from a trap. He slammed her face first against the trunk of a nearby tree, breaking her nose and two teeth, pulling her arms behind her and binding them with paracord. He turned her around and pushed her against the rough trunk, knocking the wind from her. Another length of cord was placed around her neck and around the tree trunk. He used a stick to create a makeshift garrote, choking her nearly to unconsciousness.

Behind Page's eyes a red-black curtain fell. Then the pressure on her throat eased just enough for her to draw breath. Blood filled her sinuses and throat, causing her to cough and spit blood. The man moved in front of her. She was torn between wishing for unconsciousness and pleading for answers. She opened her mouth to speak, but only gurgled and sputtered.

The man removed his goggles. Floodlights suddenly filled the area from nearby trees, illuminating the scene for an audience Page would never know was there. She looked into the sharp, merciless eyes of her killer and all hope left her. The man was cold as ice, methodical as a detective, and determined as a stalking predator. An anger rose in her, deep and primal. Driven by the scent of blood, pine, sweat and urine. With a last desperate act of defiance, she spat in his face, aiming for his eyes. The spittle landed in a red glob on his cheek, sliding down to drip against his green shirt.

He smiled.

The smile froze her. A garbled scream rose in her throat, the release of which caused her to choke and gasp again. The man slid a thin bladed knife from his belt, then made a quick, deep incision in her throat. Then, slowly, like a scientist performing the world's most interesting experiment, he wiggled his fingers into the wound with expert precision. He grasped her tongue with his long fingers and pulled, sharp and hard. Page's tongue ripped along its edges, the tender membrane giving way. A choking wail, cut short by the blood erupting from her neck, was the last act she would ever make. The man continued to pull her tongue down and down, lower and lower, until it hung at her neck, wet and glistening and steaming in the crisp air.

In the control room, Josh threw up his iced latte, missing the storm of chatter that burst from the chat. Three times he heaved until there was nothing left and then he dry-heaved again, thin bile dripping from his lips. He sat back and wiped his mouth, glancing at his computer.

"Hot damn! That's more like it!"

"Boss babe aura."

"Probably the only guy the slut never gave it up for."

Josh popped a breath mint and checked the current tally. As expected, Anton was at the top of the leaderboard. He thought of the nasty surprise awaiting the hunters and grinned, pushing the nightmare inducing image of Page out of his head. This was going to be interesting.

Rafe, a 6'7" bruiser with muscles his tuxedo couldn't hope to conceal, watched the ten hunters file into the Grand Hall of the lodge. He sized them up, gauging their likely response to the upcoming announcement. Overall, he felt good about how the livestream was going and was looking forward to the outcome. While the hunters were being prepared for the next phase of the event, the elite subscribers were watching the edited highlight reels of the kills and casting their votes. The top tier subscribers, the ultrarich few who could afford to indulge in this bloody spectacle all the way until the end, were placing bets on which of the ten would take home the ultimate prize: 5 million dollars and bragging rights they could never voice. It would open a lot of doors for them in the real world among those in the know.

As the Hunter Coordinator for the event, Rafe loved his job and respected the billionaire subscribers who went all-in on this hunt. He saw his role in this event as similar to that of being a manager of the Colosseum in the days of ancient Rome. Those games were ostensibly for everyone—the elite and the common man. This livestream was the modern equivalent, bread and circuses replaced by tortilla chips and hi-res screens. As much as he loved watching the hunters at work, he always felt a thrill of excitement and danger when it was time for the second round... the one the hunters were never informed about when they signed on.

The hall was decorated for a formal event with champagne and two smartly dressed waiters circulating with platters of expensive hors d'oeuvres. The hunters in their boots and jeans offered a stark contrast to the champagne flutes and gourmet amuse bouche served on silver trays. The men were in high spirits, bragging about their successes, laughing and joking about their kills, but also eager in their anticipation of the announcement of the winner. Even Carlos was in a jovial mood. He hadn't seen the kills of the others, or the way the audience responded to his mishap. As a result, he strutted around like a hero that had covered himself in glory on the battlefield.

Rafe let them enjoy their victories for the allotted time. Twenty minutes was the sweet spot. Long enough for them to relax and let their guard down.

Some of the men were a little more reserved in their festive boasting but that one, the one with the sharp blue eyes, was a little scary, even for Rafe. He saw what he did to his victim. How methodical and cold he was in his kill. Even now, his eyes roamed the others with a disdain Rafe hadn't seen before. That fucker was pure evil, he was certain. God knew what he'd do when the announcement was made. He glanced at his watch with a nervous flutter in his stomach. It was almost time...

Sylvia sat in her husband's study, feeling as guilty as a child sneaking into her parents' room when they were away. She was a striking woman; beautiful in a way that turned heads wherever she went. Feminine curves, smooth skin, and silky blonde hair adorned her. Despite beauty and the wealth she'd been born with along with that which her husband provided; she was insecure. A friend told her once it was a fatal flaw. She laughed it off at the time, but then couldn't get it out of her head for weeks.

Her husband was working late again. There was nothing unusual about that, but she had the feeling lately his overtime at the office might be covering up something else. His computer was on, and she scanned the files on his desktop, clicking on them one by one. She hoped her suspicions were just paranoia and she wouldn't find the chat logs or pictures of some scantily clad mistress.

Nothing on his desktop revealed what she didn't want to find anyway, but she was as thorough and meticulous as her husband, so she went a little deeper. She checked his saved documents and pictures. The more she looked, the more she felt her fears were ungrounded. Everything was related to business or his hobbies, which included chess and fine wines. The search history on his browser was full of book recommendations or historic sites. Nothing mentioned women.

She was just about to give up when she came across a file labeled GM. She paused a moment to consider what it could mean. Cars maybe. Or perhaps the initials of some paramour. Sylvia clicked on it, only to have a password request pop up. Her heart sank. She wasn't just being hysterical; he was up to something. With a stab of jealousy and indignation, she typed in her own birthdate. It would be just like the snake to use that as his password.

Access denied

Undeterred, she tried another guess.

Access denied, one more attempt

Sylvia felt her blood pressure rise. She would get to the bottom of this if it was the last thing she ever did!

One chance left. She dug deep into her memory, back to when they had first gotten together and shared everything. Flipping though her mental index card, Sylvia went down the list of childhood sweethearts, old girlfriends, pets, family members...

She spotted the glass turtle paperweight on the desk, the one she'd gotten for him for their third anniversary. He had a pet turtle as a child he'd spoken of back then. Its name was Rex. It was also his pet name for... She grimaced. But he would never use that, it would be too easy to guess. Now terrapin on the other hand... that was a possibility. For a long moment she sat staring at the screen. She thought she knew him so well, but here she was spying because she suspected him of something he wasn't telling her. Then again, if she knew him well enough after fifteen years to suspect he might be having an affair, she knew him well enough to figure out a password, right? Her fingers hovered over the keyboard. If she got this wrong and he tried to log in and couldn't, he would know it had been her.

As much as she loved him, she wasn't fool enough to believe he would never betray her. If he found out she'd been snooping he would be furious. She didn't think he was the type to make things physical, but the way his mind worked was scary sometimes.

Making her decision, she typed in terrapin7570, the number being his pin number.

Access granted

She started in surprise, like seeing a jump scare in a horror movie. In her mind she only half believed that might work. Now, confronted with the actuality of it, she hesitated. The file was full of other files... many other files. Too many to be pictures of him and some strange woman. What the hell did she stumble into?

Rafe picked up a microphone and moved to the front of the room. All eyes turned to him in anticipation as he began to speak.

"Good evening gentlemen. First, I'd like to congratulate all of you on your success today. A hunt is always only as good as the participants, and you have provided incredible sport and entertainment for our viewers. However, there can only be one winner. That winner will be the one to take home the prize of five million dollars and a digital copy of your winning hunt."

Whoops and shouts of approval, along with sustained applause, followed the announcement. With all the hunters' attention on Rafe, the armed men slipping into hall at the back went unnoticed.

"Unfortunately, the winner can't be determined until the end of the second round. When we say there is only one winner, well, what we mean is lone survivor. The second round will be your opportunity to prove yourself the ultimate hunter by taking out your competition."

Immediately, the men fell silent, looking at each other in confusion and growing anger.

"Is this a joke?" a hunter named Larry said over the growing mutter of voices. "You want us to hunt each other?"

"That's exactly what you have to do," Rafe replied. He watched carefully for any sign of rebellion, but the armed guards dressed in tactical gear put aside any possibility of that. They surged forward, drawing a tight perimeter around the hunters.

The disgruntled, panicked voices grew louder.

"That wasn't the agreement."

"I didn't sign on for this shit!"

"What the fuck?"

The shouts and protests grew increasingly louder and more slurred.

When the men noticed the guards surrounding them, they knew the game had shifted. Some were livid, and others paled. Their eyes darting around, seeking escape. Anton showed no reaction aside from a subtle tightening of his jaw. His eyes raked the others with a calculating look, then he turned to stare at Rafe.

With the sudden rush of adrenaline vying with the drug slipped into their food and drink, the hunters began to slump to the floor one by one. Rafe nodded to the guards, then looked into the camera positioned opposite him and mounted in the frame of one of the paintings decorating the walls.

"And to our generous subscribers, you have an hour break. Get some snacks, a bottle of wine, and place your bets before the start of the next round. Good luck to you all."

The waiters began clearing up and the guards moved the men from the hall back out to the forest. Rafe stopped one of the waiters walking by with a tray of half empty champagne glasses. He drank the last of the champagne from each, then placed them back on the tray and nodded to the waiter. The waiter nodded in return and walked away.

Rafe was pleased everything had gone smoothly, but that one guy, the way he'd looked at him... it made him shudder. It had been a while since they had a hunter both so proficient and so dedicated. It made even him nervous.

Anton woke up in the forest, still wearing his gear, still carrying his weapons. This was an unpleasant development but not entirely unexpected. He knew who he was dealing with and just how dangerous this game might be. Nine more kills would just mean nine more opportunities for the type of hunting he enjoyed most and, win or lose, he planned to make the most of it. Though he certainly didn't plan to lose. He donned his night vision goggles and slipped into the brush. A watch placed on his wrist that hadn't been there before chimed. A timer began to count down from two hours. He had to move quick. He was certain he would win this, his mind already set on taking out the weakest first and leaving the most challenging for a grand finale.

Carlos staggered to his feet. His head felt like it was full of cotton and he couldn't see a thing. It was pitch black out here. He wasn't where he'd begun when going in search of his prey and didn't know how to orient himself without proper light and landmarks. Pulling his knife, hoping it would offer some sort of protection should one of the others try to ambush him, he began to move through the forest. He was wobbly from whatever the hell was wearing off. He heard the chime on his watch as a countdown began.

Now, he wished he had actually seen some combat. It may had served him well in such a sticky situation. His survival skills were about to be put to the test. His confidence was lacking as he stumbled over the forest floor. His steps weren't as stealthy as he thought. His breathing was panicked and loud enough to give himself away. All things he should had known to control but not smart enough to realize.

Suddenly, Carlos found himself lifted off his feet, jerked up by an unseen snare. He dangled upside down trying to swing himself up to saw at the rope that encircled his ankle but didn't have the core strength he needed. Even if he had been smarter, it was inevitable that the snare trap was going to catch any of the hunters. Undetectable and silent.

He dangled there like a rabbit and clenched his jaw. He refused to acknowledge the hunter below him with the eyes colder than a viper. The hunter chuckled as he circled his victim and pushed him a bit, sending his body swaying. Carlos felt dizzy. He spit at the man. The man laughed and removed a large knife. It glinted in the moonlight. He grasped Carlos by the feet as Carlos struggled in vain. Carlos yelped as the hunter unzipped his pants and held his cock in his hand. He squeezed it while sneering at Carlos before he sliced through it quick and neat, tossing it away into the vines as a huge spray of blood showered his face. He licked it off his lips and then gutted the man, leaving him to bleed out as he snuck off quiet as a jack rabbit in the woods, looking for his other prey.

Larry was enraged when he found himself back in the forest in the middle of the night. This wasn't the way the competition was supposed to go. He still had the eyes of his kill in his pocket and hadn't expected to become prey himself. If anyone had been close enough, that person would have been dead. As it was, he'd have to find and kill nine people without getting killed himself. He shook with rage at the thought. Taking apart some bitch piece by piece had given him a rush of exhilaration like no other. He was so excited and confident his only thoughts had been of what he was going to spend that five million on when they'd pulled the rug out from under them all. If he got out of this alive, he'd make that smug asshole emcee eat steel.

He slipped through the trees, cringing inside when he stepped on a stick and a sharp crack rang out in the dark woods. A sudden beeping sound came from his left and the device on his arm answered, the red light on it flashing in time with his heartbeat.

"Shit!" he muttered.

He grabbed Larry from behind and slit his throat, letting him slump to the ground in a fountain of his own blood.

One by one the hunters fell to traps or ambush or their own ineptitude. Tom and Pete, a couple of wiry guys in their late thirties found each other in the open and decided to team up to take the others out. Their strategy worked three times before Tom stepped into a bear trap. He screamed in pain, begging for Pete to help him, but the other hunter cut his throat to shut him up. But it was too late, a shadowy figure materialized from the trees wearing a bloody mask of Larry's face beneath a pair of night vision goggles that made him look like a nightmare monster. Before Pete could run, the man slipped a noose over his head and began hauling him off his feet, the beeping at his wrist growing slower and slower with his failing heartbeat.

Pete bellowed and pleaded. He sidestepped Anton's knife once to the left and then once to the right. Then he charged Anton head on with his knife out in front of him like a wild bull, hoping to deliver a fatal wound or at least knock Anton off his feet so he could run away. He succeeded in knocking Anton off his feet and pivoted to get away, but Anton, nimble as a lion was back on his feet and had his knife back in his hand. He grabbed Pete from behind and without speaking he ran his knife from the base of Pete's skull all the way to Pete's buttocks, delighting in the way his weapon felt carving deep into flesh. Then he stabbed him in both his kidneys and Pete was down on the ground dead.

Sylvia stared in shock at the files laid out before her eyes. There were video clips of naked woman, but never in her wildest imagination would she have imagined this is what her husband was into. Snuff films, that's what they used to call them. Videos of women being murdered in the most sickening ways imaginable. With a hand over her mouth, she watched in mute horror as a man methodically cut off her breasts and stuffed them into a pouch at his belt like some grotesque trophy. Another woman had her throat slashed and then her killer removed her fingers, one by one, while she bled out, unable to even scream her last agony. Where had he gotten these videos, and what were the other files that seemed to be only lists of names and numbers?

Her mind reeled as she clicked on file after file until her brain finally realized what she was watching appeared to be 100% genuine. The footage was raw, filmed from different angles with close ups and long shots that captured every bit of the action. There was audio of the screams she knew were not those of actors playing a part. All the while, she tried to figure out what she was seeing and why her husband would have it on his computer.

She scanned the text files of names, searching for clues. Natalie Stern, 28 from Portland. Hadn't she been reported missing two years ago? Sylvia was certain she had seen a news article about it but couldn't remember the details. Ginger Arkady, 24 from West Virginia. The name didn't click but the picture looked like one she'd seen somewhere online. At the top of the page was a note: List for Game Master's approval. Files for GM—Game Master. What did that mean? Was this horror some kind of game? Was her husband this unnamed Game Master?

No, impossible. Sylvia knew her husband, he would never... Or would he? How well do we ever know the people we love? Confronted with this thought, she realized the little things she kept from him: messages with her friends, hiding some of her expensive online purchases to avoid a lecture. The one thing Sylvia knew for certain was that she had to put a stop to this, even if it meant the end of her marriage and security. She ran back to her room and retrieved her phone to screenshot the evidence. This had to be brought to the attention of the authorities. It was the only way she'd be able to live with herself.

Josh stared at the screen, unable to look away as he began shutting down the cameras and transferring the information from this year's hunt to the appropriate people before scrubbing it from all computers and chats. He was exhausted, glad the hunt was over for another year. His mind immediately turned to his escape plans. He'd be leaving the lodge tomorrow to catch his flight home and, once there, he'd finish up the semester then go off grid. No more laptops or computers of any kind. No cell phones or any connection that could lead the coordinators to him. Maybe, in time, the nightmares would go away and he could pretend, at least to himself, that this gig had been a glitch in the matrix and that he wasn't at least partially responsible for the deaths of several dozen people.

The chat was lively with the winning bettors congratulating themselves and rubbing the noses of their fellow subscribers in their wins. He felt his stomach lurch and he logged off, gathering the files together on his computer and accessing the temp server for transfer. Then he threw away his empty coffee cup and sighed a relieved sigh. Almost home free.

The guards went out to the forest and picked up Anton to transport him back to the lodge. His clothes and face were splattered with blood as he entered the Great Hall. Rafe was waiting for him there in his tux and he smiled and raised his champagne glass to Anton as the man entered, but received only a cold look in return.

A waiter stepped up to Anton, offering him a glass of his own but he waved it away.

"Any other surprises, or do I get my money now?" he asked, his voice like ice.

Rafe's smile dropped. "Congratulations on your win, Mr. De Luca. The Grayson Lodge is at your disposal. If you want your money now, that can be arranged."

"Then arrange it."

He nodded to one of the guards and the man left. "Five minutes and it's all yours. Would you like a drink or something to eat while you wait?"

Anton's eyes held only the tiniest hint of frosty amusement. "Just the money, thank you. I believe I've had enough of your hospitality for the night."

Rafe gave him a little bow. "As you wish."

The Game Master stood and stretched, tired but deeply satisfied. It had been a long day and night. The clock on his desk showed 3:00am. His wife would be asleep by now and if he was careful he wouldn't wake her. With any luck he could convince her tomorrow that he'd been home by midnight. He picked up the phone. "Charles, bring the car."

He shut down his computer and left the office, pausing for one last look at the sleeping city. The only use the people out there had to him were making him money or playing his game, and none of them ever knew it. He smiled in grim satisfaction. Tomorrow he would go through the footage and pick his favorites to savor. He collected the videos like trading cards, keeping them on a private server to which only he had access. The plebs could enjoy their cheap entertainments and sports all they liked. He had his own interests, and he thanked the fates he wasn't the only one.

By 8:00am the next morning, the Grayson Lodge was as silent as it had been full of noise and bustle the day before. Only the cleaning staff and a few stragglers remained on the grounds and they would all be gone by nightfall.

Josh relaxed on the plane with his earbuds in and his crypto wallet full. Everything had gone smoothly and he couldn't wait to get back to his modest apartment and start preparing for his finals. Now that he could see the light at the end of the tunnel it was like stepping into the sun after exploring a cave. No more darkness for him, only the sun and maybe a nice foreign beach or two awaited him now. His feeling of relief and freedom was palpable.

When his plane landed, he took an Uber from the airport and piled himself and his baggage into the apartment. Everything was orderly, as he'd left it, and he went next door to pick up his mail from his cute neighbor. He'd have asked her out for sure if it wasn't for... Oh well, women were easy to get when you had enough money, and he certainly did. He was young and had plenty of time to for relationships later, much later probably.

Josh ordered a pizza and turned on his Playstation, playing until his food arrived. He tipped the delivery guy generously and switched to a television program while he ate. Finally, he unpacked, showered and went to bed, more than ready for a stressless sleep.

It was still dark when he jolted awake, whether from a dream or some random noise he didn't know. That is until he saw the dark figure looming over his bed, the light seeping through his window glinting off the syringe in the man's hand.

The last words he heard were, "Nice to meet you at last. I think you might know me as Evan."

On the last word, the needle plunged into his neck before he was fully awake. It was only then he realized how stupid he'd been to think he could ever escape, even knowing what little he knew.

Sylvia pretended to be asleep as her husband slipped into bed beside her. Just a few more hours until morning and he would be off to work again. She managed to keep her breathing steady and even though her mind was racing. In the morning she would go straight to the police and turn over everything to them. Then the ball would be in their court. She still couldn't wrap her mind around what she'd discovered, but they would have to face the consequences, Tony for his crimes and herself the scandal. It would ruin both their lives. She was angry at him for doing this to the two of them but knew what she'd planned was the right thing. She only hoped she had the courage to do it.

Tony snuggled up against her, his arm resting over her body. He wanted nothing more than to strangle the life out of her, but knew that wasn't an option. One more chance, that's what the GM had said. One more chance to tighten up recruitment and take care of loose ends. Well, he'd already taken care of that. It would look like a car accident, plain and simple. No way to tie him to it at all. He'd be at work when it happened. She didn't know it but her phone had already been scrubbed of the evidence. No one escaped this life and no one screwed up without making it right, leaving no trail and no trace to the GM. He considered himself lucky to have been granted this opportunity and planned to make the most of it. He wasn't going to let his boss down again. There was too much riding on this.

The Game Master spent the next morning sleeping in. He'd decided not to chance waking his wife up after all and had chosen to sleep in the guest cottage instead. He left her a note he would be golfing in the morning and would meet her for lunch. A bit mundane after the excitement of yesterday, but he'd go through the files when his wife retired that evening and watch the highlight reel Josh had put together for him. He only hoped he'd be able to find a new editor with that boy's eye for composition.

When he awoke, his breakfast arrived at the press of a button and he ate heartily and with relish. Already his mind was turning over ideas and improvements for the next year. The incidents with Josh and Tony were unfortunate mistakes this time around, but were mistakes that would not be repeated. It was a shame to lose Tony, but there were no second chances in this game. If only everyone would adhere to that simple rule the world would be a better place.

He called for his car around 10:00am and headed for the golf course. The country club was empty since he'd decided he wanted to play a round alone to clear his head before having to face the responsibilities of the day. It was sunny with a mild breeze as he stepped onto the green and lined up his first shot. Luck was with him as he managed to land the ball within a few yards of the hole. He completed that one under par, pleased with himself in the way only a man who took every victory as a sign he was favored by the gods.

It wasn't until the seventh hole that his luck shattered and the ball went wild, flying into the woods. Cursing under his breath, he told his caddy to wait and went to retrieve it. As he entered the shade of the trees, it took his eyes a moment to adjust to the contrast from the bright sunlight.

In that moment, a figure emerged from behind one of the trees, a man with salt and pepper hair, hawk-like features, and the coldest blue eyes he'd ever seen. A blade flashed in the man's hand quicker than he could blink.

"No one likes a liar, Mr. Livingston," Anton said.

Nightglass
By Winona Morris

I never thought I was a freak until I found that tablet at the Lucky Thrift.

I don't know what possessed me to go in there to begin with. I hadn't been in there for ages. I think I was just missing my sister. Jackie and I used to go there together all the time. Back then, I was her distraction. It was my job to draw and keep the attention of the associates while she loaded her giant bag with clothes she didn't need or even want.

The night before I sent her a "remember when" text about the time we almost got caught. She never responded.

The place was exactly like I remembered it, complete with a dented cowbell tied with a bit of twine to the inner handle of the door. An overpowering smell of must and mildew clung to everything you brought home from the place.

I made my way to the back of the store where old electronics go to die and was about to snap a selfie to send Jackie, when a flash of modern silver caught my attention. Most of the electronics were ancient and obsolete, so the silver gleamed in comparison. The chrome was a beacon among the black and dusty fax machines and grey CRT monitors. It was a tablet, lying face down. I thought it was too good to be true and expected to find a busted screen when I picked it up. The screen was just as immaculate as the casing.

Since it was intact, wasn't dusty, and it didn't have a price sticker on it, I knew someone must have set it down while looking at something else and forgotten it. This was a high-end piece of hardware they would certainly come back for. I knew there was only one thing to do.

Steal it.

I didn't have a big purse like Jackie used to carry or even a backpack. I just tucked the tablet under my arm and walked out the door. The cowbell clunked drearily behind me. In front of the Lucky Thrift sign, I held it up and took a selfie to send my sister with a text: You'll never believe what I just did. I hoped she would message back this time since she hadn't responded for weeks.

I was late getting to the apartment, and my roommates, Joey and Kenny, were bouncing off the walls like hyperactive chihuahuas.

"You're late!" Kenny announced. He was in the kitchen standing at the counter, gazing into the cabinet as if he could find the whole meaning of the universe in our mismatched dinnerware. "It's trivia night," he added.

"I'm not late," I said. "I stopped by Lucky Thrift on the way home."

"Did you get lucky?" Joey came to the door and followed me as I walked through our living area toward my room. He stopped in the doorway as I sat heavily on my bed.

"You could say I got lucky," I said, and held up the tablet. "Found this for a steal."

I laughed at my joke, then pressed the power button on the tablet. My expectations were low. Sure, someone left it behind by accident, but the chances it would both power on and not need a passcode were slim. It powered up smoothly and went directly to the home screen.

The wallpaper looked like someone took a photo of a bright white painter's tarp covered with splashes of deep red paint. There was only one icon sitting primly in the top left corner. It appeared to be a camera lens and said "nightglass" underneath.

"What's nightglass?" I called out so Kenny, our resident tech-head, could hear me from the depths of our kitchen cabinets.

"Deep web," he called back. "Not illegal, but not for the kiddos."

"Like, hackers and shit?" I asked.

He said, "Has anyone seen my Snoopy cup?" in response.

Joey breached the doorway of my bedroom and was standing beside me looking at the tablet screen when I tapped the icon.

I expected a search bar or news feed to pop up like every other browser I've ever used, but it loaded directly to a page the previous owner must have saved.

It was a livestream.

In front of the camera, ropes restrained someone to a chair in a room that was both wallpapered and carpeted with the same painter's drop cloth as the tablet's wallpaper. The only difference was it lacked splashes of red. The person wearing a white wife-beater and grey sweatpants was the epitome of androgyny. I couldn't see any swell of breasts under their shirt, but their lips, despite being pressed tightly together, were full and pink. Their eyes were a startling blue, ringed with lush black eyelashes. Those eyes stared defiantly forward, but I could see the hint of tears trying to build.

Slightly behind the bound one was a second person. It was clearly a man, standing behind a lectern podium that held a laptop. He seemed to be ignoring the person tied down, focusing completely on the screen in front of him.

There was a live chat to the left of the display. When I first opened the page, it announced my entrance as 'HobKnight has joined the chat'. I was too focused on the person in the center of the screen to realize if anyone had noticed.

The chat rolled by so fast I couldn't read complete sentences, but I caught words at a glance. Cut, chop, burn, exsanguinate, and eviscerate scrolled by alongside gentler but odder words like shave, bathe, and feed.

"What the actual fuck is this shit?" Joey said beside me. The stream in front of me was so compelling I forgot. "That's not the deep web. That's dark web shit."

"What's the difference?" I asked.

"Dude, there is a fucking woman tied to a fucking chair and you're going to ask me what's the difference?"

"I think that might be a guy," I said, only to earn a scorching look from Joey.

"Seriously, you've gotta take that thing to the cops, okay? Some perv lost it, and maybe it can help them find him."

"Okay," I agreed, giving the bound person one last glance before powering down the tablet. "but tomorrow. I don't want to miss trivia night."

"You're such a dork," Joey said.

Kenny shouted from the kitchen, "We're all dorks, you dork."

I slipped the tablet under my pillow and we left together to go answer questions with other drunken college dorks.

The tablet wasn't even on my mind by the time we stumbled back into the apartment. I flopped down on my bed and my head thunked against its hard frame under my thin pillow. I remembered the person tied to the chair in the drop cloth covered room, and after making sure both Joey and Kenny's doors were shut tight, I opened nightglass again.

It opened into an active livestream again, in the same room. The chair, though tilted on its side, was empty. The man was still in the room, but the lectern was lower, and he sat in another chair behind it.

The chat was empty aside from one other person. "HobKnight has joined the chat" sat at the top of the motionless screen like an accusation.

The man looked at the computer for a moment, directly into the camera, as his fingers flew over the keyboard.

SnFthr: You are not HobKnight.

I panicked, unsure what to do or say. I kept staring at the screen, at the man in the background staring back at me. Suddenly, I felt like he was *really* staring at me, that he could see me as clearly as I could see him. I pressed my thumb over the lens of the camera, and the man smirked.

SnFthr: It's too late for that, Dylan. You are Dylan, right? Dylan Dover?

On the screen, the name HobKnight changed to DylDo followed by an eggplant emoji. The man laughed uproariously at his own joke, the sound deep even over the tinny speaker of the tablet.

SnFthr: Don't worry, Dylan. I can tell you your parents' names, your roommates' names, the exact address where you live, and every step you take on an average day, but you're not in any danger.

He paused, seeming to wait for me to respond. I stayed right as I was, thumb pressed over the camera lens, hardly able to breathe.

SnFthr: HobKnight however, now they might be in danger. I'm going to be very interested in finding out how you got your hands on their device. But... you still have their device, even after watching our brainstorming session earlier. That can only mean that you are our kind of people, Dylan. Are you? Our kind of people?

Still not speaking or typing, and even though the lens was still covered, I shook my head violently in the negative. On screen, the man frowned.

SnFthr: Don't lie to me, Dylan.

Then the man said, "Uncover the fucking camera, Dylan, and put your earbuds in. You don't want Joey or Kenny to hear this."

That is when I should have shut down the tablet. I should have taken it to the police right then and there, not leaving it in my apartment for one more minute. There are a lot of things I should have done. What I did was move my thumb off the camera and find my earbuds while the man in the room waited patiently.

As soon as the Bluetooth connected, my ears were full of the unmistakable sounds of sex.

It wasn't the pornographic slapping of flesh pounding flesh, but the soft susurrations of gentle lovemaking. There was an inaudible murmur of breath, words I couldn't quite make out, and the rustle of bodies moving on soft sheets. A satisfied hum melted into a sigh, then the rhythm quickened. Slow, drawn-out exhales became quickened gasps. The hum of pleasure turned into a full-bodied moan. I could hear the sound of skin against skin. The rhythmic knocking of a headboard against a wall overwhelmed the soft rustle of sheets. Instead of desire-filled panting, the unintelligible whispers turned into a single-syllable word spoken louder and louder.

"Yes. Yes. Yes."

Being young, virile, and male, it didn't take more than a few minutes for the erotic soundtrack to give me an erection. By the time the faceless person was yessing their way to an orgasm, my jeans were around my knees, and I was nearing one of my own. Unfortunately, in the seconds before release, the tone of the audio changed.

A wet punch punctuated the heightening yesses. Then, there was a scream. It was long and drawn out; the most realistic sound of pain I ever heard. While the scream never ended, there were more of those wet punching sounds. *He's killing her*, I thought, but that didn't stop the frantic motion of my hand. As I came, I heard one last wet slap. The scream ended in a bubbling breath, then silence.

Spent, I lay there for a few seconds. The man on the screen spoke, "That was a dull kitchen knife. One they used earlier to eat a delectable slab of Kobe beef. The first stab was into their left side, right under their ribs, at the moment they climaxed. And, speaking of climaxes, was it good for you too?"

There was a ping, and I picked up the tablet to see a water droplet emoji added behind the eggplant emoji on my newly given username.

SnFthr: Come back tomorrow, Dylan. We rarely have two in a row, but I have a special guest that I just know you'll love. Since you're new here, I'll even work a deal for you. I'll let you have the audio for free this one time, but I know you want to see it happen, don't you? I'll give you a single viewing for just 4K. After that, we'll talk about membership fees.

The screen went black, and I almost killed myself trying to rush to the bathroom with my pants still halfway down. I dropped to my knees in front of the toilet and puked up what was left of my soul before I went back to bed. Slipping the tablet back under my pillow, I was asleep instantly.

I dreamt I was fucking the blue-eyed person from the night before, but with a knife in my hand. With every thrust I would also stab. Blood leaked from the corners of their mouth, but they moaned that they wanted it deeper, harder.

It should have been a nightmare, but I woke the next morning with a tightness in my shorts that I needed to handle before I could get out of bed.

I scribbled a quick note on an index card and taped it to the front of my closed door. Something we all did when we wanted to be left alone:

GO AWAY I HAVE THE PLAGUE

While sitting on the edge of my bed, listening to Kenny and Joey get ready for their day, I pulled out my phone to see if Jackie had responded to any of my texts.

She had not.

It didn't surprise me really. We might have been close when we were younger, but once she moved out, she slowly quit trying to keep in touch. She could go weeks before responding to a text, if she ever did at all.

I thought about how people change and about how to get four thousand bucks.

There were so few hours to come up with that kind of money. My bank account barely had five hundred bucks, and this was a once in a lifetime chance. I knew SnFthr, whoever he was, would not be offering this opportunity at this low of a price again. Sure, he said I could listen for free, and what I heard the night before did things to me I never thought possible. I couldn't pass up the chance to see it in action.

I always thought snuff films were a myth, like waking up in a tub of ice with one of your kidneys missing. Nothing could stand in the way of watching it live.

When I was sure my roommates would not pop back in for something they forgot, I turned to the most trustworthy source of money I could think of.

I called my parents.

It took some negotiating, with Mom and Dad both on speakerphone. I told them about how our landlord not only raised the rent, but it was bad timing because both Kenny and Joey were short on their shares. I couldn't cover it either, because one of my classes called for some books that hadn't been on the initial syllabus, and I didn't have a thing left over to spare.

I had to promise I would look for somewhere cheaper to live and have a serious talk with the guys about responsibility. Dad ended the conversation by telling me he trusted I would pay him back. He would be writing up a payment plan and I better follow it if I knew what was good for me.

I was out the door almost as soon as my banking app pinged with a notification of the deposit. My bank was only a few blocks away. They could give me a prepaid Mastercard for $4000, but the physical card would take a couple of weeks to show up. I assured them all I needed was a digital card, and if they could keep it separate from my primary account, that would be great.

SnFthr knew everything about me already, so I wasn't hiding from him. If the FBI found nightglass and followed the digital rabbit trail back to me, something like a digital bank card wouldn't protect me. I was only trying to hide what I was really paying for from my father.

While locked in my bedroom pretending to be sick, the rest of the day dragged by slowly.

I didn't have a time for when everything would start. 'The brainstorming session' was in progress when I got back from the Lucky Thrift the night before, so I opened the tablet a little before that time.

DyLvr has joined the chat.

My name was different, but otherwise the setup was the same. Unlike the barefaced androgynous person from last night, the bound person in the foreground wore a cloth sack over their head. They thrashed and fought against the restraints holding them to the chair. The chat was going wild with suggestions both gentle and violent as SnFthr moved from his spot behind the lectern to stand beside his guest.

"Esteemed associates," he spoke to the camera. "We can now proceed with tonight's special presentation. Our timetable will be accelerated this evening since I have previous engagements I must attend to. We are going to proceed down the same path as we did with our guest yesterday. Except, without the wine and dine part of the evening. I don't think our current guest is going to be agreeable to that."

Reaching out, he removed the cloth sack from the person's head, and suddenly I was looking at a face I knew.

Silver duct tape was wrapped around their face, pinning down their brown hair. Glistening streaks of tears smeared both cheeks, liquid still running from their eyes. I saw their nostrils flare as they tried to breathe while panicking with their mouth covered. With their face uncovered, they looked around frantically for help, but saw nobody except SnFthr and presumably the camera set up in front of them.

SnFthr reached out and gently brushed a strand of hair off of their forehead before returning to his lectern and laptop as a man entered from offscreen.

"Take our guest to the restraint room," he said to the man before turning all his attention to his laptop.

The tablet dinged as a private message window popped up on my screen.

SnFthr: Do you like your gift, Dylan? A fighter, that one. I think tonight's entertainment is going to be a bit more *hardcore*, shall we say? So, what will it be? Do you just want to hear them scream, or are you going to put Daddy's money to good use? Since you know tonight's guest on a personal level, I'll even send you a private video file. Yours to keep forever. Nobody ever gets that.

A large green button popped up beside the private chat window. White text on it simply read: PAY.

That was my last chance to back out. Even if I left the app and never opened it again, I wasn't innocent anymore. There was already blood on my hands. Even if I went to the cops immediately, I knew it was too late for the person being prepared offscreen. Getting off on what I heard last night was sick, but there was something even more perverse in the fact that I was already hard at the thought of watching what was about to go live.

It wasn't just a stranger this time. It was Jackie. My sister whom I had been trying to reconnect with recently. My sister, who never responded to my texts. But I never stopped trying. Once we were close, and I wanted that back.

My sister was about to be raped and murdered for the enjoyment of corrupt people on the internet, and this was my last chance not to be part of it.

I clicked PAY.

Unicorn
By Colt M Henderson

Kevin was waiting on the porch for a stranger to show up and trade some cash for a baggie of white powder. It was supposed to be a new type and was cheaper than what he usually bought. It wasn't easy to find, but after a little digging on the dark web, he managed to land a deal. Win-win, in his mind.

A flashy sports car pulled into his driveway and a well-dressed man got out. After getting up, Kevin approached the man in his baggy sweat pants and stained shirt. They were a few feet apart when Kevin finally greeted him.

"Hey man, what's up?"

"Are you Kevin Long?"

"Yeah, I am. Are you Slanger5000?"

"I have a package for you." The well-built, middle-aged Korean man ignored the username.

"Cool, what do I owe you?"

"Five."

"Five?"

"Five."

"That's more than my regular guy."

"You indicated you wanted the new stuff. That's the new stuff price."

"Fine." Kevin pulled out his wallet from his pocket with some folded bills. After counting out the remaining amount he handed the money to the dealer. The dealer counted out the cash and turned towards his car.

"Where are you going?" Kevin called out as the man approached the back of the car and retrieved a briefcase from the trunk. "Oh."

The Goliath to Kevin's David walked up and handed the small briefcase over before nodding and walking back to the car. Kevin stood there, the warm evening air rustling through his yard, his eyes stuck to the car's tail lights.

"What the hell is this?" Kevin looked at the briefcase. This wasn't the normal packaging. Usually, goods came in a crinkled-up baggie still warm from being in someone's pocket. It was a bit swanky this time around, but then he'd paid for it he supposed.

He shrugged it off and went inside. After placing his new briefcase in his man cave, he went upstairs. It was the perfect time of night; his family should be sleeping so the real fun could begin. Behind each of the three doors he found someone slumbering. He silently hovered over each one to check for the telltale rhythmic breathing, concluding they were dead asleep.

His descent down the stairs was marked with excitement. Kevin planned on getting some play time in on his gaming system. It was his first night off in two whole weeks, so he was going to enjoy it. Snacks, drinks, his drug of choice, and a big screen television were begging to be consumed.

Back in his man cave, he opened the briefcase. "I didn't want a brick," he said to himself. He shifted the fasteners and the top popped open. Inside was one small baggie of white powder.

"Damn it!" he said through clenched teeth. He was ripped off. The tiny little package looked so lonely in the spacious case. He should have known better than to trust some random off the internet, but he was always one to take a gamble. Especially for the *good stuff*. "This better be the best stuff I've ever had."

Baggie in hand, Kevin plopped down in his recliner. He examined the fine powder. It looked right, but you never really knew until you tried it. He wouldn't be surprised if it was overly cut with trash. He held up the clear bag and gave it a little flick before licking his finger and plunging it inside. His gums went numb after running the substance over them and he grinned, excitement kicking in.

The stuff was better than his last bag, so he eagerly broke it up with an old credit card into thick lines. The first burnt his nostril, sending that familiar blast to his forehead. The rush he loved. Then his whole face went numb. It traveled down his spine, pulling his body back into his chair. He welcomed it with a wide smile.

Suddenly, something went wrong and his body began to overheat. Beads of sweat formed on his brow and ran down his face. In seconds he was drenched and breathing heavily. The heat kept rising, but he was frozen from numbness. His mouth went dry and an intense migraine encased his skull.

A terrible scream crept into his ears, but he couldn't raise his hands to muffle it. His surroundings soon melted into nothingness, engulfing him in darkness. From the void, trees sprouted and the scream faded. It was as if a spotlight shone on them. He couldn't help but imagine he'd chased the white rabbit behind Alice down that famous hole as the sounds of a jungle filled his ears. His couch, tv, his surroundings all morphed into the dark forest rooted in his mind.

Kevin grew paranoid of the looming sounds and ducked behind a tree.

Across from him, an archway of intertwining branches formed over a stage of packed dirt and scattered patches of grass. All was quiet, as if the woods were awaiting a grand entrance. A dark silhouette formed, a blurred outline of a figure with two little rounded ears. Then, the back of a fuzzy little teddy bear appeared with a puffy round tail.

Kevin approached it curiously. The furry little forest creature had a way of calling to him. When he was in arms reach, a loud snap came from beneath his foot as he stepped on a twig, breaking it into two. The bear spun around, bearing a face of anger as it sprinted towards Kevin. It wasn't the cute cuddly face he'd expected.

Kevin's demeanor changed; he was in defense mode as he ran at the small bear. When he reached striking distance, he threw his first punch at the once charming beast's angry face. His momentum won out and the bear flew violently into a bush. It growled at him as it struggled to its feet. Then, an unexpected sound radiated from the little furball, a human sounding scream.

When the beast stood up to its full height of five-foot-five, Kevin shot out a few jabs, landing all of them. The teddy bear backed up, its face melting into a pout as if ready to cry. It bum-rushed him, arms outstretched, attempting a bear hug. He grabbed the fluff of the incoming stuffed animal and threw it into the trunk of a tree.

As Kevin started to kick the downed child's toy, another oversized teddy bear jumped him from behind. It wrapped its soft paws around his neck and started to squeeze. Kevin grabbed the arms of the beast and pulled it over his shoulder like a ragdoll. With all his might, he flung the bear. Head over heels the little creature flew, hitting a tree trunk before limply sliding down.

A third one, smaller than the other two, approached him from the side, but even though it wasn't attacking Kevin, he ran at it. His foot connected with the back of the teddy bear's head with a karate kick, sending it flying face first into the two on the ground. It roared at him in return. Kevin braced himself for an attack that never came. The three bears just cowered there, groaning. Kevin thought it was a ploy and wanted to keep the upper hand while he still had it.

In the corner of his eye he saw a thick branch resting against a tree like it was put there just to aid him. He frantically swung it with a strength that could win him a world series. Heading straight for the trio, the first meek bear was easily swatted away with a single bash.

The bigger one tried to fight back, only to take a few powerful swings to the head before collapsing. Seeing its fellows down for the count, the smallest tried to run. Kevin cornered the tiny beast. Each swing increased in strength until the makeshift bat cracked. Stuffing flew through the air like fluff being yanked from a chew toy. Kevin picked up the sharpened end of the branch and backtracked to the others.

They stood, ready to tackle him—a final attempt to fight back. It was an ambush. However, they were no match for the sharp end of Kevin's splintered stick as he stabbed one in the gut, causing the other to back off. Its stuffing spilled from the gaping hole as Kevin retracted his weapon. He continued stabbing the bear over and over, filling the air around them with fluff in a fit of blind rage.

Kevin stopped as he sensed a presence behind him. He quickly spun around and plunged his weapon into the last threat. It growled as Kevin removed the branch and plunged it in again. All the bear's movements ceased. All that was left were tattered remains of fabric and scattered stuffing.

It was a short moment of victory.

A horde of bears flooded in from the darkness. He was surrounded. The sharp point of his stick would never be able to take them all down. Still, he fought all the same. He fought until he received a final blow to the face from a massive, powerful paw. It knocked him out but he continued to fidget and jerk, as if he was fighting a war in his mind.

Groggy, Kevin slowly came to. "The teddy bears," Kevin whispered as he looked blearily around. His vision was still glazed over as he imagined a room covered in cotton and fabric.

Instead of a jungle, his eyes were met with a sea of carnage in what was once his man cave. The multicolored room, once adorned with treasures and collectibles had fluorescent lights dripping in red. The bodies of bears were replaced with that of his parents and brother. He cried out. A memory of chasing down the smallest teddy bear came to mind and he cried out again.

Kevin was yanked to his feet and escorted past the bodies of his dead family. When the cops tried to pry a statement from his lips, his only response was, "It was teddy bears."

Dead Man LIVE
By Thomas Stewart

I put the knife down on my table right next to a rusted hacksaw. Turning my PC on, I smile at the glint of the camera light. It's the only one visible in the otherwise indiscernible void that is my bedroom. The monitor comes on, and I see myself staring back at me.

I raise my hand to touch my face, feeling just how smooth it is, remembering it. It won't be that way for long. My eyes glance at the knife again.

My hand twitches. I want to pick it up right now. Just do it all *right now...*

No... No...

Not yet...

Patience...

I move my hand to the mouse, guiding it towards the livestreaming app: *Dead Man LIVE*. My hand moves slow; my heart speeding up. Sweat falls from my forehead in bullets.

I click the app and the light changes from green to red, signaling it's primed. I close my eyes, taking one last moment to savor the sight of my face before I click "REC". My eyes divert back down to my assortment of weapons.

I hear the ping, letting me know the alert is being sent to all my subscribers. I know it'll only be a couple of seconds before the show has to start. Opening my eyes, I find the chat room is full. Everyone is chatting so fast that I can't begin to read any of it.

I take a breath and introduce myself. "Hey guys. My name's Cory Kelvin. I'm here today to beat the Dead Man record. The record stands at ten minutes. I plan to beat that. You all know what to do. Every time the red light buzzes in the corner, I have to cut myself.

Every ten buzzes, I have to remove a part of myself. Are you ready to begin?"

The chat members collectively start cheering "YES!". I take one last deep breath before giving a thumbs up, signaling the beginning of the game. It takes less than a second before I hear the first beep. I bring up the small Swiss army knife and start cutting across my clavicle, all the way down to my sternum. As I'm doing so, there's another beep. So, I cut another line perpendicular, crossing the last cut I made.

I cut deep. Blood runs in rivers down my chest and stomach. My breathing is slow, and my heartbeat is a crawl. It will allow me to keep cool so I won't blow the game too early. I can't fuck this up. I can't afford it...

My *family* can't afford it!

I hear the buzzer ring three more times back-to-back. I make three more cuts. This time across my chest, abdomen, and one down my cheek. I watch the chat go crazy. They ask if I wanna keep doing this, tell me where I should cut next, and opinionate what part of me I should remove first. They tell me I look soft, that I won't make it anywhere near the record mark.

Their words hurt, and the scars sting so much worse. None of this, however, compares to what's killing me inside. The responsibility on my shoulders. The price of failure bearing down on me. This *has* to happen.

I hear the buzzer ring about eight more times. I make five of the eight cuts, three of which are across my face. On the seventh, I take the hacksaw and start sawing off my pinky finger. The pain is excruciating beyond measure, but I hold my breath and do my damnedest not to let my face twist. I have to stay strong, or I lose.

The timer is at 10 seconds now. I'm a third of the way there. I can do this.

The buzzer is going haywire now. I can barely keep up with how many times it's rang. My chest is already slashed to ribbons, like I've been attacked by a wolverine. I've removed two more fingers—a thumb and a middle finger. The buzzes are near-nonstop.

I upgrade to the butcher knife. The blade is sharper, longer, and sinking deeper and deeper past my flesh, through sinew, all the way down to the fucking *bone!* I can just barely keep the tears contained in my eyes. The monitor is distorted through their welling.

The chat tells me they want to see me cut my penis off next. They call me a little pussy-boy. They tell me I'm doing the world a fucking favor with what I'm doing now. They tell me I'm making the world a better place with my death.

I want to say this hurts me. To an extent it does. The thing is, though, they're right. At least, for my family, it will be alright.

I just have to last another 16 or so seconds, and my family will be set financially for the rest of their lives. I lost my job three weeks ago, and I can't get another one. *They* won't let me get another one, nor can I get unemployment. We're about to lose our house. And *everything*.

I have to keep going. I just have to. The pain doesn't matter. Their words don't fucking matter.

All that matters is the $45,000,000 my family will get once I complete the challenge.

I manage to make it to the 20 second mark. I'm *gonna* make it. My family will be set for life. My face and my body are all disfigured now, but it's fine. I'll make it, and my family will be fine.

My eyes start fluttering. My arms feel weak. My legs wobble, getting weaker and weaker.

I can't stay much longer. Everything's starting to feel ice cold. I can feel it all fading.

I can just barely see the timer, and it's past the 37 second mark. I've made it! I can keep this up just long enough to set a brand new record. I might be able to even double the payout like this. I've severed off all the fingers on my left hand, my nose, and even one testicle. That one hurt the absolute worst, and it caused the most blood loss.

I'm almost out completely. Through squinted eyes I can see the timer make it to the 45 second mark. Finally, I sink the blade into my throat. My eyes ultimately close. My final thoughts are of my family, smiling as they move into a brand new house. One that's nicer than the one we have now, nicer than I could ever have afforded to give them. They'll have every bit of the life they never could with me. For this, and this alone, I die a happy man.

The Facilitator Part 1
By D.L.Garvin

Derek White was (by all appearances) your average middle-class businessman. He had a wife, two kids, a dog, and an up-scale four-bedroom home. He lived in a quiet neighborhood in a rural area about an hour's drive from New York City. He'd always been a good businessman, having earned degrees in both marketing and computer programming. He had made several small fortunes running online businesses. At least three of those were set up to run on autopilot. Never having to do much more than check on them once or twice a week, they raked in thousands.

They paid for his home in New York and a condo in Florida. He had the newest cars and several expensive big boy toys: an RV, numerous motorcycles and ATV's. At least one for every member of the family. He had several boats, including his treasured top-of-the-line bass boat, as well as jet skis for the whole family and a 70 ft yacht.

Besides his toys, his wife enjoyed the finest clothes, lavish jewelry, and regular spa days. At least three or four times a year he would take the family on vacations whenever the kids were out of school. They were regulars at all the big theme parks and resorts. They didn't want for anything and were living the American dream.

But there was a side of Derek no one knew about. A very dark and sinister side. Derek had another web business. Only this business was on the dark web, a place not meant for the faint of heart.

This dark side of him started in college as he was learning about programming computers. He made extra money while in school, building and repairing machines. He also built and maintained websites for local small businesses. He was fairly well known in the local IT world. Then one day he received an anonymous email with an invite and a link.

Hesitantly, he clicked on the link that opened a PDF file.

The file read: Welcome. Someone close to you has extended you an invite to access the deep web. If you decide to accept, please download the Water Fox browser and go to the IP address in the enclosed document.

Derek found himself on a server filled with different chat rooms, mainly geared toward hackers. Over the next year or so he made friends with several other users while learning his way around in the dark corners of the web. He was learning about hacking and just how much money could be made from it. From time to time, he received invitations to different servers where transactions were made for things that were highly illegal, such as depraved products and services. He stumbled upon a chat room where the discussion centered around something called "long pig" and was amazed how much people were willing to pay for the product.

Then he discovered the product under discussion was human meat. At first he was repulsed and sickened by the idea. How could people do this? Eat human flesh... And where did the sellers find what they sold? You can't just go around killing people only to butcher them and sell the meat to those who want to eat other people. This troubled Derek for a long time. He tried to put it out of his mind as he moved on with his life.

When he was a senior in college he met Sally, and it was love at first sight. They were inseparable for the two years they dated while Derek started several online businesses that made him enormous amounts of money. Also, unknown to anyone else, his activities on the dark web made him quite wealthy. He only accepted payments in BitCoin and by then his wallet was worth several million dollars.

Every once in a while, he would drop into the chat room where they were buying and selling human body parts, and over time the idea became less disturbing. Meanwhile, he and Sally married, moved into the house outside of New York City, and were expecting their first child. Derek had a number of investment accounts and would regularly travel into the city to go over his portfolio with the account managers. It was on one of these trips that he began to notice a significant number of homeless people in certain areas of town. It got the wheels turning in his head. He formulated a plan.

Soon he purchased a small, two bedroom home much closer to the city to remodel inside and out. He furnished it with moderately priced furniture. But the most important renovations were to one of the bedrooms. He found a contractor on the dark web that would do the work and not ask any questions. The room was sealed up airtight. The window was replaced with triple-pane plexiglass and sealed shut. Bars were installed on the outside of all windows.

A trap door was added in the floor at the foot of the bed, with a slide that led to an autopsy table in the basement. He also had a louver system in the HVAC vent installed which could be shut to finish making the room airtight. Tubing in the vent could deliver nitrogen gas to the room. The control panel that activated the door lock, vent louvers, and gas delivery system was hidden behind a picture next to the bedroom door. In the light fixture above the bed, he installed a hidden camera that connected to his phone so he could watch what was going on in the room.

The basement was set up like a butcher shop, with two large freezers, a band saw, a meat slicer, and a meat grinder. An oven was installed to dry bones before they were ground into powder.

After about six months of prep work, the kill house was finally finished and ready to go.

Three days later, around sundown, Derek drove into the city on the hunt. He had already made note of areas where the homeless seemed to congregate. Trolling these areas for his first victim took about three hours but eventually he spotted a likely target. In a narrow alley between two buildings, he spotted a lone figure sleeping next to a dumpster and using a small backpack for a pillow. Derek pulled over and cautiously walked over to his victim. When he got closer, he could tell it was a younger man who appeared to be in his early to mid-thirties. Trying not to startle the sleeping man, he said softly, "Hey buddy, you ok?"

Despite his efforts, the man quickly opened his eyes with a start.

"Yeah, whatta ya want? I'm trying to sleep here."

"Relax, friend. I was concerned, I just wanted to check on you to make sure you're alright."

"I'm fine, just leave me alone and let me sleep."

"Hold on, can I just ask you a couple of questions?"

"You a cop?"

"No, just a concerned citizen."

The man rolled his eyes. "Then get the hell outta here."

Derek thought maybe he should just leave but this guy looked perfect. Not fat and not too skinny. "How about if I give you a twenty?"

The man glanced up and looked him in the eyes. "Alright, sure, if it'll make you shut up and go away."

"Fair enough," Derek said, handing him the bill. "What's your name?"

"Gonna name your kid after me?"

Derek chuckled in spite of himself. "Just trying to get to know a bit about your situation, that's all."

"Carl."

"Ok, Carl, how long have been on the streets?"

"About a year."

"Sorry to hear that. When's the last time you had a bath and a decent meal?"

"Got some scraps out of a dumpster a couple days ago. As far as a bath, I don't remember."

"What did you do for a living. How did you wind up on the streets?"

Carl's face darkened. "Getting a little personal there, bud. You one of those bleeding heart types? What do you care?"

"Trust me, I'm trying to figure out a way to help out guys like you. I know things are rough out here and would like to see guys like you get back on your feet.

Carl considered this, then said, "Since you're so interested and all, I worked in building maintenance. Company went out of business and I was barely making enough to get by anyway, so before I could find another job I lost my apartment and my car."

"You couldn't get unemployment?"

"Benefits ran out, tough economy. Now if you're done, I'd like to get some sleep."

"I'd like to help you out, Carl. You see, I own a couple of businesses and I'm always looking for reliable workers. Think you'd be interested in working for me?"

"Mister, this is the weirdest recruiting pitch I've ever heard. What's the catch?"

"Frankly, I'm tired of putting out ads and having kids show up with no experience and less brains. I was driving by and saw you here and thought I'd try a little experiment. If you work out, I might be willing to look for other guys that have gotten a raw deal, see if I can help a few out. It might not be much, but it's a start."

"You gonna come back in the morning and pick me up?"

"No, I own a place near here. I thought you could get cleaned up there and get a good night's sleep, make a fresh start tomorrow. What do you say?"

"I say, where do I sign up?"

"Great, grab your stuff and I'll tell you what I have in mind."

On the way to the house, Derek told Carl that he had several rental homes and needed a maintenance man. He would be staying at one of the houses that was unoccupied at the moment.

He offered Carl a meal, and the guy said it had been a long time since he'd had fried chicken. So Derek pulled into a fried chicken place and ordered a bucket. Carl devoured it as soon as they pulled out of the parking lot. By the time they arrived at the house, he had polished off three drumsticks, two thighs, and a breast, along with downing a large drink. All without realizing he was eating his last meal.

They soon pulled onto the driveway of a small, unassuming house in a quiet neighborhood. Derek shut off the car. "Come on, I'll show you your new place."

The two men entered the house and Derek flipped on the lights. "Well, this is your new home, at least for a while."

Carl's eyes darted around the room, taking in the tidy normalcy of it. "Nice."

"Thanks, I just got done remodeling it. Let me show you around."

Derek gave Carl a quick tour of the house, then suggested he take a shower before bed. Carl gladly accepted the offer and took the longest shower he had ever taken, savoring every minute. When he was done, he came out of the bathroom in the robe that Derek left for him. Derek sat at the kitchen table with a laptop open in front of him.

"Beer?" he asked.

"Absolutely," Carl responded, trying not to appear too eager.

Derek pulled two brown bottles from the fridge and set one down on the table. He twisted the top off the other and took a long swig.

Carl sat down, picked up his bottle and did the same. "Man, this tastes good. It's been a long time since I've had a drink."

"There's more in the fridge if you want another one later. There's breakfast stuff in there too." He pulled a key from his pocket and laid it on the table. "I got a little work to finish and then I'll head out. I'll be back around seven to pick you up and have you sign a contract for the job. Sound good?"

"Sure thing. If it's all the same to you, I think I'll hit the sack. Can't wait to sleep in a real bed again, it's been a long time."

Carl finished his beer then headed to the bedroom. Derek tapped on the app connected to the hidden camera in the bedroom on his phone. He watched Carl slip under the covers and turn out the light. Derek packed up the laptop, and by the time he checked the phone feed again Carl was snoring softly. Satisfied that his victim was fast asleep, he put his plan into action. He quietly walked to the panel beside the bedroom door, engaged the system that controlled the doors, and secured the man in the room.

He pulled the lever to the gas, filling it the room with nitrogen, all the while watching from his phone. The man woke up coughing and gasping for breath. He jumped out of bed and rushed to the door, only to find it was locked. He tried to break the window, only to find that it couldn't be broken. He begged at the door, pleading to be released. The more he exerted himself, the faster he used up what little oxygen was left in the room. It didn't take long before the lack of air overtook him, and he passed out in a heap in front of the door.

Derek waited and watched until he was sure the man was dead. He then pulled the lever once more, closing the valve, then flipped another switch opening a vent that led outside. He waited some time before entering the room once he knew it was safe. Derek pulled the dead man over to the trap door and pushed him down the slide that led to the autopsy table in the basement.

He met the body down in the basement, and there in front of him was the next and most difficult challenge. He had never butchered an animal, much less a human being. He'd already researched videos on the dark web for a bit of help. The first time would be difficult, but it would get easier, he was certain. He saw the victim not as a fellow human being, but as a means to an end, anything to help ease his conscience. After five hours, and a couple times pausing to vomit, he made it through the process. All the meat was packaged and in the freezer. The bones were in the oven drying out. He would later grind them down into powder and dispose of the remnants in the garden outside.

He conducted his new enterprise in the basement. He named himself "the facilitator" and listed his product for sale under "long pig" like all the rest. It only took a few days to sell everything in the freezer, making him a hundred and fifty thousand dollars. With such a good payoff, he'd repeat the whole process a couple of times a month maybe. It didn't take long before his new BitCoin wallet was worth millions.

As time went on, the butchering became easier and faster. He could process a body in just over two hours. This side business went on for a year until he finally slipped up. Someone saw a friend get into the car with Derek and notified the police. It turned out rumors had been going on for months about people in the homeless community going missing but the police had turned up nothing.

An investigation began, assigned to a detective named Smith. He pulled the rest of the reports and start looking into the cases for a connection. He spoke to several people who worked at a shelter in the area, and found out about several homeless individuals who had mysteriously stopped coming to the shelter. Three were last seen talking to a well-dressed gentleman in a late-model silver BMW. One witness even had a partial license plate of the vehicle.

Alarm bells went off in Detective Smith's head, and he knew he had to find out what was going on. Could this be someone genuinely helping people get off the streets? Or could they be dealing with a serial killer targeting the city's homeless population.

A check of the model and make of the car, along with the partial plate, led Detective Smith to one Derek White, a thirty-seven-year-old, independently wealthy, businessman who made a lucrative living as an internet programmer/entrepreneur.

The following day, Smith made the hour-long drive to White's home. Upon pulling into the driveway, he made note of both the silver BMW and a black Lincoln Navigator. The interview lasted an hour and, naturally, Derek denied any knowledge of the disappearances. When asked about the two vehicles, he confirmed the BMW was his and the Navigator belonged to his wife. White seemed to have all the right answers to the detective's questions. But Smith wasn't a hundred percent convinced. His gut told him Derek was hiding something.

He looked into Derek's tax returns and compared them with his spending, which was well above his means. Red flag. A search of property records provided information on his home outside of the city and his condo in Florida, along with a very small house in a quiet neighborhood on the outskirts of town.

Service data for the home showed electric, water, and internet services. All billed and paid online. Smith and another detective decided to visit the house and check it out. Upon arriving, there were no vehicles in the driveway. Several knocks on the door elicited no response. The mailbox held only junk mail.

Smith noticed the bars on all the windows and a pricy security door. All the house's windows were frosted and barred, denying him a look inside, odd for a low crime neighborhood. During a quick canvas of the surrounding homes, neighbors admitted to rarely seeing anybody at the house.

The detective organized a stakeout and the next evening after dark, Derek's Lincoln pulled into the driveway. Derek stepped out of the driver's side of the vehicle and from the passenger side, a scruffy-looking middle-aged man stepped out. Together they entered the residence.

The house was quiet for hours, and then Derek left the house and drove away but the other man was nowhere to be seen. Detective Smith and his partner knocked on the door but there was no answer. Having probable cause to believe the man inside might be in distress, they called for back up and broke into the house.

A search turned up nothing unusual other than the fact that the man who had entered the house earlier was completely absent. The only thing they found was a nearly empty bottle of beer on the nightstand in the main bedroom. When they came across the locked basement door, they broke it down and were shocked to see the blood encrusted butcher tools, 2 freezers full of human body parts, bags of white powder, and a fresh set of bones drying in an oven. Tin cans containing silver and gold jewelry and teeth with gold fillings were placed neatly on shelves and there was a small kiln that had been used to melt down the precious metals.

A separate unit was sent to Derek's house to arrest him while the detectives called in a forensic team. A search of the house found both the trapdoor and the control panel, leading the officers to slowly piece together the events that had taken place in this elaborately designed kill house.

But the jackpot of the investigation was Derek's laptop, which the police confiscated that night and that forensics studied with a fine-toothed comb. Lucky for the police, but unlucky for Derek, he'd kept meticulous records of all his transactions. Dates, addresses, and names.

Investigators found DNA from at least a dozen victims in the basement. Even though they believed Derek had murdered many more than that, he never confessed and was charged with only twelve counts of murder. His sentence was to life without parole, but the investigation was far from over.

Detective Smith had Derek's clientele list but each name had to be investigated and the names were coded. It took months, but eventually Smith got his hands on the full and accurate list. One name in particular jumped out at him. He handed the list to his partner.

"Is that who I think it is?" his partner asked in disbelief.

"Yep, Alexander Wilcox, billionaire and extreme adventurer." He grinned like a wolf on the hunt. "Oh boy, is this going to be tricky, but so very satisfying."

How Dark Can It Get?
By Nora B. Peevy

One.

Linny and Kirsten sat in their booth at McDonald's, sipping their ice coffees and looking at their watches. It was almost 9pm. The boys were a no-show. They shook their near identical blonde ponytails and adjusted their matching gold chokers with their initials.

"That's what we get for going on HearthThrob, Lin," Kirsten said.

"No. That's what we get for settling too soon. That Marco guy was hot, but I knew something was off when he asked us to talk offline in WhatsApp right away. Dead giveaway he's a creepozoid." She rolled her green eyes and sat up straighter as the door dinged and two tall, dark, and handsome men in suits came in. "Hey, Kirsten. D'ya think it's them?"

They both sat up straighter and adjusted their tops to reveal what little cleavage their seventeen-year-old bodies had given them, quickly checking their teeth in their smartphone reflections before putting them in their purses.

"They're coming this way." Linny took another sip of her coffee."Excuse me," one of the men said, "Are you Linny and Kirsten?"

"Yes." They smiled at each other, trying not to squeal.

"Daniel and Marco asked us to pick you up and take you to their place. Will you please come with us?" The taller of the two beckoned. The other looked slightly bored, as if he had somewhere else to be. He kept looking at his watch and around the joint, taking note of how many people were there, which was zero except for the night crew.

Linny and Kirsten had followed the boys' instructions carefully. Dress understated, go to an empty restaurant, order something ordinary. And do not talk to the help. Yup. They'd followed the rules and now they were going to be rewarded by their dreamboats of two boyfriends. They tried to restrain their squealing as they got in the black SUV with tinted windows waiting outside for them. The locks snapped and the girls had time to look around. The ceiling of the car was a starry night scene.

"This is pretty sweet. Tell the guys thanks for picking us up."

Silence.

"Do you know where you're taking us?"

Silence.

"Hey, Kirsten. They're not saying anything." Linny slid down in her seat, an uneasy feeling growing in the pit of her stomach. She started to hyperventilate and suddenly the SUV seemed too small. "Can you pull over to the side of the road a minute, please? I think I'm going to be sick." Linny kept her head down between her knees and Kirsten rubbed the back of her friend's neck.

"My friend said she's going to upchuck, morons! A little consideration?" That's when Kirsten started checking for the window controls or the door locks and found ... nothing. "Hey, why aren't there any door or window controls back here, huh? Is this some kind of extra child protection? I'm getting a bad feeling about this. Umm ... date's off. You can let me and my friend off at the next stoplight. We'll just call a cab. No worries. Comprendo?" She paused. "Hey, why aren't you answering us?"

One of the creepy guys leaned over, grinned, and puffed a circle of cigar smoke at them. He turned up the radio. It played some Latin pop neither girl knew the words to.

"Kirsten! This is bad. Really bad. I think we made a mistake. A bad mistake. I wanna go home," Linny whined, snot and tears running down her pretty, tanned face.

"Shh! They're on their phones. I'm trying to hear what they're saying over this shitty music." A beat. "Damn it. I can't hear anything with that noise. We're gonna be okay, Linny. I promise. We're gonna be okay. Just lay your head in my lap and take deep breaths, okay? Calm down. Remember how my mom always says getting upset in stressful situations never helps?" She stroked her friend's hair. "Hey, hey Linny."

Linny was now silent as a doll.

"Pretend we're going to a party. That's probably where we're going anyway, right? I mean ... these guys obviously have money and those two dudes we were talking to were always bragging about partying on the weekends. It'll be fun. We'll go to the party and we'll call your mom and dad from there, okay? Easy peasy. Nothing to worry about. And maybe we'll have fun and even have a story to tell rich bitch Tiffany and all her other clown shit friends at school on Monday, right? Yeah. Monday. I have a calc test on Monday, don't you? Ms. Francis. She's the worst, isn't she?" Kirsten continued to ramble on about anything and everything as the SUV turned down darker and deeper roads that were less paved, until finally, the two girls were jounced around like a bunch of watermelons in the back of a truck.

"I-I can't breathe. N-need my inhaler," wheezed Linny.

"Oh shit! Linny! Do you have it with you? Where is it?" Kirsten rolled her friend over on the seat, frantically searching her jean shorts pockets until she located the yellow rescuer inhaler. She popped off the top and shoved it in Linny's mouth. "Okay, two big puffs coming. And inhale!" *Puff.* "And inhale again." *Puff.* Linny rolled off Kirsten's lap to the floor of the vehicle and Kirsten hit her head on the back of the headrest, losing the rescue inhaler. "Nice driving, asshole! She's got asthma, you dingus. If you even care!"

The door opened and a gun was pointed right at her chest. "Whoa, whoa, whoa! This is not what I was picturing for a first date.

Okay, okay. I'll play nice, okay? So will Linny. She's on the floor. She's just a little wheezy. Linny get up," Kirsten hissed at her prone friend, who was slowly adjusting herself upright and also gasped at the sight of the guns.

"What's with the gun show, cowboy? Did Marco put you up to this? Is this some kind of prank?"

"This is no prank. You're here at the request of The Five Dragon Tails."

"The what?"

"All you need to know is you've unfortunately stumbled into something you shouldn't have by playing around on the dark web."

"Nuh-nuh-nuh-nuh." Linny shook her head.

"Wait. We weren't even on the dark web. We were on the dating site, HeartThrob," Kirsten said.

"Which leads to the dark web sometimes for stupid women dumb enough to swipe left on men too good to be true.

"You mean Marco isn't real? And his friend Daniel isn't real either?"

"Oh, they're real alright, but they're more interested in your father's investments in Ascension Health Associates and health files. They want DNA files on their customers so they can work on their human cloning project. They're much more interested in that than they are in two bratty teenagers like you. You do as we say and we might let you live. They want the ransom money for you two." The two unnamed gentlemen laughed and roughly yanked them out of the car, frog marching them to a dirty shed in the middle of nowhere.

The shed opened to two grimy mattresses crusted with semen, blood, and other unidentified fluids. To the left of the mattresses was a cage tall enough for a Great Burnese Mountain Dog. Kirsten and Linny were tossed rudely to the ground inside and the door slammed and locked behind them. They crawled to the bars and started crying.

"Please let us out. Our fathers will give us anything you ask."

"That's exactly the idea. They'll give us anything we ask when they see what we're going to do to you."

"And just what are you going to do to us, you disgusting thugs? We are American citizens and we have rights, you know," Linny screamed.

The darker haired of the two cackled then came to the front of the cage. He took his cigarette out of his mouth and put it to Kirsten's pretty unmarred hand. The sweet scent of apples burning filled the air and Linny and Kirsten both wanted to vomit. Kirsten's hand felt like a thousand ants were biting it at once. She cried out defiantly. "You won't get away with this!"

"Yes, we will. And for starters, we're going to teach you little American girls how to cry pretty for the camera."

Through their tears, that's when Linny and Kirsten saw a video camera set up in front of the dirty mattresses. They started bawling harder.

"That's a good start, but you should save your crying for the camera and what we have planned for you later. Right now, eat." He passed two burnt grilled cheese sandwiches through the cage's slats and two apple juice boxes. The girls took them, unaware they were drugged. They were so hungry they scarfed everything down, and soon were sound asleep.

Two.

Linny was the first to wake up. She found herself tied up on a sweat-stained mattress, facing a camera. The red light was off, so it wasn't recording yet, but it was facing her and that was enough to give her the creeps.

"Help! Somebody help me! Help!" She cried over and over.

Slowly, Kirsten came to in the dog cage, her muscles aching from having no room to stretch. Her eyes became huge when she saw her friend stripped and tied on the mattress in the middle of the room. A bunch of studio lights clicked on by themselves. Linny blinked, blinded by the hot lights. She struggled against her binds. "Please let me go! I haven't done anything! Please! I'll do anything you want. Just please let me go!" She fell onto her side, weeping uncontrollably.

"Let her go, you creepy bastards! Let my friend go! You don't know who our fathers are or what they're capable of." Kirsten beat the meaty flesh of her palms against the bars of the dog cage as hard as she could. The tinny echo fell on silent ears.

A door opened and black dress shoes walked over to the cage.

"Indeed, we do know what your fathers are capable of and who they are. Ascension Health Associates. They're worth millions. And you are worth millions. And they'll give us the DNA profiles we ask for to save their precious daughters, won't they?"

The tall, lanky businessman in the crisp suit bent down. He was now all right angles. He smelled like her father's aftershave and the scent made Kirsten want to cry it was so familiar.

"Please, just let us go and we'll get you anything you want. Please." Tears ran down Kirsten's now dirt-stained cheeks. Her breathing came in great huffs.

"Awww. Now where would the fun be in that? You girls are going to give us what we want anyway. And we're going to teach you a lesson about not talking to strangers on the internet and going to

107

meet them in public before you really know who they are. *Tsk, tsk, tsk.* Didn't your parents teach you anything?" His rictus grin lit his eyes in a maniacal funhouse way and he tilted his head to the right like a parrot studying an ant. "Miller! Turn the camera on! Let the games begin!" He rose and clapped the dust off the knees of his dark suit as he cackled. "Let the games begin," he whispered at Kirsten, his fingers trailing on the bars of the cage, causing a hollow sound that rang out in the empty room.

Linny and Kirsten looked about them in the now well-lit shed. They saw tables off to the right with various surgical instruments, a chainsaw, a meat carving knife, rubbing alcohol, salt, and other household items. They shivered and their eyes met. Linny's bottom lip quivered and her nose was running, but she couldn't wipe it because her hands were bound behind her. In front of the blood and semen-stained mattress she'd been slung on was a great scarred and bloodstained wooden chair with thick leather arm and leg restraints.

"Miller, why don't you escort our young visitor to the chair for round one, please." Guy one gestured to the chair and then got behind the camera, adjusting the lens and then coming out from behind the tripod to adjust the lights as needed.

"Please state your full name and age for your lovely web audience."

"M-my audience?"

"Yes. This is being livestreamed and recorded. You have thousands of followers watching your show today. You're so lucky. Each and every one of them will have a chance to call in and participate. Isn't that exciting? So, state your name and your age for the camera. And try to look pretty."

"W-wait. I never agreed to participate in anything. What am I participating in?"

The tall man in the dark suit came out from behind the camera and backhanded Linny. "*Tsk, tsk, tsk.* I apologize for the rocky start to our viewers. It appears we have a camera-shy participant. Without further ado," he gritted his teeth and glared at Linny, "please state your full name and age for your viewers' pleasure."

Linny's lip was split and bleeding. "Li-linny Del Monacco. Age s-seventeen."

"Ah, so young and nubile, isn't she, audience? It's nice to get a fresh and ripe one every once and a while." The tall and dark-suited man stepped out and grabbed her tit. "Yesss ... so firm. If you could only feel how plump and firm she is. She's going to be a fun one."

"Stop it!" Linny struggled to protect herself but couldn't get away. Instead, she sobbed harder, her head down.

"Awww. Look, the little slut wants to cry now when just a few hours ago she was ready to meet a complete stranger off HearthThrob named 'Marco.'" Probably would have spread her legs for him, am I right audience? Am I? A little vixen like this?" He took his left hand and grabbed her crotch suggestively. "Yes, I do think the kitty is straining to be let free. Should we? Let's see. I'll wait for the callers to light up the lines. Miller, if we get three calls, we'll play free the kitty, okay?" The tall man kept his hand firmly on Linny's crotch while she struggled to scoot away and he chuckled all the while. "No use in struggling, dear child. It'll go faster if you just give in, and you might even like it." He winked.

The phones lit up, red lights blazing in a row.

"Boss, that's more than three. I think they want to free the kitty."

"And so we shall." The tall man strode over to the two tables to select his tool of play. "What should we use, Miller? My hands? Yours? Or ... something a little more creative for our viewers?"

"Something a little more creative," Miller said, leering in front of the camera for a second or two.

Kirsten screamed loudly and hid behind her curtain of blond hair.

"Shut up, bitch! We haven't forgotten about you," Torres taunted, running the large stainless-steel scissors along the bars of the cage so they echoed in the empty, dank shed. *Clink, clink, clink.*

Linny tasted bile in the back of her throat. Her chest heaved and she glared at her captor as he approached her. "You don't scare me," she said through gritted teeth, tasting her own sweat on her upper lip. She wanted to piss herself, she was so scared, but she wouldn't dare give them the satisfaction. She held her head up straight and stared into the camera, emotionless.

Torres began cutting the buttons off her shirt and she could feel the cold steel against her skin with every slicing motion. She wanted to kick and punch and fight and scream. Where was her father? Her mother? Somebody? Anybody? They had to notice she was gone by now. A single tear ran down her face.

"Aw, look. She's crying," Torres said as he ripped her shirt off her with dramatic flair, exposing her lacy pink bra beneath. He snipped both straps and her breasts hung free, strawberry sized areolas tensing in the cold of the shed. He grabbed a nipple and tugged harshly. She gasped. He slapped her across the face one way and then the other. "You like it rough? Do you?" he asked as he continued to slap her face and her breasts until they were raw and red, yanking viciously on her nipples, pulling them like putty a few inches away from her body until she felt they would bleed and wouldn't stretch any further.

"Linny! Stop! You're hurting her," sobbed Kirsten.

"Miller, will you shut that dumb bitch in the cage up. Her time will come. Shut her up! Now!"

Miller opened the cage and roughly tugged Kirsten by her hair, until he could sufficiently gag her. Kirsten felt suffocated and tasted cotton in her mouth. She tried to breathe calmly so as not to hyperventilate and kept her eyes on her friend, but Linny wouldn't look at her. Linny leaned forward in the chair against her restraints like a limp rag doll, breathing heavily, her hair hiding her face, sweat dripping down her back.

"Now for some more fun. Let's see what the audience wants. Caller number six gets the lucky choice of deciding whether we should whip little Linny first or pull out her fingernails before cutting off her jean shorts. Which shall it be? Let's light up those phones, people! We haven't got all night. Oh, wait, but we do," he cackled. He turned and gripped Linny's cheeks, scrunching her lips into a pout and kissing her, slipping his slimy tongue—which tasted of the taco he'd had for dinner before he'd picked her up—past her lips.

Miller chuckled as he answered the phone line. "Caller number six?" Pause. "Yes?" Pause. "Alright then. Thank you for calling in."

"What did they say, Miller my man?

"They said you should give the girl a pair of pretty stripes across her chest before we see what's down below." He smiled wolfishly, his lips cracking and bleeding. "You want me to hold her, so she doesn't struggle?"

"Noooooo! You can't do this! Please!" Linny attempted to claw out of her restraints, but Miller held her shoulders back against the hard wood. His hands were rough, dry, and skinny.

Torres sauntered over to the table like the snake he was and grabbed a black cat o' nine tails. He smacked it in his hand in front of the girl's eyes and she jumped for good effect in front of the camera. He slowly ran the leather down her cleavage to the button of her jean shorts. "So sorry I have to do this, darling, but duty calls," he apologized as he raised the cat high above his head and the leather came down across her breasts with a great *snap!* that bit into her tender young flesh, leaving a long red welt that oozed blood. Her blood spattered to the floor in fat droplets as he raised his arm and the cat came down in the opposite direction, drawing more of her blood. She wheezed in pain, snot flowing freely from her nose now and she bellowed like a wounded animal.

"Awwww. Will you look at those pretty titties. All red and ripped now." Torres cupped them in his hands. "Such a shame when good flesh goes to waste." He bent down in front of them. "Let daddy kiss them and make them better." His slimy tongue flicked out and roughly licked the blood off her boobs. She shuddered and felt the vomit crawling up the back of her throat.

"Have you had enough yet, darling?"

"P-please stop hurting me. I'll be good. I'll do whatever you want."

"Awww. I wish I could, but you see, your daddy hasn't called in with the money and the information we asked for. So I guess we're going to continue playing a bit longer, you and me. You're having fun, aren't you?" He held her head up by her long hair. "Aren't you?"

Linny only blubbered in response.

"I said 'aren't you?' Answer me when I'm talking to you!" He backhanded her and her head rocketed against the wood of the tall chair.

"Yes."

"Yes what?"

"Yes sir," she blubbered.

"Now that's better. Because you were such a respectful girl, I'm going to give you a reward. I'm going to let you suck me off before I take you from behind like a real woman, and you're going to like it. And if you don't, you're going to pretend you like it anyway. And if you dare to even think about hurting me, you just remember that I have a knife to your throat, little kitten. Now open wide and don't bite down and remember to suck me off real hard and swallow for the camera."

Linny gagged at the sour taste and smell of him sliding in and out, tapping the back of her throat and violating her this way. When he was done, she swallowed and Torres grinned like a snake. "That's my girl. I like a girl who knows how to suck. And you don't even need any training. You already give A+ head. You must have had a lot of practice with the boys." He winked and zipped up his pants.

He turned to the cameras. "Next caller gets to pick what happens next to this delightfully accommodating slut."

Tears ran down Linny's face. Her mascara and eyeliner were smudged. She had raccoon eyes. Her hair stuck to her hot and sweaty face. Beads of sweat dripped down the small of her back and she itched. She shifted in her seat, struggling to change her position and not think about how bad she wanted to scratch. Her breasts burned where she'd been whipped, but worse was the humiliation she felt and the anger welling up within her like a constant companion. She was going to survive this, and he was going to get his.

"Miller, the phones are lighting up. Why don't you pick up? You schmuck! Sleeping on the job, and just when things are getting interesting too. Geez." Torres leered at the camera again. His entire head was drenched in sweat. He smelled rank, like a goat.

"Uh huh. Uh huh." Miller nodded. He held a receiver to his ear. "Sure thing, boss. You got it."

Beat.

Miller put the receiver down.

"Well, what excitement do we have in store for our girl now?"

"Caller said she should lose her fingernails."

"NOOO!" Linny struggled in the chair, howling at the top of her lungs. "You motherfuckers!"

"Ain't my orders, sweet cheeks," Torres said as he held her face and popped her cheek with his right hand. "It's what your audience wants. They just want to see the pretty lady perform. Look into the camera and smile."

"No."

"Smile, bitch." Torres forced Linny's mouth into a smile as she sobbed. "That's better. Only happy faces on camera. Now I'm going to do this for the audience. It's not me, but I gotta do it," he jeered. "Well. I might like it a little bit. Miller, could you give me those pliers over there?"

"No. N-no. No. NOOOOO!" Linny screamed and bucked, but she was buckled tightly to the wooden chair by the straps at her wrists and ankles. There was nowhere for her to go.

"*Shhh. Shhh.*" Torres stroked her hand. "You have such pretty hands. Like a butterfly's wings. Such a shame we have to break them. *Tsk, tsk, tsk.* If only you'd stayed at home where you belonged, but you had to come out tonight. You just had to come out to meet..." He pulled a fingernail out with the pliers and she screamed. "Ol'..." he yanked out another one, "Marco." And he pulled another one. "Are we having fun yet?"

By now Linny was drooling and her eyes were rolling back in her head. Her breathing came rapid and shallow. Her skin was pallid. Her head drooped to the right.

"Awww. It looks like our songbird is fading a bit. We need to make sure she stays with us for the rest of the show. The show's not over until daddy says it's over. We're just getting started."

Kirsten was blubbering and shaking like a piece of paper in the wind in the cage. Her eyes were huge and brown. Torres walked over. "What? You have a hard time watching your friend suffer? You want to take her place?"

Kirsten quickly shook her head. "I didn't think so. I've got something special planned for you, though." He leaned against the dog cage for a minute. "It's a shame. Your daddies could stop all this with just a phone call and a quick deposit of information and cash. I guess they don't care about you the way you think they do, huh? Such a pity. Such a shame, girlie." He bent down and took hold of her hand that was grasping the bars and squeezed it tightly, just to watch her flinch. Then he laughed maniacally.

"What do you say I bring you a furry friend to keep you company in there? Hmmm? Would you like that?"

Kirsten made a muffled response and shrank back from the bars, shivering.

"Oh, don't worry. He doesn't bite. He's more of a lover, but only when I command him to be."

Another muffled plea escaped her. She shook her head violently.

"I think your friend Linny will find out soon enough. Is she a virgin? I certainly hope so. It'll make this even more exciting for Rocco when it happens. Miller! Bring in Rocco! And get that girl out of the chair. Give her something to eat and drink. I want to keep her strength up. I'm not done with her yet. We're going to make this last as long as we can."

"Yes, boss."

Miller disappeared and came back a moment later with a Great Burnese Mountain Dog, well-groomed and well-hung. He escorted the dog into the cage and slammed the door shut. Ten minutes later, he came back with two subs wrapped in butcher paper, two bags of chips, and two cans of Sprite. He tossed them in the cage and then went to fetch Linny off the wooden chair.

She shied away from Miller's touch when he went to unbuckle her.

As he bent to unbuckle her legs he said, "You should just do what he wants."

"Why?"

"Because it's only going to get worse from here on out. I've seen him do things to girls that you couldn't even imagine. He gets off on it. It's more than a job for him."

"Why are you doing this?"

"Because I owe a debt. Quit asking so many questions. Get in the cage and eat and rest while you can, okay?"

"Miller, are you talking with our guests? What have I said about talking with our guests?"

Miller flinched. "Don't talk to the meat."

"That's right. Get her in the cage with the other girl. We're going to put on a really good show in half an hour. I already have a client who's paid top dollar to come and sit in personally to watch." Torres leered. "Guess daddy dearest doesn't care about his sweet meat there after all. That's okay. Sooner or later the hospital will cave and give us their patients' DNA samples. They can't go on like this for more than another day or two without too many people asking questions and it getting leaked to the news." He slapped Miller on the back. "We're gonna be rich and the Chinese are gonna clone the hell out of a bunch of Americans."

Torres walked over to the cage and knelt down in front of the two girls and the dog. "Enjoy your meal, honeys. It's probably going to be the last one you have. Either you won't have teeth before the night is over or you'll be dead. We'll see what the viewers want."

Kirsten spat at him. "You're a real piece of work, you know that?" She scowled.

"Oh, baby. I do know that and soon you will too, but first I'm going to let old Rocco break you in for me.

"What?! You can't be serious. Please. I d-didn't mean it. I'll do anything to get out of here. I'll be a g-good girl. I'll—"

"Oh, I know you're going to be a very good girl for daddy. A verrry good girl, aren't you? You're going to do everything I tell you to do because you want to go home to your big mansion and your bitch cunny of a mother, right? You wish she were here right now to cuddle you and make things better." He laughed, reached in between the bars and squeezed her right boob hard. "Finish eating. Second act starts soon. I'm sure Rocco will love you. Won't you boy?"

Rocco stood on all fours, which was a feat, considering how tall he was and how small the dog cage was. He wagged his tail in satisfaction as Torres patted his head through the cage bars.

Kirsten bawled, her mascara streaking.

"Aw now, don't cry. Rocco will be gentle with you. He's gentle with all the new girls, aren't you, Rocco?" Torres pulled a filmy red teddy out of his back pants pocket. "I almost forgot. Here's your costume."

"I'm not wearing that," Kirsten sniffled.

"You are, if you want to go home alive. Your choice. You can go in a box, if you want to. Means nothing to me. I just care about the money and the information. Now. Put. It. On," he said through gritted teeth as he continued to smile that creepy smile that made Kirsten want to crawl inside of her own skin and disappear.

"Kirsten, please just do what he asks. I can't. I just can't." Linny burst out crying. "For me, okay? I can't do anymore right now and maybe our dads will see this and call."

Kirsten's tears rolled silently down her face now in large rivulets of black makeup. "As if. My dad probably is having dinner with Evelyn tonight and won't be back until late. I doubt he'll even check his cell phone. And do we even think this is being broadcasted on the news?"

"Oh, my pet. It is. Just not the normal news. It's being broadcast on the dark web news for all our clients that have eclectic tastes. You two are proving to be a honeypot for us. So put the damn teddy on or I'll put it on for you and you won't like what happens before I dress you up, dearest." Torres winked at Kirsten. Miller, standing behind Kirsten, gave her a pitiful smile and stared at the floor.

"Miller, go check the equipment and make sure we're ready to roll. Then get Candy in here for Rocco."

"Wh-who's Candy," Kirsten asked as she stripped out of her clothes and put on the flimsy red teddy. It barely covered her ass and left nothing to the imagination. She was cold and her nipples stood erect.

"Mmm. So nubile and perky. The viewers are going to love you. I'm going to let Rocco warm you up before the main course. That's me." Torres winked. "And Candy is ... let's just say ... Rocco's fluffer."

"Wh-what's a fluffer?" Kirsten's eyes got bigger as a tall straight-haired blond in dominatrix boots and a cage dress opened the cage and removed Rocco.

"A fluffer is someone who gets the showman ready for the main act."

"And wh-what's the main act?" Kirsten gulped, having somewhat of an idea, but hoping it wasn't what she was thinking. She clung to Linny tightly.

"The main act is Rocco with you. Are you a virgin?"

"What the fuck? I'm not fucking a dog!"

"But are you a virgin?"

"That's none of your business." Kirsten clung tighter to Linny who was sniveling against Kirsten's arm.

"As a matter of fact, it is. Because if you're a virgin and we announce that on camera, the callers could have different suggestions than normal. So, I will ask you one more time before I check for myself. Are. You. A. Virgin?" Torres looked pissed enough to eat iron.

"Y-yes."

"Aww. Will you look at that? Daddy dearest is going to be so proud of his little girl taking it like a champion." Torres cackled. "Miller, she's a virgin. Put it out on the chat board and see what type of requests come in for the big performance. Anal, vaginal, or oral. Or perhaps all three? Or maybe we cut a hole in her stomach and Rocco takes her that way? Make that option. And hurry up before our little performer has too much time to think about it. Great," said Torres.

He opened the cage door and yanked Kirsten out by her arm. She howled in protest and dug her heels in but found herself being dragged by her hair, her knees scuffed and bloodied on the cement floor of the shed, to the filthy mattress in front of the camera.

"Miller, roll the camera." Torres kept a firm grip on Kirsten as he put a collar and a leash on her. She cried uncontrollably, snot running down her face. "Oh, stop your sobbing. It's so unsexy and we'll lose millions if you keep that up. If you don't stop it, I'm bound to think up something even worse for you, which I still might. I have at least six warm bodies waiting backstage, ready for a nice piece of ass, and nothing rakes in more money than a good gang rape of daddy's perfect little virgin. So, you decide. Stop crying and take it from Rocco like a good girl or be the naughty whore and take it up the ass by six grown men. Your choice."

Kirsten stopped crying, but her chest still heaved as she drew in great breaths. Torres jerked on her leash. "That's my pet." He stared directly into the camera. "Now, ladies and gentlemen. For your viewing pleasure tonight, we have daddy's little virgin. So pure. So ripe and fertile for the plucking and she's never been tasted by anyone. And we've got Rocco, my Great Burnese Mountain Dog here ready for some action. As you can see, Candy has kept him good and stroked and he's feistier than a nest of hornets, so what will it be? Should Kirsten get fucked up the ass, the cunny, or suck off Rocco, or all three? You decide. Get your wallets out people, because this is a special case that doesn't come around every day and the phones are already going wild. Five minutes and the highest bidder gets the final decision."

The phones lit up and rang faster than the pounding of Kirsten's heartbeat. Linny clung to the bars of the cage, her eyes red and wet as she watched her friend. "I love you," she mouthed.

"Okay! Times up! Miller, what do we got?" Torres gave another jerk on Kirsten's leash and she choked, coughing and gasping for air.

"Oh, I'm sorry honeybun, did that hurt?" He did it again with a sadistic grin.

"Anal," Miller said.

Kirsten wailed and Torres backhanded her. Her nose began to bleed. "Shut up and look pretty at the camera." He tore off the flimsy red teddy. "This was just eye candy anyway. Now that the show's on, it'll just be in the way." He cackled and grabbed one of Kirsten's boobs, squeezing it hard. She squealed in pain. "Oh, you think this hurts? You haven't experienced anything yet, my little lady. Now smile for the camera as Candy brings Rocco over here."

Silent, hot tears poured down Kirsten's face as she knelt on all fours, staring into the camera. Her arms and legs shook and she took great, rasping breaths.

"Now, just for the camera, one more time, sweet cheeks," Torres said as he spanked Kirsten and she jumped. "You ARE a virgin, aren't you?"

"Y-yes," Kirsten whispered.

Torres backhanded her again and sent her head whipping to and fro. "I'm sorry. I don't think our audience members could hear that. A little louder, please, lovey." He grinned sardonically at the camera, yanking on her chain. She choked and coughed again.

"Yes! I'm a virgin!"

"A virgin, and Daddy didn't bother to call in and save his little girl's most precious gift. I guess he really doesn't love you." Torres bent down and grabbed the back of Kirsten's head, giving her a long kiss with a lot of tongue. He tasted like cigarettes and liquor and Kirsten wanted to puke. He smelled like stale sweat and breath mints. "Well. Not for much longer. Candy, position Rocco."

Candy positioned Rocco behind Kirsten. Torres yanked on Kirsten's leash. "Ass in the air like a good little cunny for me, okay? This'll all be over sooner than you think. And who knows? You might like taking it up the poop chute. Some of them do. Those dirty, filthy girls. Are you a dirty, filthy girl? Hmm?" He yanked on her leash again.

"I-I don't know," Kirsten wailed, quivering.

"Rocco, mount!"

The dog did as commanded and mounted the girl and she howled and thrashed, screaming in pain, tears of anguish running down her face, snot streaming from her nose. The dog panted and humped her and in less than five minutes the whole experience was over. Candy came back and disengaged the two and led Rocco back to the pen, where Linny shrank into a ball in the furthest corner from the dog.

"Did you like that, audience? I have something else for you now. This one is called 'Operation'. I get to play myself and you get to watch. And the more you like what you see, the more donations you call in. And daddy dearest, if you're watching ... all you have to do is call in, give us the money we've asked for and the DNA samples for our experiments, along with the patient files. It'll be over quickly ... more quickly than your daughter is going to lose the rest of her virginity tonight, I promise. And the same goes for the other girl. Or we can keep them here as long as we desire and continue our fun little games. Your choice. But if I were you, I'd make my decision soon because things are about to get much worse for dear, dear Kirsten here. Now Kirsten," Torres said as he jerked on her leash, "crawl over to the surgical table for me like a good little girl."

Kirsten started to crawl over.

"Ah, ah. You're forgetting something."

"What am I forgetting?" Kirsten blubbered. Her hair hung in sweaty strands around her face.

"Say 'Yes, Daddy.'"

"No."

Torres kicked her in her left kidney with his boot and she gasped as the searing pain overtook her entire being. "Say it, you little bitch. Say it or I'll kick you again." He jerked on the leash.

"Yes, Daddy."

"That's better." Torres walked with her to the table and helped her up. He put her wrists and ankles in restraints and finished by buckling a leather strap across her forehead.

"Open your mouth."

"Why?"

Torres smacked her in the face again. By this time, Kirsten's face looked like raw steak.

"Because I told you to. Now do it."

She did and Torres put a ball gag in her mouth. He smiled and patted her cheek as more tears flowed down her face. "Just so you don't bite off your own tongue. If anyone is going to silence you, it's going be me. Right?" He paused and looked at Kirsten expectantly. "I said right?"

"Riff, Aah-ee," Kirsten said awkwardly from behind her ball gag. She tried to turn her head to see what instruments lay on the surgical steel table beside her, but she could only see out of the side of her eyes.

"Miller. I need a break to piss and eat. Shut the camera off for a bit. She's not going anywhere." Torres slapped her left tit and it jiggled wildly as she howled behind the ball gag that tasted of old rubber. "Oh, sweet peaches. The things I have in store for you." He adjusted his crotch. He was getting a stiffy just thinking about the show later, wondering how long these two could survive and if their dads would call before the big finale.

Typically, clients called before the snuff part of the snuff film, but these two bastards... It was like they didn't give one damn about their kids. He was a father himself, and he'd never let one of his children suffer like this. That's why he monitored their internet usage so closely. Because he knew there were sick, depraved assholes like him out there on the web, right at this moment. There had to be at least ten people, or more, dying every minute for the sadistic, twisted pleasure of some rich fuck who had every toy known to man.

Torres headed to the bathroom and Miller was already in there taking a leak.

"Hey, boss. You think we're getting close to being done for tonight?"

Torres unzipped. "You going weak on me, Miller? I hired you because I thought you had balls. You want to end up in front of the camera instead of behind it?" Torres sighed as a steady stream of piss went down the drain. He shook himself and put himself back in his pants. "Ah. It feels good to drain the snake after all that hard work, you know?" He clapped Miller on the back. "Don't be too hard on yourself, Miller. These people have everything. Money, power, prestige. We're just showing them that they're not the only ones in charge and giving them a taste of their own medicine. Besides, I like that hot dish Kirsten that's out there. She's got those small little titties with the big nipples and those pouty lips. I can imagine them doing some real classy work around my dick, if you know what I mean. See you out there." He winked, his hand on the bathroom door. "I'm going to get a burger. You want anything?"

"Nah. I'm not hungry. Just a Coke would be okay."

"Okay, suit yourself, but you know how this line of work always wets my other appetites."

Three.

Kirsten lay shivering on the table, nude, her nipples erect. Torres loomed over her, leering for the camera as he surveyed his assembled tools.

"It's so sad that Daddy won't call in and just give us the patient information we want and the money. Doesn't he love you? Or maybe he's being coached by the FBI and they're trying to find us. But by the time they do, you're going to be nothing but dead meat, baby girl." Torres caressed her cheek and Kirsten shied away from his touch. He guffawed with pleasure, adjusting his crotch.

"Gave me a little tingle down there." He spoke, addressing the camera but looking at Kirsten. "Now, callers, listen carefully. We're going to do some light plastic surgery on these perky boobs here." Torres squeezed Kirsten's left breast until she screamed and tears ran down her face. She balled her hands into fists.

Linny sat traumatized in the cage, rocking back and forth, her hair hanging in front of her eyes, so she couldn't see, hugging herself.

"You have two choices," Torres continued, gesturing to the table. "A: a potato peeler. B: A belt sander. Now I'm not going to tell you which one I think would hurt worse, but I have my own hypothesis, and I guess it'll be proved shortly. Okay, callers. Light up those phones!" Torres grinned at the camera as Kirsten shook with fear, blubbering.

"Aw, honey. Don't be afraid. It'll all be over soon, and you'll look so pretty in red. Red brings out every girl's eyes. My mother always used to say that." Torres slapped his knee. Miller tried not to puke as he continued answering the phones.

The red lights blinked on and off faster than Christmas lights as the calls came in. After a few minutes they stopped. "B-boss, I think we have a winner for $50,000 here."

Torres slapped Kirsten's titty. "Somebody paid $50,000 for you, baby girl. Ain't you special? Let's see what it's gonna be. Miller?"

Miller read from the piece of paper with shaking hands, "Belt sander."

Linny screamed in the dog cage and Kirsten's howls were muffled by the ball gag, but still loud enough to be heard on camera.

Torres took off his suit coat and rolled up the cuffs of his shirt sleeves. "Belt sander it is then. Let's get this party started, Miller. Will you do the honors and plug her in, please?"

Miller did as he was told and handed Torres the sander. It made a terrible buzzing noise as Torres pressed the "on" button. He lowered it to Kirsten's breast and her eyes widened and she squealed like a pig as the sander took off her nipple and quite a bit of flesh as he worked it back and forth. By the time he was done her left breast looked like raw hamburger and then he started in on the right. By now, Kirsten had blessedly passed out from the pain. Blood was dripping off the table in rivulets. The sander was coated in it and so were Torres' hands and his white dress shirt. Beads of sweat stood out on his brow.

"Now this, ladies and gentlemen. This was fun." He grinned sardonically. "I feel like a kid in a candy store." He picked up a surgical steel knife from the table and proceeded to saw through the minced meat of Kirsten's left breast. It hung like a jiggly chicken breast in his hand as he held it up to the camera. Then he tossed it over his shoulder. He did the same with her right breast.

"Miller, get the smelling salts. Wake this piece of ass up. I want her awake for this next part. You all at home watching are going to love this. Now listen closely, Daddy. I'm going to give you five minutes to call in on one of these lines with the money and the information on all the patient's DNA or your daughter's going to have some more reconstructive surgery. Ya hear me. You got a choice to make. Hundreds of strangers and your wealth or your sweet precious blood and flesh. I'm guessing the FBI is going to have a

The Baby Mama Show
By Joshua Singleton

Jess worked the evening shift as a cashier at Goof's, a hardware store in rural Georgia, in the middle of nowhere. It was her second job, and she liked it a whole hell of a lot more than being a McDuck's cashier during the day. She was against working so late, but she needed the extra money for college and her baby, due in three months. Her boyfriend Drew was bringing in pretty decent money too for the past few months, with whatever job he had. She didn't know what it was and didn't really give a fuck either. He always tried to do everything but apply for work, and Jess tried not to stress herself out too much about it.

Anyway, Goof's was a ghost town after 6 pm, and she got off at 9 pm. She used that time to do her schoolwork and sit in a desk chair provided for her by her manager, since she was visibly pregnant. As she sat and did her work at her register, while eating BBQ chips and a ham sandwich, she noticed a blinking camera just below the screen of her computer. It was distracting — a constant blinking red dot every two seconds, some sort of black webcam, fastened to the neck of her computer, facing directly at her, even though her computer was at an angle on the counter.

"What the fuck is that? Eh, probably something else to make this ghetto ass store even more ghetto. Cameras or not, people are still gonna steal shit," she said as she chewed her food.

She didn't really get any schoolwork done because of stressing about the camera and getting one or two customers every few minutes. As the clock struck 9 pm, she counted all the money in her register, clocked out of work, and went to pee before leaving the building, as usual. In the restroom mirror, she brushed her long brownish-blond hair while seeing a black object in the corner of her eye. Jess sat on the toilet seat after lining it with toilet paper, while nervously looking at the black object in the top corner of the wall. It was another black webcam, staring at her with the same red blinks every two seconds.

"First, everybody at this damn job constantly hits on me, I barely get paid, and now they install a camera in the women's bathroom. Wait 'til I tell Drew about this shit." Jess said under her breath. After she finished, she closed down the store and left.

It was raining, and she was alone as she walked to her black car, invisible from the lack of bright parking lot lights from the old hardware store. As she opened her car and got in, all she could see was the green light of her LED radio system and another red blinking light below it. It was dark, but it looked like the same black webcam in the bathroom, as well as the one at her register. She paid it no mind, since all she was concerned about was getting the fuck out of there, and rightfully so, feeling her baby kick in her stomach from her uneasiness.

Jess made it home to her apartment and parked, rolling her eyes at the light show coming from Drew's gaming PC in their living room window. "I still don't know how he got the money to get that expensive ass computer but can't put gas in my car. It's bad enough he doesn't pick me up from work."

As Drew heard Jess slam her car door, he glanced towards the front door in shock, frantically closing a tab on his computer. He got up to greet Jess at the door.

"Hey, babe!" Drew said with more enthusiasm than usual, as Jess walked in, confused by his tone and greeting.

"Hey, babe. You sound like you hit the lottery or something."

"Nah, I'm just happy both of my babies made it back home safe." Drew chuckled, scratching his shoulder-length dreadlocks. Jess wasn't impressed, as she lowered her brows and cocked her head to the side, staring at him with smoky green eyes. "Hurry and get comfortable, babe, I cooked dinner and ran you a bath!"

Jess still had her brows lowered in confusion and disbelief as she replied, "Dinner and a bath? You've been acting really weird lately, Drew. Also, you never say anything about where you work. As far as I'm aware, you drive nowhere either?"

"Honestly, babe, it's just a remote call center job. It's kinda boring, and I just wanted to be low-key and start bringing money in. I'm just trying to do better for us. I'm sorry about all the lights, too. Maybe I should have bought a cheaper computer."

"Mhm, I hear you. It's okay, but I've got my eyes on you, Andrew Mitchell. Thank you, I'll be ready in just a minute."

After she kissed him and went to change into her pajamas in their bedroom, Drew sighed and then sat back in his chair, pushed up his glasses, and opened that window again on his computer. He used the Deep Web to go on a site called "The Baby Mama Show.com." He accessed a layout of camera footage on a black and green website background like something out of the 80s. The camera footage named where the cameras were located: Jess's register, Jess's bathroom (job), Jess's car, Jess's bedroom, Jess's bathroom (home).

On the "Jess's bedroom" camera, Drew, and thousands of users watched her get undressed. The live chat on the right side of the window filled with dozens of green-colored comments per second as she removed her undergarments. The comments and donations increased when her face and stomach were in view. Drew's heart started racing as one comment read, "Beautiful. You're a lucky man, Andrew."

Some other comments then read, "Jess is a bloody legend in the pregnancy category, already smh."

"Make her another sandwich!"

Identity Theft
By Megan Russ

The body has been found. It's time for me to move on.

It's like this every time. I can only stick around for so long before someone finds evidence of my crime. I cannot stop, and why should I? It is the perfect crime. They never suspect a thing. Plus, there is the bonus of giving those lazy pigs something to do every once in a while.

I busy myself stripping my cords from the wall and packing up my system while I listen to the news broadcast. "The identity of the victim is unknown. However, early information leads theorists to speculate that this latest murder is part of a string of strange cases that extends to seven states."

"Ten," I growl as I snap the lid of the metal case shut with more force than needed. "It's ten, and they know it." I heft the case from the desk I've used for the last three and a half months. I pick up the remote and click the television off before making for the door of the small apartment. The one bedroom served me well, a den for me to pursue my passion. I take nothing but my trunk, nothing else is mine.

Usually I have another target picked out before moving on. I expected to have more time here. Who could have expected that another monster was stalking this city? My hiding place was perfect, which I suppose is why the beast had taken his victim there. Then the dumbass tried to play the good Samaritan finding two murder victims. I would laugh if it were anyone else's dumpsite he stumbled upon.

The ass-crack of dawn is upon me, but my favorite fix is just a few miles away. Their Wi-Fi will do for what I need. I head through the drive-through and grab myself an extra-expensive, extra-shot, super-charged latte. Then, I spin my van around into a spot near the front of the dimly lit building. The green lady of the logo smiles down at me like she approves of my actions as I pull my laptop onto my knees and boot it up.

My fingers stroke the keyboard softly as I imagine the things I'm about to search. Depravity hides just beyond the glowing screen. I pull my privacy screen over my window and settle in for a long few hours. I sip my coffee and let the familiar rush of heat and caffeine flood my system. A universal truth is coffee equals life—man or monster.

I need to find someone sooner rather than later. But finding the perfect match takes time, having to stalk and find their patterns. Will they be missed? I try to make sure their disappearances will go unnoticed. Sometimes it works. Sometimes there is an extra-nosy neighbor who is on vacation the week of my stalking.

The screen goes dark as I engage my scrambler. My fingers spring across the keys as if little gerbils power pistons in my knuckles. The relentless tap-tap fills the dark van, until I find the right chat. Until I find the right stream. There. There they are.

Fresh flesh, fresh faces, fresh names. All unsuspecting of what I have planned for them.

I zoom in on their names and quickly type them into a small note on the bottom left of my screen. Five of them are in this chatroom. Two of them are on camera doing things that make me squirm in my skin. It itches to be free, like my muscles are ready to shed my flesh and embrace the monster within. But not yet. I have to stalk. I have to wait until the time is right.

I rip my eyes from the depravity on the screen and bring up the next window. My worm has already drilled through their security. A scrambler is nothing against the virus I had ramming their firewall the moment I entered the chat.

Knock knock, motherfuckers, the actual monster is here.

I need to find the right one. With five potential playmates, I can only hope that one will fit the bill. The closest one might be convenient, but convenience and guarantees are not the same thing.

Within moments, I have all five profiles in front of me. I scroll through pictures while turning down the speaker to ignore the whimpers and moans. There's work to do, preferably without distractions.

My teeth grind together. The perfect candidate is on my list. The right profile. Perfect age, build, and lifestyle. They will slip through the cracks just like they are now. My fingers slide over the fluorescent screen on my lap. My skin itches to feel them, to touch their flesh with mine as I peel it while their screams fill the night air. But it is not meant to be, not yet. They are too far away.

Their names go on a list for the future. Who knows when I might feel like visiting the good ol' PA.

There's two. Both will do, but I need only one. They live within fifty miles of each other. I like the younger one, I love when they have fight in them. Though the other fits the profile, they look a little saggy. Both will be stalked to make an educated choice.

After all, one should never rush into murder. That is how one gets caught.

I will dream about that ideal meat sack in Pennsylvania tonight. But there is nothing for it. I cannot go that far without attracting some kind of notice. Being predictably unpredictable is necessary if I am going to keep doing this forever with modern technology constantly breathing down my neck. I can't attract unwanted attention.

Well, no more attention than ten murders attract. But I'm one step ahead of them on that one. With no hands, teeth, or face, it takes weeks to get DNA back, and without something to compare it to there is nothing but the evidence left behind by the time they get to wherever I was before.

They really should stop announcing my victims on the evening news. It gives me plenty of time to move on.

After downloading my victim's information, I tap the GPS on the dash. Santa Fe is a lot closer than Boswell. I make one more circuit around the green-lady's skirt and order a sandwich along with my fix. Even monsters have to eat.

Seven hours and a few pit-stops later, I pull into the no-tell motel along the I25 on the western side of Santa Fe. Every major city has one of these babies. And this is so far removed from my last spot that no one in Tucson will think to look here for a while. By the time they do, it will be too late.

In the morning, I'll scope out the first address, but I'm itching to get to know my quarry. After checking in and double locking my door, I pull the drapes tight and turn on my scrambler. Upon opening my laptop, the hum of the fan fills the small room before the clacking of keyboard keys staccato through the night air.

The television is clicked on when the site finally loads. The whimpers and moans echoing through my speakers are drowned out by the show. I keep the sound on to get to know my prey. And like a moth to a flame, there they are. I had a feeling they did this often.

I make note of the decor behind them, the things they think others would never pay attention to. They do not know that the monster has eyes for everything, not just them. My fingers stroke over a few keys, and the cam-feed fills my screen. My eyes slide over their form for a brief moment before my face twists into a grimace. If they refrained from such vile acts, they would never be on my radar. Not my ideal candidate, but they will do in a pinch.

Perhaps my prospects on the other side of the city will be a better option. Fifty miles is nothing out here in the desert. It is the other side of the city, as the locals call it. The suburbs surrounding Santa Fe are part of the sprawling oasis just as much as the skyscrapers in its center. In order to blend in, I always have to stay up on the latest slang and local terminology.

My eyes scan the background on the screen. While blurry, I can still make out old family photos, and the image of a dog. Nothing new, nothing of them. It is hard to tell through the screen, but I swear cobwebs are fluttering in the breeze of the ceiling fan. I grin and sit back on the creaky motel bed.

I set up my worm to see if my other name is online. Their username is absent from the current chat, but there are always others.

Within moments, my program dings through the speaker. A new chat, a new feed and new people pop up on my screen. I smash my finger onto the mute button as a scream splits through the speaker. With any luck, my temporary neighbors will think I'm watching porn.

With eyes fixed on the central screen, where a girl is being tortured, my heart rate quickens and goosebumps spread across my arms. My fingers itch to do something while my skin ripples with the need to move and feel. I slide the computer from my lap and stand, running my fingers through my hair before I pace the small room. My eyes flick to the screen, and I decide my first check will be on my new friend across the city.

I rush to the keyboard, keeping my eyes on my target as my fingers fly across the smooth plastic. With each click and combination of keys, my next victim's life spreads out before me. Bank accounts, savings that are nonexistent, and a pile of debt a mile long. School records slide quickly across the screen, along with a high school transcript with no graduation date. This should sadden me, but it is the truth of this dark side of the world. Most are uneducated or over-educated with nothing better to do. They slip through the cracks because people stopped caring about what they were doing. Next comes the criminal record.

It's shocking to see a pair of arrests. Usually these people scoot under the police radar. That is until their body is dumped in a field to be found a few months later. I scoff. Two minor drug charges are nothing compared to what is happening on the next tab over. I grin. Good, there will be no parole officer wondering where they went.

They are perfect in every way. Young enough for me to enjoy, but old enough not to be missed. I set my program to drill through their security and get me more. Then I turn off the lights and try to get a few hours of sleep. I have to wake up early.

After all, it is the early bird that gets the worm.

The New Mexico sun is just as bad as Arizona's. Not sure why I thought another desert was the best way to go, but it is too late now. Maybe next time I should skip a few states and go somewhere green. Colorado is nice but has too many others to compete with, so perhaps go north for a while. I hear Montana is nice in the summer.

My ball cap is pulled low on my head, and I glare from under the bill towards the front of the liquor store. My quarry has interesting tastes. It was the ATM first thing, then the grocery store, but they only came out with a single bag. Now they have gone to a hobby store, something with a large dice on the front window. It is best for monsters like me to avoid places like that. Now it is the liquor store and they've come out with the largest bag so far.

Loaded with bags, they head down the road in the direction they came from. I keep to the other side of the street, while my gaze beneath my sunglasses is on them. My head turns and twists as though I'm a tourist gawking at the peeling stucco of this random downtown street.

I patiently stalk my prey, while my skin feels like it wants to peel off and race after them. I cannot have that, so my pace quickens as they turn a corner and I lose sight of them. A smile graces my lips as I jog across the street and find my new friend leaning toward a window.

Not wanting to attract attention, I stroll past. My eyes graze over my prey, and my fingers itch to reach out and slide across the graceful curve of their back. I keep my hands in my pockets, but my eyes find what they are watching through the window. The muffled sound of orchestral music assaults my ears, and I am glad for the thick glass and sturdy door that keeps that cacophony locked up.

My spine stiffens as I glimpse the small crowd of innocents that play beyond the smudged glass. Like the relentless rise of the sun each morning, it is uncontrollable. My new friend grins before turning away from the window and coming down the street, where I stand examining a menu stand in front of a bistro.

I glance back at the building before following my quarry. They are too young to have a child learning music inside. They have no children listed on record. I suppose I picked the perfect target to get them off the streets and out of the world before they can corrupt more life.

They climb the stairs to their second-floor apartment and I watch as they disappear inside. Knowing they are secure, I return to my van parked in the next apartment complex. I need to see if my drill has accomplished what's needed. It is time to start my plan.

I do not simply remove my prey from this cursed earth. I destroy everything that was theirs. My grin widens with each keystroke. Frantic eyes dart from one window to the other as I set up the slow stream of cash from their account to mine and a few others. Who would think anything of someone giving to charity? It's a tax write off after all.

My laughter fills my van as I set my laptop aside to continue its work. I turn my baby on and head for the motel. With my new friend online, it's safe to leave and return to my temporary lair. Oh, how much fun I am going to have playing with this one.

Usually, I am secure in my current identity while stalking my next victim. It has been a long time since I've had to stalk prey while watching over my shoulder for someone to recognize me. I'm hopeful the FBI and its goons keep their noses to the west. With five of my friends spread throughout California, they should look that way before east.

I flip on the news out of habit as my laptop is set up on the bed. They are talking about me again. It's nice to be recognized. The ancient coffee maker brews some grounds as I drop onto the edge of the bed to watch.

"Authorities are still investigating the murder of Taylor Emit. Friends of the deceased claim to have seen Taylor at the park, the store, and coffee shop in the weeks after his time of death. Authorities claim that these sightings must be mistaken, and that the friends are recalling times they saw Taylor before his death. However, recent security footage given to our studio by a confidential source clearly shows Mr. Emit walking around and placing groceries in his cart." The broadcaster continues as the feed cuts to a grainy black and white video of a young man grocery shopping.

I cackle and fall back onto the bed, holding my stomach. This is perfect. What better way to get away with my crimes than for false information to be floating around?

"According to our source within the San Diego police, they have no knowledge of this tape and have not confirmed its authenticity. But you make your own call, people. Is this not Taylor Emit marching around in the store? Yet according to that date stamp, this is three weeks after Mr. Emit's estimated time of death." The broadcast switches the view back to the reporters sitting behind their desks. "What do you think, Emily?" the man turns to ask his companion.

"Well, John, it certainly looks like Mr. Emit." She taps a manicured fingernail to her chin and turns to pretend to be looking at the images behind her. There is nothing behind her but a green screen, but to the audience it looks like she's looking at Taylor's image beside the grainy black and white. "It certainly does look like the same man."

"It certainly does," I say with a broad grin. "Taylor was a fun one. Nice and young and fit, plenty of fight in him," I announce to the broadcasters.

I stand and stretch, ripping my gaze from the television to look at my laptop. Three alerts are blinking at the bottom of the screen. My grin widens as I pluck it from the side table and settle it onto my lap.

"What do you have for me, baby?" My fingers slide across the keys like a fog over the moor—quick, light, and almost silent.

The first alert notifies me of a police situation in Tucson. I scan it. They found the apartment and evidence of someone recently living there, but of course the only fingerprints belonged to the original owner. I exit the window and bring up the next.

One is a notification of my account transfer and scrub. It is the last window that brings a grin to my lips. I scan the information and, with a few more strokes of my best friend, the program is back at work.

My drill has infiltrated my new friend's accounts. All of them. Banking, DMV, social media, dating apps. Fake and real profiles are all listed. Anything linked to their five email accounts.

"It might be time to start the game." A sigh leaves my lips as I lean back against the cracked and stained headboard. "Just because I'm rushed doesn't mean we shouldn't have some fun," I say to my laptop as I slowly slide my hands down each side of the screen.

There's a black screen with the live feed. I keep my eyes on the cam-feed from my prey. They have changed positions, closer to the screen for a better view. My flesh tingles with the thought of peeling that face from bone, chopping those depraved hands from arms. I envision smashing a rock into those pearly whites and destroying any hope of identification.

One can never be too careful.

I look at the chat and link with their name. Upon opening, a conversation is started. They cannot do it themselves. My username is hidden. I have their username and their real one. Which to use... It is always best to start off formally.

"Good afternoon, Alex." I hit enter and wait. Their eyes twitch from the live feed to the chat window. They do a double take, and their eyes narrow. I grin. "Good to know I have your attention. I would love to have a little chat, Alex. When you have time."

Slowly their movements stop, and their eyes fix on the chat box. They dart around to the others on camera, all watching the live stream. They can't see the chat. It's private for now. They scan each of the other four on camera. None are typing, but I am. Alex cannot see me. I'm a ghost in the dark. The unseen predator in a room full of monsters.

The camera picks up the slight shake in Alex's hands as a message is quickly pecked out with index fingers. Just another reason to kill this piece of shit. Key by key, the reply is crafted.

"Who the fuck are you?"

I roll my eyes at the originality of Alex's intimidation method that follows. Alex threatens to track me down and have me arrested. Laughable. At an agonizingly slow pace, the threat to empty my accounts is hurled at me next. Ironic. I finally compose my reply while Alex works on another poem of vengeance upon my family.

"How is Thunder?" I use the name of the dog in the images in the background.

Alex's face twists into a mask of fury before the feed goes dark. Their username goes red and then vanishes from the chat. I smile. They will be back, they always are.

The first battle is won. But this is a war.

I set up an alert to notify me the next time Alex's VPN scrambler comes online. It might be a few days. I'll have time to research and possibly take the first steps with Jordan. It's always good to have a failsafe. The older of my two candidates will have to wait until tomorrow. It's time for some takeout and bingeing the latest anime.

Even monsters have to eat.

Jordan might be the better choice. They are walking with their head bowed and avoiding eye-contact. A few errands are quickly finished before Jordan retreats behind the thick door of a bungalow set away from the neighbors by a good fifty feet.

I take in the neighbors' houses while my laptop beeps in its passenger setup. I glance over and hit the enter key twice before looking to Jordan's neighbors once more. My eyes catch the movement of curtains closing in the front window of the house to the left. More research is required, but Jordan, while slightly older, is still within my acceptable range.

Maybe I need to take someone older. Throw those profiling FBI pigs off my trail for a little longer. I think of changing my process for a moment, but why mess with a good thing?

I switch my programs to drilling into Jordan's accounts, and I head to the motel. I get a ping the moment I open up my laptop. Alex and Jordan are both in the same room. How fortuitous. I get my setup going and slide into the chatroom like a phantom. Alex and Jordan are grinning at the action on the screen. Their faces twist in pleasure as the feed continues.

If only I could have them both. Alex may be fun to torment once I play with Jordan. I am sure Alex will just find a new dark site to visit, but until then I can have two friends.

I open two windows, Alex and Jordan, in different chats. I cannot have them think I'm cheating on them.

"Good to see you again, Alex." I grin as the cam-feed suddenly goes black.

I swallow the laughter. Some spook like deer, while others fight like lions. When Alex notices the leak in their bank accounts they will fight back. Until then, I can focus on Jordan.

"Jordan, did you know your rose bush needs watering?" I watch as Jordan's face follows the same sequence of movements that Alex's made the night before.

At least Jordan has the manners to type with both hands. A furious response flares in the box. "Show yourself, cocksucker."

"Oh, I love when they have some fight in them." I pretend the news broadcaster on the television is smiling at my quip.

"And why would I do that," I type out, "when it is so much more fun to watch you squirm? Are you enjoying the show?"

"I was until some freak decided to interrupt." Jordan's brows are knit together. I wonder if the keyboard is still in one piece after watching the movements through the feed.

"Now, now, no need for name-calling. I might impress upon you that each time you say something rude, I will subtract one." I smile as Jordan leans away from the camera and squints at my message.

"One what?" Appears on the screen.

"You'll see."

"Who are you?"

"A relevant question. I don't know who I am. Perhaps you can help me find out."

"Why would I want to do that?" Jordan's scanning the other cameras as I reply, searching for the other user. Nuh-uh, you can't see me.

"Because if you don't, I'll subtract two." I screen share and show Jordan their own live bank account.

With widened eyes, they move to respond with as much fervor as before. I worry about their poor computer. The other users are so busy watching the main feed they take no notice of the cam-feed with a scowling face hovering over a glowing keyboard.

"You're threatening me, you motherfucker? I will end you in every universe."

That's a new one. I respond, "That's one," and one million is removed from Jordan's account.

Jordan jumps up and spins away from the camera. I cannot hear the scream, but the body language is clear. Even for a monster, one million dollars is a lot. But Jordan can stand to lose more.

"What is your favorite coffee shop?" I ask in the chat.

Jordan looks at the screen and steps closer. Eyes narrow as they reread the message to make sure they are seeing correctly. Jordan sits down and types a reply.

"What sick game are you playing?"

"Answer, or I'll take two," I warn. I'm a fair beast.

"The place on 3rd," is the reply that quickly comes to my side.

"Perfect. I'll see you tomorrow." I close the chat. The window showing the depleted bank account follows a blink later.

Jordan's eyes widen again, followed by lightning-fast typing. They watch the screen for a response that will never come. A grin reaches across my face as I see them grab the computer setup and shake it, face twisted in a scream. Another key pounding message that will go unanswered. They torment themselves for a few more moments before the feed goes black.

Once Jordan is out of the chat, I read the messages. Can't seem too desperate now.

"What do you mean?" I smile at the message. "Answer me, you prick!" I tap my chin, wondering if I should subtract another million for the insult. The answer is yes, Jordan has to be taught a lesson. Disobedience of any kind will not be tolerated.

I'm up an hour before dawn and parked outside the coffee shop on 3rd when they open their doors. Not my usual fare, but the greedy-green-lady cannot be everywhere. For one, this place is walk-in only. I slide out of the van and get my fix before retreating to my mobile lair.

The smell of caffeinated gold fills the van as I scan the web for any new alerts. I doubt Jordan will show up early, but I know for sure that, out of curiosity, they will show up. My programs to do their work while I move the van to the lot of the fast-food joint across the street and park between two employee cars with my back end facing the coffee shop.

I can hide in plain sight while watching the coffee shop on my laptop through their own security feed. With a grimace, I sip my coffee. This is not oat milk. The sour taste coating my tongue tells me it's goat milk. This is why I'm loyal to the overpriced, dumb-named drinks that the green-lady's elves serve.

The sour, caffeinated concoction makes it way down my throat as I watch patrons enter and leave the coffee shop. The feed from the outside camera shows cars as they roll past or park in front of the shop. A familiar lithe frame steps around the corner and pauses.

Jordan's eyes scan the street, the cars parked in front of the shop, and even upon the rooftops. Oh, come now, Jordan, I'm not the CIA. If that were true, you would have just vanished without a trace.

They are better than I am, yet I'm doing their job more often than not. It makes me wonder how long until they get involved. The CIA might connect the dots that the FBI has missed.

The CIA knows its monsters.

Jordan walks past the coffee shop and scans the inside with wild eyes. I grin at the anxious image in the cam-feed. Jordan keeps going to the end of the street on shaky legs and glances back.

At the corner, Jordan pauses and waits a moment before turning around and doing another pass in front of the coffee shop. Three more similar courses follow as Jordan walks up and down the street, watching for anyone coming or going. I have to applaud.

"At least someone isn't too eager of a beaver. Don't you worry, Jordan. We will play soon," I purr. I wait until the door to the coffee shop opens and Jordan orders their regular. I make a note of it and close up my laptop.

My door opens and I slide out like a puma on the hunt. I stalk around the van and toss my empty coffee cup in the trashcan on the corner before heading into the coffee shop.

Jordan is sitting at the back table, eyes wide as they scan the crowd. My eyes stay on my phone screen, bored and uninterested. The image is appealing. The camera shows Jordan's hands shake as they reach for coffee. Zooming in on the feed, there are some peppermint sprinkles on top of the intoxicating concoction.

At the counter, the barista looks at me with dull eyes, already bored, already done with today, and the sun has barely risen. Maybe I should remove her from this world instead. No, that would be wrong.

"What can I get you?" she asks before yawning.

"Can I get an extra mocha-pumpkin-peppermint espresso, large, with peppermint shavings and chocolate drizzle on top of the whipped cream?" I order with a smile.

"Sure, that will be thirteen ninety-seven." I hand over a twenty and tell her to keep the change. "Can I get a name for the drink?" she asks with a slight smile at the edges of her tired mouth.

"Jordan," I state, making sure to spell it correctly for her.

"We'll have that right out to you," she says, handing the cup and receipt off to one of her coworkers.

I move aside and glance at my screen. Jordan watches my back as I weave my way towards the front door. Searching eyes are soon drawn to the next mote of movement. At the front bar that overlooks the street, I lean back and cross my legs for a moment. Just like everyone else, I'm waiting for my coffee.

When the door to my left opens with an ear-piercing ring, I slip out into the morning air to head down the street instead of across to my car. My eyes are glued to my phone screen as I wait.

"Jordan," a barista calls out. My Jordan flinches but ignores the call, it is a common enough name after all. "Jordan?" The person holding the steaming cup calls again. "Jordan with a large extra mocha-pumpkin-peppermint espresso?" I watch as the form on the other side of my screen looks up. Wide eyes scan the cafe, looking for me. How sweet.

Jordan steps across the tiles on shaky legs and takes the cup extended over the counter. Eyes scanning the cafe again, no one but the confused barista is looking anywhere near them.

I laugh and circle around the block while Jordan escapes the coffee shop and rushes down the road out of camera shot. I look up as a form barrels around the corner and right into me. A tidal wave of brown and white foam sprays into the air.

"Oh my God," Jordan shouts as we both tumble to the ground. I roll away and look up into stormy-blue eyes. "I am so sorry. Are you all right?"

"I think so." Laughing, I push myself to my feet.

"Are you sure?"

So kind, so concerned about me. Yet at night, Jordan prowls the dark web looking for a score.

"No harm, no foul." I brush the dust from my clothing. "Although the same cannot be said for you." I gesture at the large brown stain spreading across the band logo on Jordan's shirt. "Can I buy you another coffee?"

"God, no."

I raise an eyebrow at the sudden outburst.

"Oh, sorry. I just—um—I have no idea how I even had that coffee. I didn't order it. Honestly, I think I have a stalker," Jordan rambles.

"A stalker, like romantic or creepy?" I ask with a smile. Jordan shudders. "Ah, sorry friend. Do you want some company on your way? I can keep an eye out for your stalker."

"Really, you would do that for a stranger?"

"I'm Taylor," I say, holding out my hand.

"Jordan."

"There, we aren't strangers," I say as we shake hands. "And walking with a new friend on a nice morning is as good as anything else. If I keep some creeper away from you while I'm doing it, it's just a bonus." I shrug.

"Sure, why not?"

And that is how I got to know Jordan on a personal level. When we stop in front of the bookshop they work at, we split ways with the promise to meet up for drinks.

My skin crawls, walking away. The thought of Jordan in that bookstore all day, around people, it should be forbidden. After all, they have plenty of money, even after last night. The bookstore is a front for how Jordan makes money at night. It is only a matter of time before I will be in charge and everything else will fall into place.

I pull my van into the park down the street from Jordan's home and walk to the bungalow, letting myself in through the back. Room by room, I examine the inside of the house. There isn't an indoor camera system, and I've already hacked into the exterior security while still in the van.

The CPU set up in the master bedroom makes me stop to appraise it, and then roll my eyes.

"You would think someone who can afford this and has millions to lose would invest in a few cameras." I gesture at the empty crown molding. "But you have a shag carpet in your living room, so you aren't the smartest cookie." I continue to ramble to myself while familiarizing myself with the house.

The best spot has to be chosen. "Perhaps the master bedroom with the proof playing right there on the massive computer screen," I muse, spreading my hands wide like a director taking in a shot. "Yes, perfect." I clap my hands and practice as if Jordan is in front of me.

"It might not be your screen debut, but it will be a smash." My fists swing like I plan to do when I bash Jordan's pearly whites.

It's all set up. Candles, a chair, rope, even a ball-gag. I'm a romantic at heart...if I have one. I'm pretty sure I have one.

The door creaks open and keys hit the bowl in the entryway. The lock of the deadbolt slides into place. I love being locked in. There's a heavy sigh and shoes are kicked, hitting the wall.

A grunt reveals the light from the bedroom has been seen. There is a clatter in the hallway. Ah, the bat hidden by the umbrella stand. Too bad it is tucked under the bed for my use later. The tip of an umbrella slides into view first—like the flimsy aluminum can do anything to me. Jordan emerges into the doorway with wide eyes.

"When you told me you had a stalker, I knew I wanted to help you feel better."

"What the fuck?" Jordan scans the setup. Bare feet squeak on the floor as he tries to spin and run away.

"We are going to help you feel better!" I roar, grabbing the back of his shirt and hauling the tall man back. It is so easy to tip someone backwards.

Jordan sprawls back, the umbrella skittering across the hardwood far beyond his reach. I straddle his hips and grab both his arms. Jordan glares up at me, convinced he will be able to overpower me. Men and their power trips.

My eyes shift, the whites overtaking the colored iris I've stolen. Jordan struggles more. The smell of piss fills the air as he starts to wail. I clamp my hand over his mouth and grin, my teeth sliding over the incisors that belonged to another. My lips split as they curve over razor sharp fangs.

"Ah, this will be so much fun. You're a fighter. I love fighters." With my hand wrapped securely around his mouth I lift and slam his head into the floor with a loud crack.

Jordan's eyes roll up in his head. I hiss and drag his dead weight to the chair. The game is about to begin. He's strapped in, nice and tight. The bruises will give the cops something to study. Jordan groans as I crank down on the ropes around his torso. A sick monster like him deserves no mercy.

He will receive none.

A loud screech fills the room as I spin the chair to face the computer screens. My fingers dance across the keys. I'm running out of time. My skin itches to feel Jordan's. The stress of finding a new face has driven this one to wear out quicker than usual. My reflection is in the dark screen as I pull up Jordan's crimes.

"Did you know Zoom backgrounds work on other applications?" I cackle as I continue to work.

I glance over at my own laptop, hacking into his system and pulling up everything needed while simultaneously erasing any sign I was ever there. Windows pop up on his multiple screen setup. I shake my head. Jordan may not have proof that he personally touched a child or a woman, but the material floating on his hard drive is enough to send three people to prison.

"And they call me a monster," I hiss, glaring at Jordan over my shoulder.

Once I know the feed is live and secure, I stand and wave to make sure I'm covered in a black censor cloud. I pull a mask on and black clothing for good measure, those censors can be hacked after all. Although, nothing would confuse the FBI more than a dead man torturing a man for the same crimes. It is that kind of snuff that attracts the CIA.

I can't have that.

"Wakey, wakey, eggs and bakey!" I pull back and slap him so hard his neck pops.

Jordan groans around the ball-gag as his eyes flutter open; stormy-blue marbles that will be mine soon enough. I bet he's lured many women in with those soulful eyes. They will be mine and I will only use them to hunt other monsters. Those blue depths are focused on me, narrowed with a rage only death can bring.

Jordan thrashes in his bonds like a butterfly in a net. I sit back and allow the cameras to capture his struggle. He screams around the ball when one shoulder pops. I click my tongue and shake my head. He glares at me, teeth gnashing at the ball.

Yes, eat it please!

I reach to my left and click the play key. Jordan's eyes flick to the screen behind me, he cocks his head then looks back at me. The screams and whimpers of tortured women and children filter through his speakers. I pluck the pliers from the desk and spin them in my grasp. After stepping towards him, his eyes flit from the screen to me, widening with each step.

"You like to watch little girls get mutilated? You like watching innocent women be murdered?" I point to the blinking red light. "Well guess what, there are monsters like me that enjoy watching filth like you be tortured too."

I grab the hand of the arm he carelessly dislocated. Releasing the rope, I yank his arm from the chair to wave at the camera. He howls behind the ball.

"Say hi to all my friends out there." I drop his wrist, and the arm drops with another pop. Jordan tries to scream; this is why I use the gag. "Now, now, Jordan, you won't have that hand much longer, you should wave while you can." His eyes widen again, and I strap his wrist in place once more.

"Don't worry, it won't go to waste. I'll make sure to do better things with them than you did." I tap his fingers with the pliers, and he winces. "I see you've watched some feeds with tools. Good, none of this should come as a surprise then." Before he can react, the pliers are gripping one of his fingernails and pulling.

I lean closer as he screams through the ball-gag. "Such a lovely sound." I pull the pliers up to look at the bloody scrap of keratin. I wave it in front of his face. "You didn't want this, did you?" I grin toward the camera, although they cannot see me.

I wave the fingernail before the audience. A few familiar usernames are in the chatroom. Not all are visible. Like myself, my long distance friends know it is best to stay hidden. A few are trying to tell me what to remove next, but this is not their snuff feed, it is mine.

Jordan whimpers as I tap his other hand with the pliers. I slide behind him and hold up different tools to the audience behind his back. My eyes narrow, following the chat thread. They are too excited for the little glass tube in my hand. I set it down and collect a handful of bamboo slivers.

"Did you know that the human hand can have three-thousand nerve endings per square inch?" I slam the first sliver under an intact nail. "It just shows how important our hands are to daily life," I muse, and insert another. He struggles but I press my free hand down on the top of his wrist. I grin at him from beneath my mask.

Jordan's whimpers are like music to my ears. It's nothing compared to the years of torture he's watched others endure, encouraged through chats, or possibly performed with these hands that will soon be mine. My anger surges and I grab a finger and bend it backwards. Jordan's eyes fill with fresh tears as he squeezes them shut. He howls and thrashes under my touch. I lick my tongue across my fangs. The pain fuels me, my white eyes flash to the screens.

"Ah look at that, the girl there. Isn't that your name in the chat, encouraging the beast to remove her eyelids?" I point with the blood-covered pliers.

Jordan's eyes snap open and to the screen. He shakes his head vehemently. I tap the bloody tool to my chin and lean towards the screen as though to read the chat.

"Nope, that is you." I shrug. "What a wonderful idea. We wouldn't want you to miss anything." I grab a razor from the table. "It will be that much easier for me to take your eyes without the lids."

I crank on the rope, holding his head until Jordan is looking up at the ceiling. "I mentioned all the nerve endings in the hands." I smile down at him and slide the razor over his eyebrow. "But did you know that there are so many nerves in the face that science cannot accurately quantify it?" I slide in front of him and put a hand on his forehead. "Try to hold still, I know it will hurt." I cackle with laughter.

Jordan screams behind the ball-gag as the thin metal lowers to his orbital socket. The screams turn to roars as he tries to fight. I stop and smack him, blood trailing into his right eye from the incision. Each time he blinks, his sclera peeks through the new opening.

"Do you want to lose an eye?" I wave the razor in front of him. "Don't you know I could poke your eye out with this thing?" I laugh again and return to my gruesome deed.

With a roar from Jordan and a giggle from me, the eyelid is torn from his face and flung toward the camera. It smacks against the screen with a wet splat before fluttering to the keyboard, where it lays like a shriveled insect. Jordan's muffled screams fill the room as the other eyelid soon follows.

"There, now you won't miss a thing!" I slap his blood-streaked cheek and turn to the camera as though presenting a prize car on a gameshow. "We are almost out of time folks. What do you want to see most?" I lean forward. "Oh, so cruel. Ooh, brutal," I say with a giggle, reading out the chats. I will be doing none of it, I cannot leave any trace of the torture on the main body. The rope marks should be the only evidence.

"Wow, Jordan, these guys really want to see you suffer." I turn around and lift the fillet knife from the table. "I suppose I can indulge in a few simple requests. Did you know that there are two hundred six bones in the human body? Twenty-seven are in the hands. All those nerves and bones. More than enough to have fun with."

Slowly, like fishing for a splinter, I drive the end of the blade between his index and middle finger.

"How many women and children did these hands harm?" I ask, but Jordan cannot answer.

He can just stare with lidless eyes as I peel back the flesh from his hands and press the blade between each joint from the tip to the carpals of each finger. The bones hang loose, supported and held only by the dozens of tendons and tiny muscles that work the hand.

"Can you wiggle your fingers for me?" I ask like a concerned doctor.

Jordan groans, his eyes rolling. He stopped screaming when I started on his second hand. It could be blood loss. I glance at the drenched tarp beneath him. Or it could be shock. It's probably shock; I am careful not to catch any major vessels.

"Did you know there are two-thousand nerve endings per square inch on the lips?" I tap the razor against his sagging mouth. Jordan jolts and stares at me with desperate blue eyes.

"This is the end of the show, boys. I'll show you all the proper way to skin a face." Jordan starts to scream again. I grin beneath my mask. "There is some controversy among our kind about how to best preserve the flesh with the least amount of trauma. After all, we want the longest wear time possible." I address my audience like a teacher.

"Remember to cast your votes for where all of my new friend's money should go." I point down to indicate the window that just popped up on my viewers' screens. "This time I am offering three choices. The Victims of Abuse and Trafficking Relief Fund is my favorite, but you vote for whatever your conscience feels deserves his money best. If all three get enough votes, I'll split the money." I give a thumbs-up to my viewers and return to my bestie.

I move around Jordan to make sure he is center stage.

"I know most like to cut from here," I place the razor at the base of Jordan's neck. I can feel the frantic fluttering of his heartbeat through the steel of the blade, resting just a press from his carotid artery. I tap the blade lightly, causing him to flinch and whimper. Jordan's eyes roll wildly as he tries to track my movements behind him.

"But I find it risky to start from here. They like to fight here at the end. All cornered animals try to bite, remember that friends. The major arteries and veins are right there. We cannot have them dying before what we need is removed. So, too much risk of death, and the mess! Arterial blood spray can travel five feet. We don't want extra messes to clean up." I run my finger along Jordan's jaw.

"Others go right here. And while it seems like a natural place to start, you also want the skin on the neck for the best retention." I grab Jordan's hair and press the razor into the top of his head, just behind his hairline.

"I like to start here and work my way back to create a natural seam, but that isn't the end. One moment while I make this first cut. Try to be as straight as you can with this one. And remember, the flesh here is like the hands, you don't have to cut too deep to get results."

Jordan whimpers as blood drips down his forehead and from the tip of his nose. I grin as my skin shudders and crawls with the sensation of the blade slicing through his scalp. My whole body aches for this.

"Alright boys and girls, we aren't done just yet," I tell the camera. I can see the vote counter ticking up as well as the active feed in the chat. My followers are excited to see this part. It has been a while since one of us has had time to do this.

"We need to loosen the skin around the important parts. Since we already removed the eyelids, that is one chore done. It is an easy feat to cut around the nose. But be careful not to get the eyes, sometimes it is easier to do the nose before the eyelids, if you have the choice. But you greedy fuckers just wanted to make sure he watched." I chuckle and pat Jordan on the shoulder. I kneel and narrow my milky white eyes at him.

"This is the fun part." I reach up and remove the ball-gag's strap.

Jordan's mouth is slack from the effort. He might have dislocated his jaw, there were a lot of pops I'm not sure of their origin. He fought hard. But now a puddle of drool spills onto his lap. A weak moan escapes his lips.

"I leave this for last, because if they fight back now there is a chance of getting bit, and I hate being bit." I grab Jordan by the cheek and slide my fingers between his flesh and teeth, forcing his mouth wider. "We have to remove all these attachments, or we risk losing the lips. And you have such a pretty mouth. I bet many ladies believed your lies," I growl in his face.

I insert the razor between his teeth and the top of his lip until the blade pokes through the incision made around the base of his nostrils.

Jordan's scream fills my ears. Weak, raw, primal. His eyes roll up into his skull as I finish my job and step back. His lips and cheeks sag away from his jaw like the jowls of a hound dog.

I step behind him and insert my fingers into the seam. Jordan jerks and croaks out a screech as the sound of Velcro fills the air. The copper smell of blood fills my nose anew as inch by precious inch I peel the scalp toward his face. I stop at his ears and the son of a bitch vomits.

"This is why we don't rush this part. We have to cut the ears from the inside or they will tear." I make quick work of the cartilage and continue to peel.

When I have rolled the scalp all the way to the hairline, I come around the front. Blood and bile drip from his lips.

"Almost there, Jordan. Just hang on for me a few more moments." I add sugar to my voice, "Are you glaring at me? I can't tell." I grin beneath my mask. "We're almost there." I look over at the camera. "What do you all think? Like a band-aid or do you all want to spend a few more minutes with me?" I wait. My fingers itch to be done with the process, but my love for drama demands giving the audience one last choice.

"The ayes have it." I grin at Jordan. "I really hope you stick with me until the end."

I reach behind him and grab a pair of garden sheers. Blue eyes frantically dart between me and the tool. Bracing my footing, I wink at him then grab the flesh just above his eyes and twist my hips pulling my weight and his face away from his body.

A squeak of agony escapes Jordan as I peel the flesh down to his chest like a rogue hangnail that got away from me. I chuckle and raise the clippers. Blue eyes still flutter in bloody sockets. It must be disturbing to see the inside of your own face. I cut the loose flesh and flap it in front of his twitching body like a flag. I drop the clippers on the tarp and grab the other end of the skin and hold it up to the camera.

"And that is all for today, folks. Be safe out there. And remember the real monsters are the ones who hurt innocents." I tap the command to disconnect the feed and turn to Jordan.

"Now for the finale." I pull the mask from my face and notice the chunks of flesh that come away with it.

Jordan's jaw opens and closes as he watches me step closer. I wipe a hand over my face, removing the old me like clay.

He sees my true form.

The monster beneath the mask. A skull with fangs for teeth and empty eye sockets that see the truth of a soul. I gnash my teeth at him before standing up straight and placing his face over my own. Soulful-stormy eyes watch as my body changes. My shoulders broaden, and I shrink a couple inches. I shudder as my new form takes hold.

Jordan stares at a copy of himself. A version lacking eyes. I grin down at him and squat to his level.

"Ah, it's always nice to be someone new." I grin. "But something is missing." I look around the tarp and pluck the two brown orbs from the mess. "I'll trade you."

I like it here. I have until Jordan's body is found, and that will be a long time, hopefully.

"A connection has been made in the Facer Case," the news broadcaster announces. I lean forward, liking this new nickname. What channel is this? I'll have to send Sarah a thank you basket for the moniker. "All of his victims have one thing in common. It took the CIA and FBI profilers looking at all the cases to realize these men and women are all sexual predators. After reviewing their computers, each was found to be in possession of illicit material."

"Perhaps the Facer is doing us all a favor." The man beside her chuckles.

"I guess if you're a monster, you better be on alert. There is a bigger monster out there now." Sarah laughs and nods at her co-anchor.

I grin and shut off the television. Jordan's face smiles back at me, stormy-blue eyes sparkling.

"Maybe one day they'll get me on identity theft."

Danny Boy
By Jeffrey Caston

It *seemed* like a good idea at the time.

In fact, it seemed like a *really* good idea.

At the time.

Go to Hawaii, Danny had thought. *Let the company pay for 10% work and 90% vacation.* He worked too much as it was. He rarely got any time to himself, much less having the chance to get on a plane and actually go somewhere.

Then an opportunity, out of nowhere, fell into his lap.

Danny's employer, a nationwide shipping company, planned to send two employees, Maria and Leah, to an industry retreat that would roundtable issues facing the companies charged with delivering goods to a consumer-hungry American populace. Four days of ostensible working and industry discussions sprinkled in with luaus, drinking, and soaking up rays on pristine Maui beaches.

In a seeming stroke of misfortune, both Maria and Leah had to back out. Maria had contracted a nasty flu and Leah claimed a 'family emergency', though everyone knew, in reality, her fling with Daryl in accounting (the worst kept secret in the office) was—yet again—causing Leah abrupt marital problems.

So, Danny's manager offered him the trip in their place. Because of audit and tax concerns, Danny's wife or kids couldn't go with him. That was fine as far as Danny was concerned. His wife was helping her dad recuperate from open heart surgery and really couldn't get away. She had taken their daughters with her to Ohio since his father-in-law doted on the girls.

That left Danny with four days to spread out across two adjoining suites the company had reserved for Maria and Leah.

It *should* have been amazing.

It wasn't.

Or at least it hadn't started out that way.

Danny got to the airport early. But then the flight was delayed—for four hours. Some mechanical problem. He finally got on the plane. But he'd misread his ticket. It wasn't business class, but coach. No leg room. Then the plane started to fill up. Right away *that* became a nightmare. Two sorority girls took the seats ahead of him and talked incessantly the moment they sat down. A young, harried mother dropped into the seat behind him and to the right. *Directly* behind him sat her demon-spawn, masquerading as a five-year-old. The little twerp felt it his God-given right to kick Danny's seat-back, heedless of Danny telling the kid to stop, arguing with the mother, and finally imploring a flight attendant for help. All to no avail, leaving the brat to thump its little juvenile foot into Danny's seat-back.

The whole. Fucking. Flight.

Danny finally landed in Hawaii, only to learn there was *another* plane with its own mechanical problem, which delayed Danny's flight from taxiing to the gate.

And to top it all off, the cabbie taking him to his hotel blasted some sort of 'music' that consisted of a random collection of discordant sounds overlaid by screeching gibberish.

The entire experience left him in quite the sour mood. He grumbled his way through getting cleaned up once checked into his suites. Exhausted and discombobulated from the time change, he staggered down to the ground floor, where he found an independent coffee shop adjoining the lobby.

He'd spilled most of his in-flight coffee—twice. That little spot of fun came courtesy of the brat's incessant kicking that vibrated both cups out of his hand. The inadequate supply left Danny in desperate need of a java recharge.

Danny entered the coffee shop, sighing to reset his emotions. The shop had a simple set up with a cash register and a commercial espresso machine. Danny saw only one employee, a tall man with sandy blond-hair that might be between 30 and 40, though his chiseled jawline, broad shoulders, and narrow waist made him appear much younger. His radiant hazel eyes made contact with Danny's muddy brown orbs. He walked to the service counter.

"Aloha! I'll be right with you, sir," the extraordinarily handsome man said with a low, masculine voice that somehow also managed to sound melodic. "My counter person is on break."

"No problem," Danny said.

Thirty seconds later, the man stood in front of him at the register. His name-tag identified him as Jeffrey. He'd inexplicably become even more good-looking in the five steps between the espresso machine and the register. He'd always heard Hawaii was populated by gorgeous people. Danny was suddenly very glad to be at the conference alone—and being in the shop alone. Unwelcome images of Leah succumbing to yet another impulsive lady-boner and ripping Jeffrey's clothes off then jumping his bones pushed into Danny's mind's eye.

I hate this guy already, Danny thought.

"What can I get started for you, sir," Jeffrey said with a subtle but genuine smile, displaying perfect white teeth.

Of course, they are, Danny internally grumbled.

"Um..." Danny mused, looking at the menu. "What's the strongest drink you have?"

Jeffrey blinked. "Hmm... Java addict or a long trip in?"

"*Looong* trip in."

"Okay," Jeffrey said. "I would normally suggest the house brew. We have some of the best Kona coffee on the islands, but I have something special for you. It has our house blend mixed with white coffee beans and a few other varietals. *Very* high octane. It'll perk you right up. Sound good?"

"Sure," Danny said, though he felt less than certain.

"Coming right up, sir," Jeffrey said. "Can I get you anything else?"

"No, that's all," Danny said, then thought better of it. "Well, sure. Some advice, maybe. I'm here for a conference, but it doesn't start until later this afternoon. Is there somewhere I can get something to eat?"

Jeffrey's expression became pensive for a moment, then those hazel eyes glittered.

"Oh sure, yeah. About four blocks away, there's Mama Jamie's Kitchen. Local institution. They serve all kinds of delectable Hawaiian dishes."

"Okay..."

Jeffrey's excited expression lit up his face. The man probably moonlighted as a cover model for those Harlequin books his wife read. "You have *got* to try their lau lau! Best you'll ever have. Promise. Oh my God, I would donate a kidney for their lau lau right now." The younger man smiled again, though this time it had an almost predatory quality to it, like a shark's.

Loud loud? Yikes. Sounds too weird. I'll look for a burger joint or something.

Danny's response, however, was more polite. Just how he was raised. "Thank you, I'll look for that. Four blocks. Thank you, young man."

"Sure. Hope you enjoy your time in Hawaii. That will be five dollars."

It was at that moment, when Danny pulled out a crisp five-spot, that he noticed a tip jar.

Ugh... Tipping culture.

He wasn't a fan to begin with, but had he a single in his wallet he might have parted with that. But he didn't, so Jeffrey would just have to be content with his stunning looks and the washboard abs Danny suspected lay under his tight-fitting polo. Danny handed over the money, then deposited his wallet back in its proper place—his right back pocket. Jeffrey's smile faltered the tiniest bit with his apparent realization that his services hadn't earned him a tip.

He'll live.

"Very good, sir. Hawaiian Sunrise Special coming right up." Jeffrey whisked back to the espresso machine and began assembling Danny's beverage. They made eye contact a few times. As he was pulling espresso shots, he mixed in a white powder from a clear plastic container marked 'Da White Coffee Grindz'. Odd spelling, but Danny gave it no further thought.

When it looked to be done, Jeffrey palmed the open top of the paper cup and set it on a counter. He aligned a black plastic lid over the top and snapped it in place.

"Here you go," Jeffrey said. Another smile with perfect teeth set off with a flawlessly tanned face. "Hope you enjoy. And if you're in the hotel here, I'll be interested to hear what you think of lau lau! Aloha!"

"Thank you. I'll do that."

Yeah sure... Not.

Danny made a mental note to at least do an internet search to figure out what the hell Loud Loud was, just in case he ran into the annoyingly handsome barista somewhere and needed to intelligently sound as though he tried it. He remained grateful he was alone at the conference too. If Leah had been in that coffee shop, met Jeffrey, *and* had the adjoining suite. One of them would have seduced the other and subjected him to hours of panting, the thumping of a bed, and crying out for God during raucous sex. Oof. Talk about Loud Loud. That was a frustration—and a lack of sleep—he didn't need.

But right now, he just needed his coffee, even though Jeffrey had made it.

Danny left the coffee shop and let the outside rays tickle his skin. It felt good. He sat upon a nearby park bench and took a sip. It was delicious. Jeffrey could add coffee creation to his list of talents.

Ugh. So maddening.

It didn't stop Danny, however, from taking another sip. Then another. It didn't even bother him that he was drinking a hot coffee on what—to him—was a very hot day. In fact, the coffee felt almost euphoric going down. Another sip. He was hoping that promised caffeine would hit him soon. He needed it.

The heat seemed to be getting to him first though. A lightheadedness made his body sway, like sail in a light breeze.

Wow... This climate... I better...

Then Danny's world went dark.

Danny awoke freezing. Colder than he'd ever felt before.

Through chattering teeth, Danny took stock of his surroundings. He was in a tub. The tub in his own hotel room. He recognized its basic décor and his toiletries that he'd left on the counter.

The water was freezing. Dozens of ice cubes bobbed atop the chilly water's surface. He tried to sit up, but a lance of pain stabbing into his back brought him up short. He cried out, which told him something wasn't right. Danny *never* cried out in pain. He was too tough for that. Even when he'd blown out his knee in high school football, he'd managed to keep it together. But he was older now and the deep-seated agony hit him a lot harder.

Danny gritted his teeth and calmed down. He slowly raised himself within the tub. It hurt, but he managed it. His breaths came in short, hard gasps. He grunted as he eased one hand behind him and probed at his back, the source of his pain. He cried out when his fingertips brushed something off center of his spine. He'd thought maybe he'd somehow injured his back. He knew better than that now.

Tender, rough lines passed along his tactile sense. Danny recognized the sensation immediately.

Stitches.

He had stitches in his lower left back. The realization made the room spin.

What has happened to me?

Danny was a smart guy. He worked hard. He knew when he had a problem before him. Despite the pain and disorientation, he went into problem-solving mode.

I need my phone. Get to my phone.

Danny always had a strong work ethic and could push through most anything. Taking it slow and easy, he managed to rise to his feet and exit the tub. He needed to find his clothes. That was the most likely place he'd find his phone.

He staggered to the main room. His clothes lay upon the bed, neatly folded.

His phone was in the right front pocket... just where he'd left it. If only he could remember where he'd left himself.

Danny shook and his back ached as he positioned the phone in front of his face. He plopped onto the bed, unable to summon the strength to stand an instant longer. He powered it up and waited for the home-screen. Within seconds, it chimed with notifications popping up for voicemails and texts. His family and employer probably checking on him. The home-screen clock told him it was six hours later than when he'd gone down for his coffee.

He was about to check the voicemails and texts when a new chime came, sharper and higher-pitched.

And one he'd never heard before.

Danny opened the notifications menu and found someone had sent a video clip.

Scared and intrigued, he tapped the screen to open it. A short buffering later, and Jeffrey's face popped up on a screen and a video started.

The annoyingly handsome barista sat at a table. The clutter of sounds from human activity filled the background.

What the...?

"Hi, Danny, Jeffrey here. I'm at Mama Jamie's having lau lau—my favorite! Look!" He raised a fork with a speared chunk of some kind of meat with a dark green layer that looked like boiled spinach clinging to it.

"So delicious!" Jeffrey said. "Wish you could try some. I told you that I'd donate a kidney for a plate of this... but never said whose!" Jeffrey turned one eye to the camera and winked.

Asshole. Fucking ASSHOLE! Rage built as Danny realized what had happened and why he was having back pain.

"Lucky for me, I had access to one! Thanks a bunch, buddy. You'd be amazed at what kind of stuff you can sell through the dark web." He took a bite and his eyes rolled back ecstatically.

"Oh my God, dude, you gotta try this! Don't blow me off this time. I would totally share the money I got selling your kidney to a dark web organ harvester... but..."

Jeffrey took another bite of his 'Loud Loud' or whatever the hell it was. He paused again to chew. Though he hated the man and wanted him to die, Danny remained fixated on the video.

"Anyway," Jeffrey said as he finished chewing. "I would totally share the proceeds from your kidney sale, but... well... I don't want to. Oh, and one other thing... a little life advice... always tip your barista!"

Jeffrey winked again and then the video ended.

Danny sat there, stunned, lamenting how easily and unexpectedly he'd gotten tangled up in the dark web.

Jeffrey
By D.L.Garvin

Jeffrey had always been a strange kid. From the time he was born, he was never a picky eater. That always pleased his parents, since there's nothing more frustrating than a picky eater. Eventually, they became concerned when he started eating weird things like bugs, worms, and lizards.

Although they were concerned, they imagined he would eventually grow out of it. To their dismay, the older he got the more bizarre his taste got. Fish guts and exotic grubs were often on the menu.

Jeffrey's compulsion with bizarre foods led him to write horror stories about wild and crazy foods. His book series became insanely popular and the royalties from the books afforded him a very comfortable lifestyle. He was able to travel the world, trying the most exotic foods from each country he visited. This experience was constant fuel for his stories, with each book being more bizarre than the last.

He sampled every kind of bug imaginable, dozens of different types of grubs, and fish parts that would turn the stomach of the strongest person. In fact, he took pleasure in making other people sick to their stomachs. It was to the point that it had turned into a full-blown fetish. Nothing excited him more than someone hurling their lunch after watching him eat some gross food. Every time he would go out to eat, he would try to find the fullest restaurant possible and then order the most disgusting thing on the menu. As he ate, he would constantly watch the crowd for that one person to start looking a little green.

As soon as they blew chunks, it created a chain reaction. The more people that spewed, the more excited he would get. When he finished, he'd stand up and bow to the hurling masses, then pay for his meal and walk out with a huge smile on his face. He would tell himself aloud, "Job well done."

This went on for years. It finally got to the point he was banned from every restaurant within fifty miles of his home. His culinary exploration kept taking him further and further afield. He finally reached a tipping point, the travel time no longer worth the effort, especially when he stopped getting the desired reaction. It became a major letdown that resulted in him withdrawing and falling into a deep depression. He became a recluse, barely able to have any contact with the outside world.

His writing started slipping and his book sales plummeted. He sat in front of his computer for hours, staring at the blinking cursor. All he wanted was to eat something gross and then watch the reaction when someone barfed at the sight of him doing so. Friends tried to console him to no avail. He made desperate pleas on social media for people to send him videos of themselves barfing, only to be denied. This just depressed him further.

Then he discovered something.

He discovered the dark web. It led to a deep dive. He found a chat room that bought and sold every kind of rare and exotic food on the planet. Jeffrey was quite literally like a kid in a candy store. He began ordering foods that were so rare that many of them even he had never heard of. In most cases, this did not deter him in the least.

He sampled foods from all over the planet from the gastric smorgasbord he discovered. The only thing missing was the reaction he so desperately craved. The fetish that he couldn't live without. As luck would have it, there was absolutely nothing one couldn't find on the dark web. One late evening he was cruising the deep web while enjoying his supper—a large bowl of live witchetty grubs from Australia with a side of escamol from Mexico, topped off with 2 slices of toast with a healthy slathering of Vegemite. He stumbled upon a server that hosted every type of fetish video you could ever imagine.

He searched through the topics: feet, hands, hair, big girls, little girls, warts, scars, on and on until his heart skipped a beat. He found "Emesis Videos".

"Eureka!" he shouted. It was the treasure at the end of the rainbow.

The next week he spent in the basement, in the dark, glued to his computer from the time he woke up until the time he went to bed. Hours and hours of vomit videos. From liquids of every color imaginable to different sizes of chunks. Fruity bits of cereal came out like a rainbow across one person's room. Another person blew a flight of expelled rice that resembled a swarm of maggots. Each video was more exciting than the last.

It seemed as though there was no end to the ways and amounts people could puke. He did have his favorites that he would re-watch over and over again. The rice flight was one of them. He watched it 20 to 25 times a day. He just couldn't get enough. Jeffrey was in heaven. Endless videos and the e exotic foods delivered straight to his door kept him happy.

He would never have to leave the house again. It couldn't have been more perfect. But, as the old saying goes, too much of a good thing can become a bad thing. And that's exactly what happened.

One evening Jeffrey was sitting in his dark basement enjoying a heaping plate of tuna eyeballs and deep-fried grasshoppers. A cold can of peanut butter porter beer to wash it down with sat before him. He was rewatching one of his favorites, then it happened.

The projection was like a fire hose of bright white chunks of cottage cheese. First, he had an uncomfortable feeling. Then came a distinct gastric rumble, followed by profuse sweating. Then came an eruption not unlike Mount St Helen's in 1980. The convulsive explosions continued for over an hour until his stomach had no more to offer. But the violent convulsions didn't subside.

Suddenly, he felt a pop in his abdomen, followed by a gusher of blood mixed with chunks of meat. Jeffrey had convulsed so violently it ripped his stomach wide open. He collapsed and died in a large pool of his own vomit and blood.

It was days until the housekeeper arrived and found his body. She called 911, and after hanging up she looked around the room, hand over her nose and mouth, trying not to add to the existing mess.

They don't pay me enough to clean this up. I'm outta here!

Pay it Darkward
A Novelette By Jeffrey Caston

Day One

It's like something you might find on
the dark web. :D

Marcus Moxley looked at his computer screen, unsure how to proceed. He'd started chatting with a woman who—according to her profile—lived in Tacoma like him. He was desperate to make a connection but wasn't sure how to respond.

Just play it cool. Like anything else. Fake it 'til you make it.

So he tried that, typing his response then waiting.

LOL.

You know I don't really even know what the dark web is. I mean, is it even real?

Whaaa! You don't know what the dark web is? Are you ancient or Amish? Lol

I mean I've *heard* of the dark web obv, but what is it really? Does it really exist or is it just urban legend?

LOL. Pretty sure it's real.

Okay... but then what is it?

It's just a place that's basically like a black market that stays off the radar of the regular web. Stuff you wanna do or say or buy. All kinds of illegal taboo stuff, for sure. Or at least pretty shady. Think... uh... if ur mom would disapprove or you would go to jail for it, chances are it's on the dark web.

I suppose...

You didn't answer my real question tho

Oh? What question?

Well, two questions. Sorta. Are you ancient or Amish?

Oh! LOL. Neither. Promise.

Prove it?

How?

Meet me for coffee?

Wow. Really? U wanna meet?

Absolutely.

Marcus's heart-rate entered jackhammer territory. He didn't know what 6-6-6TerrorBabe looked like. But he didn't want to screw up a potential match or meetup, so he'd agree. Obviously, he would. After only a moment's hesitation, he returned his attention to his keyboard.

Cool. Sure. I'd like that. You pick the time and place.
Great. Tomorrow work? 8 pm?
Sure.
K. Look forward to it. See you then! Here's the address...

Day Two

Marcus looked at his phone for the third time to check the address. Something had to be wrong. This was definitely not a coffee shop. Was it a trap? A murder house? He confirmed the address in front of him was the same as what 6-6-6TerrorBabe sent. But it just couldn't be right. She'd invited him for coffee, but this place... This place looked like an abandoned warehouse.

Except...

Two things put his mind at ease. First, he noticed a yellow plastic placard with black lettering spelling "COFFEE" above an arrow pointing downward at a set of heavy, metal, industrial doors. Embarrassment crept up his cheeks for not having seen the sign earlier. Second, a man, well-dressed in a dark tailored suit and an impeccably tied glossy silk necktie resting on the front of a gleaming white, crisply laundered shirt, opened those industrial doors. He held it open for the glamorously dressed woman hanging on his arm.

Okay, well it might not be a coffee shop per se, but unless these two are well-dressed contract killers, this probably isn't a murder house.

Three more women entered through the still open door while Marcus gawked at it. All three wore more casual attire. Following them was someone Marcus could have sworn he'd seen on TV as a city council member. If *that* guy felt comfortable, no way it could be a murder house.

Maybe a pop-up coffee shop? Maybe 6-6-6TerrorBabe, whoever she might be, was running it and it was just a temporary shop.

Point was, it clearly wasn't a trap set just for him. It was something to do with coffee it seemed.

So, Marcus entered the building.

He followed the crowd of people. The hallway, giving off a creepy vibe from the sputtering, half-dead fluorescent bulbs, ratcheted up his anxiety again. He considered turning back. There was just so much that felt odd, too unknown to him. But, he also knew that he needed some adventure and excitement in his life. Playing it safe, not being spontaneous, being fearful of the new and the unknown, was what prompted his split-up. His girlfriend, Alicia, dumped him six months prior.

If I want a different life, I have to live a different life.

Marcus continued, pressing on and resisting the urge to turn away when he heard cheering and thumping music. He detected spotlight beams moving about. Five seconds later, he entered a large open space. Throngs of people crowded together, forming a rough box enclosing the center of the room. Tentatively, Marcus moved forward. When he neared the edge, he realized what the people were surrounding. They formed a perimeter around foam mats laid upon the floor. Marcus sensed money exchanging hands between people in the crowd. Shouts, jeers, and clapping mixed with the music to create a reverberating cacophony. Off to one side, against a wall, three metal canisters stood upon a folding table. Stacks of red and white cups formed towers next to them.

Um... is that the—

A commotion to one side interrupted Marcus's train of thought. It took him but a moment to discern the reason for all the excitement. A man knelt upon the mat, bare chest heaving with panting breaths. His skin glistened with sweat and one eye was swollen shut. But there was another person sprawled supine on the mat, bloodied and bruised, clearly in far worse shape than Mr. Swollen Eye. Two more men approached and began dragging the unconscious Mr. Bloodied off the mat.

Jesus, I am so in the wrong place...

Marcus took in a slow, deep breath. He wasn't going to fight anyone. He'd run away if it came to that. He'd never been much of a fighter. He wasn't a wimp or a pushover, but he had better skills in conflict avoidance than conflict ending. Maybe 6-6-6TerrorBabe used the term "coffee" as some code he was supposed to have known about but didn't. Hardly mattered now. He was here and he would see it through, unless shit hit the fan.

But how am I supposed to meet this woman?

A slender blonde, wearing a white blouse, a black pencil skirt, and matching black jacket, walked to the center of the mat.

With a voice projecting like a stage actor, the woman spoke and the excited crowd quieted.

"Wow," she said. "What a fight that was! That was just the last of our mid-card bouts. Maybe next week Mr. Dorn will come back and take on another challenger. What do you think?"

The crowd cheered as Mr. Dorn/Mr. Swollen Eye left the mat. They might have been excited, but the atmosphere dried Marcus's throat. *What in the world did I get myself into here?* he wondered. *Some sort of fight club? Does anyone expect* me *to fight?*

But the blonde lady seemingly in charge wasn't discernibly paying any attention to him. Nor was anyone in the crowd from what Marcus could tell. Her next statement confirmed that.

"So, are you ready for your main event?"

"YES!" the crowd boomed in one giant voice that reverberated and echoed through the industrial space.

"I don't know," she said, "y'all don't sound too sure." She held her arms outstretched to her sides with her palms up. "Lemme ask one more time. *ARE YOU READY FOR YOUR MAIN EVENT?*"

Marcus didn't participate in the response. But everyone else stepped up their affirmation. "YEEESSSS!" they shouted. Rhythmic clapping emphasized their excitement.

"All right then," the blonde lady said. "Here's your champion Diana 'The Hunter-Killer' Simmons! Show her how much you want to see her beat some ass!"

The crowd erupted once more. Marcus toyed again with the idea of trying to duck out. But something he could not put his finger on rooted him to his spot near the front of the crowd. He stood still in the second row of the throng forming a human ring around the mat. He still had a clear view of the fighting space.

A tall, lithe woman, with raven-black glossy hair cut in a bob a few inches below her jaw, strutted in through a pathway formed by spectators clearing the way. She had a pretty, though severe, face bearing a harsh expression. But she projected a magnetism Marcus found sexy. Her outfit, which decidedly didn't appear well-suited to a fight of any sort, left little to the imagination. A black tube top covered her torso from just underneath her armpits down just past her breasts, highlighting her washboard abdominal muscles. Tight black shorts starting just above her hips traveled down only so far as her upper thighs. A woven mesh, the type of material used for fishnet stockings, covered the rest, from the base of her neck down to her ankles. The mesh also covered her insteps and the soles of her otherwise bare feet. Sinewy, compact muscles rippled under her taut skin as she rolled her shoulders and bounced lightly in place.

"Diana is your Extreme All Goes Champion," the blonde lady explained. "She's held that title for a while now and she's undefeated in her title defenses..."

Wow. That's... that is immensely impressive, Marcus thought. Given the two bruiser looking guys he'd just seen, he could scarcely see how this Diana could be undefeated. Unless it was a women's league. Marcus wasn't sure.

"Diana has snapped, tapped, or napped every man, woman, and anyone brave enough to face her. Each one took an epic ass-beating along the way."

Hmm... okay. Scratch that. Co-ed fights? Real fights that were co-ed? Marcus reeled as he considered. He was nothing of a fighter himself, so he lacked personal experience. Obviously, Diana the Champion had to be pretty formidable. He knew he certainly wouldn't be able to match her. He felt no shame in that. All thoughts of leaving... well... left him. He was too intrigued now to scurry away like a coward. And truthfully, seeing this raven-haired warrior-woman stirred something exciting within him.

As if reading his thoughts, Diana the Champion made eye contact with him. She smiled. Then—most surprisingly—she gave him a wink that took him aback.

Was this...? he wondered.

The blonde announcer's continued introduction interrupted Marcus's train of thought.

"But tonight, we have a special treat for you. A mystery of violence. A thriller of mayhem. A title match of unpredictable, unknowable, and unpreparable fight action. Diana, why don't you explain tonight's challenge and your eleventh title defense?"

Diana the Champion's gaze lingered upon Marcus a moment longer and her smile became more mischievous. She broke off when she addressed the crowd.

"Tonight, I put my title up for grabs for anyone with balls big enough to take me on. Any comer. Any style. Any size. Whoever. I don't care. I will beat anyone. So who's up for it?"

Diana the Champion wasn't looking at him. Instead, her eyes scanned the crowd. She didn't seem to be directing her challenge at him, but he could feel her confidence like waves crashing toward him.

"I'll do it. Bitch, you're going down tonight!"

Across from Marcus's position, other spectators jostled and stumbled as another woman pushed her way forward to reach the edge of the mat, flanked by a tall, muscular man with tow-head blond hair.

"I challenge you for the title!" she barked.

"Oooh!" The crowd murmured. Marcus took in this challenger's appearance. She stood confidently, with a physique even more impressive than Diana the Champion's. She was shorter, but had a more heavily muscled frame. She, too, wore no footwear Marcus noticed as she stepped onto the mat. Blue and white spandex shorts and a blue tank top covered her frame. Her bare shins bore bruises of varying shapes, sizes and colors. Strips of off-white tape wrapped her hands and wrists, sort of like what Marcus had seen boxers use under their big, cushioned gloves. The challenger wore no such gloves. But she carried a stony, hostile game face, staring down Diana the Champion.

Diana the Champion kept her back to the challenger. Her right index and middle finger slipped under a thin strip wrapped around her left wrist. Marcus quickly realized it was an elastic hair band. Diana the Champion remained facing Marcus as she pulled the strands of her bob behind her head into a stubby ponytail.

Diana the Champion's eyes met Marcus's again. She puckered her lips and mimicked giving him a kiss. She winked again. Only then, did she deign to speak to her brave challenger.

"Wow. Bitch? Wow. Okay," Diana the Champion said. "Well, here's the thing, honey..."

Diana dropped her hands, having secured her hair from the sides of her face. She turned, putting her back to Marcus, facing the challenger.

"...after I get done with you after a minute or less into a fight, when I tap *you* out like a little *bitch*..." Diana said, voice dripping contempt.

"Ooooh! Ooo-hoo-ooh," the crowd murmured.

"...It's just *not* gonna satisfy my bloodlust. And I *really* need to satisfy my..." Diana looked back at Marcus, "...urges," she continued, turning her attention back to the muscly, bruiser lady challenging her. "So, I can't fight you..."

"You fucking said—" The challenger went red-faced in protest, pointing an aggressively hostile finger at Diana the Champion.

Diana held up her hand to shush the challenger, who didn't get the message.

"—any challeng—"

"Honey, this is the part where you shut your mouth and listen," Diana the Champion said. "I can't shut your mouth *for* you... yet. But I'm talking, which means you're not. Champ's prerogative."

"OOOH!" the crowd reinforced Diana the Champion's taunt. It worked. The challenger narrowed her eyes and grimaced. But she did so quietly.

"As I was saying... Hearing you scream and beg for *my mercy* will be satisfying, but not enough." She wagged her finger at the challenger. "I'll fight you, but only on one condition. Your boyfriend there fights with you. I'm gonna knock his ass out first, *then* deal with you. Sound good?"

The crowd gasped. The challenger's face slackened for a moment, but then recovered her composure with a smile and a laugh.

"Both of us? At the same time?" the challenger asked. "Okay, fuck yeah, bitch. It's your funeral."

"You accept the conditions?" the announcer lady said to the challenger, stepping between the two women. The challenger responded by stomping her bruised legs on the ground and punching one wrapped up fist into the other wrapped palm.

"Fuck yeah!" the challenger said. The man who accompanied her appeared even taller and more muscular after Marcus took a better look at him. His spiky blond hair gave him a sinister visage. This apparent boyfriend stepped onto the mat and joined his girlfriend's side, standing a full head taller than her. The announcer lady spoke as the imposing boyfriend pulled off his shoes. His shins too looked a bit bruised.

"What's your name, stud?" the announcer asked. "And your name, too, princess."

They gave the announcer the same unamused looks. The man spoke first. "Fredrick. Fredrick the Fearless Badass," the boyfriend said. He sounded like every arrogant jock that Marcus had the displeasure of encountering in high school.

The girlfriend got right into the announcer's face and spoke loudly. "I'm Collette. Collette the Cutthroat."

"Okay, wow. You two sound really confident, Fredrick the Fearless Badass and Collette the Cutthroat. Do you accept the champ's challenge? Fighting you both at the same time?"

The crowd hushed in anticipation. Marcus, for his part, had no idea what was transpiring or how real this exchange was. It didn't look staged. But two on one? And each challenger looking like seasoned martial arts fighters? Marcus's throat dried with worry as to what was to come.

Fredrick and Collette looked at one another, smiled, then responded in unison. "Fuck YES!"

Diana the Champion threw her head back and howled, but not a howl of aggravation or anger. It was more like a wolf's howl, the howl of a hunter pleased that the hunt was on.

The announcer lady's eyes went wide, and she regarded the challengers. "You guys sure you want to do this? That first guy looks like he's going to need a seeing eye dog after his fight."

"*FUCK YES!*" they repeated. Collette bounced in place while Fredrick rolled his shoulders and stretched out his legs and arms.

"Okay," the announcer said, "take your places on opposite sides. Champ, you ready?"

"Yes!" She pointed at her two opponents. "Prepare to be in a very dark place, you two."

Diana the Champion turned to Marcus again with a seemingly laser-focused ability to hone in on his position. He couldn't hold eye contact this time, however. He shifted his gaze between her and her two challengers. Diana the Champion seemed to read his concern. She met it with a smile and mouthed the words "no chance" while pointing at them.

"Okay, folks," the announcer addressed the crowd. "This is the final bout y'all. The final bout of the night for Extreme All Goes Fight League. And y'all know how we operate here, right? You know the rules, right? What are the rules?"

"No RULES!" the crowd intoned.

"That's right! So let's get started." The announcer threw her fist up into the air then beat a hasty retreat from the mat.

The boyfriend-girlfriend challengers rushed forward, Fredrick leading. Diana the Champion held her ground until the last second. She jumped up, meeting Fredrick head-on, placed her hands on his shoulders, and kicked Collette. Diana's heel connected with Collette's forehead, shoving her backward several feet. She stumbled, then fell awkwardly on her rump. Her head swayed and her eyes held a slight, unfocused glaze.

Fredrick roared as he grabbed Diana's wrists. But not for long. With circular flicks of her hands and wrists, Diana was free. She hopped back several steps and took up a defensive stance. Her legs looked as though they were quivering with jackhammer intensity, but Marcus soon realized Diana merely readied herself for the next stage of the fight. She hadn't retreated, but baited Fredrick away from Collette. Fredrick's girlfriend appeared in no condition to offer any help at the moment.

Fredrick took that bait, closing the distance with a few long, purposeful strides. He held his arms up, elbows in, and his wrapped fists covered his face, knuckles poised just below murderously angry eyes. Diana held her ground again, though still bouncing in place. She looked like a vibrating spring ready to snap at any instant. And then she did. Fredrick raised his right leg up, looking as though he'd swing it like a meaty club.

He only brought his knee up to waist level when Diana's left foot shot out, checking Fredrick's knee, stopping whatever attack he'd planned dead in its tracks. With a continuing, fluid movement,

Diana jabbed Fredrick in the solar plexus with the ball of her foot, exposed by pulling her toes back. Fredrick lurched forward, leaning into Diana's upswinging right elbow. The second blow to his solar plexus left him nearly doubled over.

Diana leaped up, driving her right knee under his chin while pounding upon the top of his head with the base of her elbow. The crowd reacted to the blows as intensely as Fredrick did. He staggered away and struggled to keep his feet.

Next, it was Diana capitalizing and rushing her opponent. Two short steps preceded a leap forward, one leg outstretching in a thrusting kick aimed at his head. Fredrick took that bait, too. Her kick had merely been a feint. While still mid-air, Diana dropped and bent that leading leg in front of her, then snapped it forward, kicking Fredrick in the lower abdomen. Before the large brute could react, Diana struck each side of his jaw with a combination of punches, left then right. She slid back on the mat half a step, then whirled around backward, swinging her outstretched right leg like a lean but strong stick, the bottom of her foot arcing upward as the striking surface. Diana's balletic movements mesmerized and amazed Marcus; he managed no reaction other than standing there, mouth agape.

Diana's kick connected with Fredrick's temple even though he stood a few inches taller than her. Even lacking Fredrick's bulky muscle mass, Diana's kick delivered a ferocious force that sent him spinning forward, heels over head, until his back slammed on the mat with a heavy crash.

He stopped moving. The entire exchange of blurred movement and Diana's perfectly executed attacks lasted less than five seconds. Marcus was holding his breath. He felt reasonably sure he wasn't the only one based on the hush falling over the crowd.

Then the crowd's cheers and clapping erupted with such growing intensity it created a giant wave, like those surfers hunt for. It enveloped Marcus with its energy and before he realized it, he found himself clapping along with them despite the headache and ringing in his ears.

Collette screamed with rage and rushed forward. Diana the Champion shifted her stance, almost putting her back to Collette, but stood her ground. When she came within striking range, Collette kicked, clumsily and with amateur-looking skill compared to Diana's obvious—and dangerous—grace. Diana sidestepped and countered with a kick of her own, finding purchase right in the middle of Collette's gut.

Collette grunted and doubled over. Diana dropped to the floor, catching herself on hands readied to take the fall. Her legs scissored out and swept Collette's feet out from under her, knocking her to the mat with an awkward fall, face down. Diana demonstrated why she was the Champion by rolling into a new position and grasping the downed Collette by one wrist. Diana wrenched Collette's arm back into a very painful-looking, bent position. Marcus could almost feel the ache within his own elbow and shoulder.

An instant later, Collette's eyes shot open with agony-driven desperation. With her forehead and cheeks scrunched up, eyes closed tight, her mouth shot open and from it came the most urgent, helpless, and pitiable shriek Marcus had ever heard. Collette's free hand slapped the mat three times like a rapid-fire piston. A bell, from somewhere Marcus could not discern, rang.

Diana the Champion released Collette and sprang to her feet. Collette cradled her wrenched arm close to her body and tried to roll away. But not before Diana managed to plant her toes into Collette's left cheek and push her head away, bouncing it off the mat.

"Tapped you out like a little bitch," Diana the Champion said. "Like a little *BITCH*!"

The crowd erupted with jubilation, throwing their fists in the air in time with their whooping cheers as they chanted Diana the Champion's victory.

"Di-ann-ah! Di-ann-ah! Di-ann-ah!"

"Di-ann-ah! Di-ann-ah! Di-ann-ah!"

"Di-ann-ah! Di-ann-ah! Di-ann-ah!"

The announcer met Diana, still the champion, in the center of the mat and raised Diana's hand. "Here's your *WIN-NER*," she paused, "and *STILL* your Extreme All Goes Fight League champion... *DI-ANN-AH*!"

Fresh cheers, which Marcus joined, erupted.

"Di-ann-ah! Di-ann-ah! Di-ann-ah!" the collective voices said, even louder than before.

"Di-ann-ah! Di-ann-ah! Di-ann-ah!"

"Di-ann-ah! Di-ann-ah! Di-ann-ah!"

Marcus found himself carried away with the communal reaction. However, it was only him that got another wink and mimed kiss from Diana Still the Champion.

Not long after, the crowd thinned, leaving the underground fight venue in a slow procession. Marcus felt no desire to join them. There had to be something to Diana's personal hints and overtures. She must be 6-6-6TerrorBabe. She must be. Why else give him that personal attention unless she was and wanted him to stay? Was this all just a prelude to more?

Marcus didn't know, but he'd come too far to just slink away, and he intended to find out. If their 'date' was done then so be it. He felt more alive, more adventurous now than he ever had. Whatever happened now would happen.Hopefully, whatever happened would involve a closer view of Diana and that intoxicatingly exotic and dangerously alluring mesh suit covering her body.

Maybe he'd even feel a bit of it if he was lucky.

Diana wasn't going anywhere else either.

He tried to keep eye contact, but her lithe figure, covered by that body-suit mesh, was impossibly irresistible. It stirred feelings in his body and mind that became a heady sexual intoxication.

All activity died down, just he and Diana remained at the site. While he was at the edge of the mat, her still in her victory position centered in the room, their eyes finally met again. She smiled. Genuine. Knowing maybe, but (maybe not?) caring. They shared the space only with the odd creaks of the building and blows of random gusts of air indicative of an abandoned space.

"6-6-6TerrorBabe?"

She nodded in acknowledgement. "But you can just call me Diana now."

"Cool."

"Well?" Diana asked, "What did you think?"

Marcus's first inclination was to characterize it as 'interesting.' But he caught himself before giving that word breath beyond his thoughts. "Interesting" was a wholly inadequate label and a denigration to Diana's accomplishment. It simply wouldn't do.

"Amazing," Marcus gushed with a smile. "Utterly amazing. You're amazing. You're unbelievable. I'm excited and intrigued and amazed and... I don't even know what else. I want to process this all, but I can't. But what I do know is that you are, as I said, really amazing."

Diana's smile widened and she strolled toward him, slowly, hips swaying just a bit. Marcus thought he might lose his mind. She beckoned to him as she took a hard turn and started walking to the folding table that had the three metal cannisters. Marcus, obedience ingrained in his psyche, followed. He kept silent as Diana pulled two paper cups from the stacks.

"So did you like it?" she asked.

"Yes," Marcus said. No point in denying it. He was the furthest thing in the world from a fight fan, but seeing Diana in action created stirrings he could not articulate. He knew he needed something more than a simple 'yes' to make an impression. To be worthy of any further attention. "It was... unlike anything I could conceive. I mean I've heard of MMA and all that, but this... Where it was so primal, so raw and unadulterated. And personal. To see it up close, experience it..."

Diana nodded acknowledgement as she poured a dark liquid from a cannister into each cup.

"And all this when I thought we were just going to have coffee," Marcus said.

Diana turned and held one of the cups out to him. "We are having coffee," she said, friendly mirth leading a short laugh. Marcus took one of the cups and sniffed at it.

Sure enough, the smoky, chocolatey aroma of a craft coffee wafted up to his nose. A sip confirmed it wasn't some garbage grocery store brew.

"Okay then. Here we go. Having coffee after you utterly and definitively stomped two people, one of whom could have been my high school bully. Wow." He took a sip of the delicious coffee. "Where did you learn to fight like that?"

Diana the Champion shrugged. "Lots of places. College clubs, martial arts schools I would go to during summers. I even did gymnastics as a kid and learned to adapt some of that into fighting."

"Wow. How many fights have you had? The lady said 'still' the champion."

Marcus could still discern her smile despite the coffee cup covering her face during another sip. It was the mischievous gleam in her eyes.

"Those two dumbasses...and I'll count them together as one since they weren't exactly much competition, were my seventeenth title defense."

Marcus's jaw dropped. Seventeen? Seventeen fights where someone was trying to dethrone her position? That had to mean there were at least a few brutal skirmishes Diana had *before* transforming into the Diana the Champion.

"I... I don't know what to say. Here I was thinking I'd meet a nice geeky girl to go with my geeky self and talk about the oh so mysterious dark web. I wasn't expecting any of this. Please don't get me wrong. This was unbelievable. And exciting. I've experienced stuff tonight I thought only existed in movies. This is so much more than some lame conversation about the dark web."

Diana held her cup in both hands at her waist. He could see her stifling another giggle from the small shaking of her chest and cheeks. She pursed her lips and looked deep into his eyes.

"But we are talking about the dark web," she said. "Or maybe more accurately 'walking the walk' of the dark web. Where do you think I heard about this? The dark web. How do you think I became the controlling financial interest—all secretly, of course—in the organization that puts these tournaments on?"

"The dark web?" Marcus offered it as a question, though he knew, in his heart, that mysterious internet phenomenon was the answer."

"Yup," Diana said.

"So, it's just like, what? A big internet speakeasy to find things that are illegal? Sort of like the alternative, goth version of the information superhighway?"

Marcus had a moment when he feared he'd gone too far, been too cheeky. Diana was, after all, pretty goth-looking herself with her dark hair, dark eyeliner and black, webby outfit.

But it took but a moment for him to realize he had nothing to fear in her reaction. This time Diana could not contain her mirth. Her head tilted back and she let loose a laugh Marcus found infectious. He joined her with his own giggling.

"Sorry," he said finally.

"Don't be," Diana said. She took a step closer.

"So, I guess, it's just called the dark web because it's illegal?"

"Not exactly," Diana said. "It's real. And it's a reflection of us. The dark web is nothing more than the infection of the human soul. We like to pretend we're always high and mighty or that we're good people. But everyone has needs that can't be fulfilled as part of a so-called civilized society. Things they are afraid they want and even more afraid to ask for. Most of the time we can keep it at bay, deny ourselves our darkest thoughts and desires. Dismiss the impetus for doing the horrific acts we sometimes wish we could follow through with. Disease influences life and death in all its forms. So, the dark web is nothing more than the disease that influences the life and death of our humanity, our effort to keep our own inner darkness at bay. And when one goes to the dark web, one ends up exposing themselves not only their own dark, taboo desires, but spreading it to someone else willing to give or receive it. The interaction between influence and desire. It's sort of like paying it forward—only the opposite of that."

Marcus mulled that over. "So, I guess... pay it... darkward? I don't know. I just made that up."

Marcus breathed an inner sigh of relief as she pulled her coffee cup away and began coughing. Not from disbelief, but from finding his suggestion humorous. A few little spasms later and the smile returned. Her eyes watered, but it was happy, joyous.

"Pay it darkward... yeah... I suppose that works as well as anything," Diana said.

"Cool."

"So..." Diana said. She eased her body closer. Intimately close. Her breasts, perky and firm, brushed up against his chest, which decidedly lacked muscle tone. She smelled lightly of sweat mixed with herbal soap. "In the vein of desires, come join me on this mat. I want to show you something."

Trepidation gripped him. He feared this whole situation was a lure for him to take some sort of beat down. He didn't want to sound like a coward, but he was afraid, especially after seeing Diana dismantle Fredrick and Collette with such frightening ease.

"I... I don't know anything about fighting. I'm not ready to..."

Diana put a gentle finger to his lips, hushing him with her intoxicatingly intense presence. She smiled. She was nearly his height and her eyes bored into him, but not with anger or hate or anything negative. It was more an enticement to something exotic and exciting. She set her coffee cup down on the table, took his hand, and began pulling him toward the center of the mat.

"No fighting. I'm not going to hurt you. Promise and cross my heart," she said, using her now free hand to corroborate her intentions with the standard gesture. "Plus, I'm not about to hurt the man I want as my boyfriend." She continued to lead him toward the site where she'd knocked out and tapped out Fredrick and Collette, pausing to let Marcus set down his own coffee cup.

Marcus's heart thumped hard, and the sound of rushing blood became prominent. Only Diana's voice sounded louder in his ears, no doubt the product of the force of her personality. He would just have to accept whatever fate Diana planned for him. He'd never be able to out-fight her, and if he fled there were enough turns and confined spaces that she would undoubtedly catch him. He hoped she had something nicer than all that in mind.

She took both his hands in hers and maneuvered them so his forearms rested on her shoulders and his hands joined behind her neck. Diana, in turn, held him around the waist. It was sort of the reverse stance he remembered from high school dances. Her firm, perky breasts were back tantalizing his chest, even through her athletic top and his polo shirt. If she'd put her hips closer to his, she might have felt just how excited he was making her. He hoped she wouldn't turn cruel and slam him on the mat.

Her lips, however, partially open and very close to his, sent a different message. Her sweet breath filled his nostrils. Their eyes locked. Marcus's mouth dried. Even if they were going to tussle somehow, he now felt like it might be worth it.

Diana, Champion and Potential New Girlfriend, whispered in his ear, "Now put your left leg between my legs and rest your calf muscle against mine."

Marcus complied. Like the rest of her, her lower leg muscle felt rock-hard. His compliance earned him a new crooked smile and a flutter of her eyelashes.

"Now take that same leg and step gently back," she coaxed.

He started to slip his leg back, out from between Diana's. But with apparently preternatural reflexes, she hooked his leg, stopping him. The discrepancy between their physical control became so obvious to him.

"No, no," she said, putting her lips so close to his ear, the slight moistness sent a pleasant jolt through his whole body. "Don't move it away. Step back, calves together. Gently and slowly."

Marcus complied again. Her leg gave way to his gentle pressure, the sole of her right foot coming off the mat. It might have seemed like she was falling, only that was clearly not the case. It was more a matter of her lowering herself to the mat, balancing with envious control with her left leg easing her down. But she kept the grip on his waist, firm but not hard or rough. He followed her arc down until she was laying on the mat, face up. Without nearly her level of grace, Marcus straddled her waist and hips and rested his torso on slightly bent arms.

"Excellent," she said. "See, your first takedown. Not so hard—or unpleasant—was it?"

"No." Marcus was getting dizzy. Not from the activity—or at least not *strain* from the activity. More like the wrangling he was starting to find oddly erotic. He'd never done anything like this before with a woman. He'd barely survived the wrestling portions of junior high and high school PE.

"Now this, what you have, is called a full mount. A very good position to be in. Does it feel good?" Though his attention was focused on her emotionally intense eyes, he could not help but also sense her fingers caressing and kneading his hips, but only for a moment, before they slid to his buttocks and lower back.

Oh yes. It feels very, very good. Oh, yes indeed, Marcus thought. If this continued, he might have an embarrassing accident and need to excuse himself to... clean up. He realized the most tragic part of that was it would undoubtedly end what he hoped would be contact similar to this... but with a lot less clothing.

"Right," she said. "So this is a powerful position to be in... in MMA that is... but I suppose..." She spoke in a soft tone. Her mischievous smile formed a perfect row of ivory and her hands, though touching his hips only lightly, continued to send jolts of electricity coursing through his body. "I suppose it's a powerful position off a mat, too. But..."

Diana pressed her hips up, mashing into his. A flash of embarrassment eclipsed the electricity of excitement. She'd undoubtedly felt his bulging erection with their contact. But she didn't seem to mind. She kept pressing up until her knees were bent at a ninety-degree angle. It felt to Marcus that her feet were flat on the mat and supporting her lower body. Diana slid out from under him and wrangled her legs around him.

"Now this," she explained. "This is me in a full guard. This evens things up. It gives me a bit of control. Lets me do stuff like this..." Her arms clasped around his head and she pulled him closer to her with her arms and her legs, trapping him in an embrace.

Their lips met and Marcus lost all control. Whatever a 'full guard' was, he couldn't see any way it could be anything but complete dominance when Diana used it. His body relaxed and he eased into her, belly to belly. The kiss was warm and soft and Marcus wanted nothing more than... more of her. Her lips massaged his and her tongue slid past teeth and lips and began probing his mouth, digging deep. Her hands felt like they were everywhere at once, as were his.

Then she started pulling at his shirt until it came off and she tossed it aside. Their groins and hips ground against one another's. Her tongue found its way to his ear and preceded a biting nip at his earlobe. A hand caressed one of her breasts. The fabric covering them had a gossamer thin quality that proved only the barest of tactile separation between his cupping palm and gently probing fingertips.

"Mmm," Diana purred. She pulled him down even closer. He rested on his elbows, letting her breasts press against his now naked chest. The sides of her fishnet covered torso pleasantly tickled his forearms as she rocked him gently back and forth, guided by her hands digging deep into the muscles of his lower back. He wasn't sure sex—where Marcus presumed this was going—was a good idea at this specific location. His place, or her place, maybe. But here—right then—seemed like a bad idea.

Diana made no further move to take off her bizarrely erotic outfit or take his pants off. She seemed quite content to swap tongue jabs, licks, and plump, wet kisses. That was great, too.

Then, before he knew anything else, Marcus's world went dark.

Marcus awoke... or came to. He wasn't sure. He also had no concept of how much time passed. His shirt was still off and his pants still on. He didn't feel any stickiness in his groin, and he was still pretty hard. His shoes had remained covering his feet. But he was laying on his back, spent. If he'd slept, it hadn't refreshed him one bit.

He rolled to his side, putting Diana in his field of view. She too looked as though she'd been asleep or unconscious. She stirred and rolled to face him as his free hand stroked her arm. He gazed into her eyes and she into his when their flesh made contact. It gave Marcus a jolt, and judging from Diana's widening eyes, their touch gave her a jolt too.

Only, this time, it didn't feel like a jolt of excitement or sexual energy.

This time, it was shock. Shock and surprise.

And it confused Marcus, too.

Diana's arm was bare. And that wasn't all. Gone was the fishnet bodysuit he'd found so powerfully erotic. He broke eye contact to look her over. Diana, however, was already on the move. With a gasp and a hand clamped to her mouth, she sprung to her feet. Though she still wore her tube top and shorts, the rest of her body bore no trace of the fishnet bodysuit. Her arms covered her chest as though she were naked. She fled the room without a word. Before Marcus could sit up, she disappeared from view.

Marcus looked after her, wondering why she was embarrassed. Had they had sex after all? He checked himself and found no residue or smell. How or when did she get undressed from the fishnet bodysuit? And if she had taken it off, where was it? Marcus glanced about but discerned no sign of it. What's more, Diana seemed as surprised as him that she was disrobed from a garment that barely covered anything anyway. Why bother? And why bother hiding it or losing it, or fleeing for that matter?

None of it made sense.

With a sense of disappointment mixing with his confusion, Marcus pulled on his shirt and wound his way out of the abandoned warehouse that housed the dark web sponsored fighting tournament.

Marcus soon learned he'd been dead to the world for over four hours, laying by Diana's side. He looked about to ascertain if she was still nearby, but no such luck. The most interesting and strongest woman he'd ever met had fled his presence. He tried not to take that personally, but it was proving quite difficult.

He pushed the thought out of his head for the moment. The night pressed down upon him with intimidating pitch blackness. His phone told him it was 2:35 a.m. He didn't have work tomorrow, but he knew his present locale was not the best part of Tacoma for loitering during the small hours of night. His car, luckily, seemed intact, him having parked it a few blocks away from the abandoned warehouse. He should have gotten another cup of that delicious coffee before he left the tournament site. His eyes felt heavy, and he struggled to focus. That would be all he needed to top this bizarre night—getting stopped on suspicion of driving while intoxicated.

Taking a deep breath, Marcus moved as purposefully as he could toward his Prius. The car recognized his key fob and beeped to unlock itself when he pulled at the handle. He flinched as the high-pitched chirp announced his presence, alone and vulnerable to whatever might be lurking nearby while daybreak remained perilously far away.

He scrambled into his car and activated it, grateful that the hybrid would make little to no sound when it started. Marcus let his vehicle beep at him, its species of scolding for not engaging his seat belt. He would gladly take that scolding now if it gave him a few more moments with which to escape. After several blocks, he acceded to the car's more insistent beeping. His heart skipped a beat when his fumbling efforts forced his eyes off the road, which in turn led to him to waver within his lane. That set off a new alarm warning him he'd drifted across the road's center line. He wanted to get away, but he also didn't want to risk a crash or getting pulled over. Adrenaline perked him up and granted the temporary focus and coordination he needed to latch the seatbelt closed and straighten his vehicle.

That adrenaline began to wear off as his dash down 6th Avenue led him to an intersection with North Pearl Street. He nodded off for a moment, then snapped to. It took significant effort. He was so exhausted. He could not recall the last time he'd fought such fatigue. Even working late at the office one night and turning up the next day bright and early with only three or four hours of sleep hadn't produced this level of weariness and lethargy. He poked at the console until it produced a blast of cold, air-conditioned air that buffeted his face. He made his left turn onto North Pearl Street towards his apartment building in the more upscale Ruston neighborhood of Tacoma with only slightly renewed energy.

Sheer will, helped by no small push of luck, saw him home safely. He exited his vehicle, then wrapped his hands around the edges of the open door when lightheadedness threatened to dump him on his ass. A few deep breaths steadied him—barely—and he managed to close his vehicle, lock it, then stagger up to his apartment. Diana the Champion and her impressive victory against two formidable opponents seemed a distant memory from years ago rather than what he'd seen that same evening. All of Marcus's attention focused on getting him into his apartment and his bed. There, he could safely sleep and give himself the rest that every cell in his body cried out for before utterly giving out.

Somehow, he managed to enter his second story apartment and trudge to his bed before falling atop the sheets fully dressed and snoring with his belly on the mattress. Dead to the world in slumber.

Day Three

Marcus Awoke.

Though his room was still dark but for a small amount of natural light penetrating between the slats of his blinds, Marcus discerned everything in his room with perfect clarity.

He closed his eyes, but still the pounding headache he'd woken up to didn't abate. The inside of his mouth tasted of dirt and rot. Swallowing repeatedly helped but did not stop that unpleasant sensation. And as if that were not enough, his forearms itched. He stared at them for a moment but found himself confused by what he saw. Clearly, there was some sort of weirdness on his forearms. It made no sense.

Marcus rolled over and turned on a bedside table lamp. Tears immediately sprouted from his eyes from the piercing light and he shut them again. He grunted then eased them open. He had to see what the deal was with his itching arms. Adjusting to the light proved a slow and painful process, but eventually his eyes acclimated.

Marcus didn't like what he saw. Not one bit.

He closely inspected his arms, shifting his gaze from left to right. He disbelieved what his eyes told him as clearly true. "What the fuck?" he exclaimed.

Dark brown lines, forming a lattice of hexagons spanned the entire surface of both forearms. They itched. He rubbed at the inner muscle of his left forearm with the heel of his right hand. No movement or change.

What he found more jarring was the gap in his memory in evidently submitting to some sort of tattoo while with Diana. That was a complete blank, and completely perplexing. Also scary. He'd experienced or felt nothing that signaled he'd submitted to any sort of ink.

"*How* in the fuck?"

Wondering what might have happened wasn't going to help. His curiosity, however, might... So long as he directed it in the right place. Diana was seemingly almost as confused as he was when she'd fled their budding tryst.

Or was she? Might it have been relief? Fear?

Marcus desperately wanted to know. His curiosity was going to be the key. If anything, it would solve the apparent mysteries of last night.

First things first, however. The tattoos itched, but they looked lighter than he expected. Wondering if it might have just been a temporary tattoo or just paint of some kind, Marcus entered his bathroom and washed his arms with hot, soapy water.

Nothing.

He tried a shower; he needed one anyway. The inside of his mouth wasn't the only part of him that felt gross. The longer he remained up, the grungier he felt.

Still nothing.

"Fuck!" he shouted, venting his irritation to the otherwise empty apartment, as though the air itself could absorb his negative emotions. With every passing moment, Marcus found his irritation growing. It wasn't like him. This situation was unlike any of the major or collective petty annoyances he'd experienced, but he prided himself in taking a calm and collected approach to life and all the problems and challenges it invariably posed.

His arms itched and he scratched at them absentmindedly. If anything, the shower had seemed to make the inked-on lattice a bit darker.

Marcus growled. *That* was also *very* unlike him. But right then it made him feel better. He inspected his arms while he dressed. From what he could see, each hexagon was perfect even though the curves and surfaces of his arms clearly were not. How could a person achieve such precise lines? Another mystery.

He put his eyes within an inch of the skin of his inner forearm, studying the texture.

Henna? Is this shit henna? Marcus wondered. He didn't know a lot about henna tattoos, but he was virtually certain they weren't permanent. He strode toward his computer and switched it on. He already had his planned first internet search while the machine booted up.

'Getting rid of henna tattoos.'

Marcus reeled as a bright flash of light stabbed through his eyes and directly into his brain. It originated in the upper left portion of his field of vision. He couldn't shake it. Even once he protectively closed his eyes, that sense of intense light remained as though it projected against his inner eyelids.

Fuck that hurts, Marcus thought. Damn.

He sat down and clasped his hands together. The light in the upper left corner of his perception persisted. Nothing made it go away, not pressing on his temple, covering his head with the front of his T-shirt stretched out from the bottom hem, nor trying to focus on a Zen-like mental state.

If you can't beat it, join it?

So he tried that. Marcus opened his eyes and looked up and to the left. Shock led to a sharp intake of breath.

A window—like those used in Windows-enable machines—appeared in his vision like a HUD on a fighter jet. Only he was in no cockpit.

What the...?

There was text in that window:

> *Henna tattoos are, by definition, not permanent and the easiest method by which to remove them is simply allowing time for the stain impregnated skin to slough off. Other conventional methods include hot, soapy water, applying a lemon juice/baking soda paste, baby oil, or hydrogen peroxide.*

Marcus dashed toward his laptop. There wasn't a page loaded, no windows, no movement or any obvious activity on the screen. Yet his own HUD window remained where it was, even when he shifted his gaze. Marcus next called up an internet search engine and typed up the exact search he'd been thinking of moments before the weird panel appeared in his vision.

The top result popped up in less than a second. That description matched the one embedded in his vision.

Word for word.

Without thinking, Marcus's eyes drifted down to his arms. The ink forming the interlocking hexagons appeared darker. A few shades noticeably darker.

A troubling thought occurred to him. One that fit the facts and could explain both his apparent henna tattoo and Diana's abrupt departure and reaction to waking beside him.

Can henna be used to poison someone?

Another HUD window appeared in his vision, diagonally placed to the lower right relative to the first. Marcus found the old one distracting. He waved away at it, like he was shooing a mosquito. The words contained within the new, lower right window appeared denser. As though scooping something up, Marcus pulled the window closer to the center of his vision. A come-on gesture enlarged it to fill his entire visual field. The text enlarged a bit, but he wanted more. Just like enlarging something on his cell phone, he pinched his fingers together, then snapped them open. The text enlarged while automatically adjusting the margins to fit the new vision-window.

He began to read:

> *Henna is not inherently poisonous. It is merely a stain applied to the outermost layers of skin. However, one should avoid so called "black henna" as that often contains additional chemicals that are either an irritant or poisonous but not part of traditional henna. Black henna will...*

"No, no, no, that's not it," Marcus muttered. "Used as a means to deliberately poison." He wanted to know if Diana had somehow poisoned him with henna or some other ink laced with something toxic.

Several text bubbles popped up, replacing the relevant but not specifically requested information.

Fucking bitch tried to poison me with her shitty, cut-rate henna. BITCH!

Maybe I should poison my husband? Lace some henna with some arsenic? Would that work?

It might. Could be worth a try.

Can I use toluene to remove henna really fast? My boyfriend will kill me if he sees this Indian stuff on me. He's such a racist. Why did I think this was a good idea?

Oh my effing god, I shoulda listened to Sarah when she said to stay away from black henna. My hand has puffed up like a marshmallow!

Oh damn. Are you sure that stuff is safe?

Maybe if I get a henna tattoo and then feign an illness from it, mom and dad will finally give a shit about me.

And on and on these thoughts and messages went. He pushed them away and they disappeared with pops as rapidly as they had appeared. Marcus took in a sharp breath when he regarded his arms again. Before his very eyes, the inked hexagons flared darker and darker until they were glowing ebony threads before easing back to a lighter shade. They settled upon a dark, russet brown that was still darker than when he'd last looked at them.

What is happening to me? Marcus wondered, full of trepidation.

He wasn't sure. But that curiosity started extrapolating possibilities. One of those possibilities brought him back to one thing from the night before. These lattices on his arms...

They reminded him of one thing...

Diana's fishnet bodysuit. She'd still worn it when they writhed around together on the mat after her fight and after they kissed. He made plenty of contact with her and that oddly pointless, yet alluring, outfit.

Oh my god, what did she do to me?

Day Five

Marcus stabbed his fingers at his alarm clock's snooze button for the ninth time. Or was it the tenth? It was too many.

He needed to get up but didn't want to. He'd spent the rest of his Saturday and Sunday cooped up in his apartment. But now it was Monday morning. As much as he lacked any desire to do so, he needed to drag his ass in to work.

His head ached terribly. That headache hadn't abated since his run-in with Diana. Marcus grunted as he sat up in bed. At least this time the change in position hadn't left him light-headed. But he now had a much different—and much more frightening—issue he faced. Two of them, in fact.

First, the alarming tattoos had a mind of their own. They were growing. Faint lines started to reach past his wrist into his palm and the back of his hand. More distinct and darker lines developed into the same hexagonal lattice and ran just past his elbow on Saturday. Then, they ran along his mid biceps on each side to the point he had the courage to inspect himself on Sunday. Now they reached his armpits. Washing and all other means he researched and experimented with proved fruitless in stopping the living tattoos' progression. As bad and alarming as that progression was, it wasn't the issue that was taking its toll on his psyche.

Far more alarming were the dark thoughts that kept trying to push their way into his consciousness. Never in a million years would he have entertained such darkly unhinged and violent ideas as those that were now occurring to him. Sure, there were the odd thoughts of wishing harm on the jerks who tried to push him around, but never had he imagined or visualized the gruesome, evil ends to human life that now flashed through his mind. These thoughts that kept pushing their way into his mind... They were *much* darker. Worse, they didn't feel like *his* thoughts with his own mental voice. Instead, it was like having dozens of people trying to get his attention with their dark desires by implanting them directly into his head. It made for the most unnerving, soul-decaying 48 hours far beyond his imagination. He lacked any means to combat it.

He tried everything. Meditation, mindless video games, reading. Nothing. His efforts in the short hours of early Sunday led him to heavy drinking, nearly finishing a bottle of bourbon. He found himself more susceptible to the intrusive thoughts while buzzed and queasy.

That left him with but one choice—enduring it. It hadn't proven easy. Alternating between bone-chilling coldness and parching, sweaty hotness kept him awake but for only a few hours of uneasy sleep.

Marcus contemplated calling in sick. He felt horrible. It would be a legit use of a sick day. But he was also pretty tough. Maybe an easy work day, spent cruising the internet instead of working in his HR position, would help clear his head. He had long sleeve shirts to hide his new, involuntary tattoos.

He pushed through getting cleaned up. Somehow he staggered out of his apartment, but his head swam, the world shifting erratically back and forth. He leaned against a retaining wall. He didn't need to visually inspect them to know the tattoos were growing. Lines of fire burrowed through the uppermost layers of skin, tracing hexagons that reached all over each bicep and tricep. His head pounded. He had so many thoughts. So many needs. There were so many things that so many people wanted desperately.

Marcus's attempt to take another step produced a near fall. He'd never be able to drive his car. Fortunately, a bus stop was nearby that would take him almost to the door of his work, if he could get there.

He steeled himself and walked toward the bus stop. He managed, but by the time he reached the metal-framed plexiglass enclosure forming the bus stop, he was ready to puke up whatever juices might be left in his stomach. He collapsed onto a bench, panting. Slouched over, he was still able to see someone else sharing the covered space. She was a brunette white woman with a well-proportioned nose and mahogany eyes that complemented her olive complexion. Any other time, her trim figure and fashionably flattering clothes would have caught his attention. But she was too pure at the moment and looking at her created a rancidly bitter film that coated his tongue. Impure thoughts that felt like bricks falling from the sky, battered away at his skull.

I should have stayed home! Marcus thought. He grunted and whined, trying to keep it all at bay. He didn't know why he felt impelled to shut out the voices, data, whatever it might be. Perhaps a last-ditch effort to keep his sanity or his humanity. But perhaps if he just...

NO! He thought. *Don't let it in.* Yet, some primal part of his brain seemed to implore the thinking and feeling parts of his mind that it might not be so bad. Letting the darkness in, that is. Besides... it was getting *so* hard to fight it...

"Awww... Uuhh..." he groaned.

"Mister, hey, are you okay? You don't look so good," the woman sharing the bus stop with him said. She took a tentative, cautious step forward.

"Fuck off, cunt," Marcus spat out. The woman recoiled as though he'd struck her. The shock drained from her face, replaced by repulsed disgust. She gave him nothing more than a silent snarl and a receipt of his own anger flashing in her eyes.

"Asshole," she muttered under her breath as she moved outside the bus enclosure, pulled out her phone, and then focused her eyes on its screen, shutting him out.

He had no idea where that rage came from. It certainly wasn't like him. The lady was only concerned and trying to help. She hadn't deserved the misogynistic epithet. No woman did. Yet he hurled it at her as though it was second nature.

"Sorry," he tried to tell her, but his voice was so hoarse he doubted she heard him. He looked over at her, hoping to apologize with his eyes. That didn't work. She stubbornly kept looking at her phone, even though her flaring nostrils and angrily furrowed brow told him she felt his imploring stare.

Fuck her, he thought. She's a cunt. Just a cunt. She should mind her own business before she gets hurt.

Marcus squeezed his eyes shut. He had no idea what was happening to him. He'd think about it more while riding the bus, which had just pulled to a stop before the enclosure. Marcus was forced to steady himself with the enclosure's stout metal frame before boarding. He felt the woman behind him. For reasons he could not explain, he separately felt the presence of her cell phone. And it was enticing somehow. The device gave off an intoxicating, salivating scent like meat searing on a grill during a lazy summer barbecue. He wanted her phone. As though he could snatch it from her and take a bite out of it, he wanted it more than any steak or the juiciest cheeseburger he'd ever had.

The woman stayed behind him. Marcus had no difficulty working out that she wanted him on the bus first so she could take a seat, *any* seat, far away from him. It's what he might have done in her place.

It won't save her. Don't let that save her. He recognized that baser thought as something primitive, dark, and a reflexive desire to punish someone who didn't like him. Any merit to their belief be damned.

Marcus rested his forehead on the seat-back in front of him. Whatever was happening to him, whatever he was trying to fight off... he was losing. His resistance started to wane. He just wanted whatever it was trying to get into his head and burrow through his skin to stop... or... maybe... kill him. Marcus thought for a desperate moment maybe death would be better.

This is so hard... I can't... I just can't.

Marcus pinched his kneecaps to distract himself from the pain and constricting pressure on his head.

Maybe just let a little bit in, he thought. If it kills me, it kills me. Anything to have this headache let up.

Marcus let the rest of his resistance crumble. His shoulders slumped and a cold sweat coated his face, back, and palms.

Whatever was trying to batter its way into his head, when it came, it brought with it blessed relief.

Just as he'd experienced in his apartment, HUD bubbles appeared in his mind's eye. So many more than the first time. He didn't need his eyes open to see them. It was a rush—a flood of dark and deadly desires and wants.

> *I want to kill my POS boss. Where can I find a murderer for hire?*

> *I want to marry my rapist. I've dreamed of that ever since my grandpa fucked me on my sweet 16.*

Where can I find a child?

Anyone wanna hook up? My husband can't get it up anymore. I'll let you tie me up! *smooch*

Help! I'm going to lose my boyfriend! Can someone point me to a video that demonstrates how to give a really good blowjob?

Wanted: Two guys with their own guns: one who can work as a getaway driver and one who can act as a lookout. I've got security and a second lookout already. Big score. Asshole jeweler who's just *begging* to get robbed. Take split evenly. Message me at @fuckemupbaddog. Peace.

Search: where to buy fertilizer in large bulk amounts without attracting gov attention

Dozens more mental HUD windows popped into his mind's eye with offers and requests ranging from kinky, to bizarre, and to terrifyingly dangerous. Bored housewives to wanna-be terrorists.

Then hundreds of similar requests crowded for space in his mind's eye.

Thousands of uncountable HUD windows shrunk to fill space in his mind, moving as though jockeying for Marcus's attention.

He focused on one of the HUD windows, the lady with the frigid, limp-dicked husband. Part of him wanted to be her man, but looking at the window and focusing on it, Marcus realized this woman lived in Cleveland. He had no idea *how* he knew that. But he was absolutely sure of its truth. Tacoma to Cleveland was a bit too far a jaunt for a hook-up. The window took on a blue glow. His attention drilled into it and learned more. The woman's name was Donna and she was a school teacher with a bondage kink. He somehow managed to access her bank accounts and knew she purchased whips, fuzzy cuffs, and a tight leather body suit. He saw her bathroom selfies posing with the equipment, but also a text chain with some friend lamenting she hadn't had the chance to use any of it because her husband found it weird.

Marcus looked about the seemingly endless supply of other HUD windows in his mind's eye. His attention gravitated towards perhaps a dozen of them giving off an orange hue.

Why? Why orange? Then a thought occurred to him.

Orange is the opposite of blue. He'd heard that or read that somewhere. He thought he'd seen it described some other way, too. He struggled to recall for a moment, but it came back to him quickly.

Orange also 'complimented' blue. Opposites that functioned well together instead of canceling each other out.

So, Marcus picked one of the orange windows. Pointing to it, he then dragged it towards Donna the Bored and Sexually Frustrated Lady from Cleveland. The two HUD windows merged, eliciting a pleasant tingle of excitement that prickled Marcus's skin.

Marcus jerked upright.

It all became so clear to him now.

There was the 'dark web' as most people understood it—a theoretical, intangible, construct based more on fear, reputation, and assumptions than anything else. But that wasn't actually it. That wasn't what the *dark web* was. Marcus now understood *that* in his bones and in his heart. Diana described the dark web as a disease of the human soul. And that disease was now infecting him. But the Dark Web, the disease, created where humanity's basest desires and needs intersected with modern technology as a means to spread it... was a much more tangible matter. And one he seemed unable to escape.

Not that he wanted to.

The Dark Web made him feel wonderful now. He wondered why he'd fought it at all. It was amazing. Powerful. Insightful. Needed. Wanted. World-Changing.

Things he'd never had in his dull, ordinary, scaredy-cat life.

But now he did.

Marcus welcomed the spread of the Dark Web tattoos growing past his armpits and over his shoulders. He gripped the seat ahead of him and lowered his head. He focused on another blue HUD, then matched it to an orange one. One blue received a map of the local parks which had the best playgrounds situated far away from CCTV cameras. He matched an up-and-coming assassin who had been dishonorably discharged from the Marines with the guy who wanted to off his boss. He sent the desperate college co-ed links to a porno actresses' how-to videos on oral sex. A recently released sex offender anonymously received the address of the woman looking to marry her own perp. The awkward boy seeking fertilizer, sadly an INCEL who was looking to die in a blaze of glory, received a connection to a Chinese supplier who would sell him some direct from the factory. He could pick it up in San Diego.

And on and on Marcus went, connecting dark desires with dark services for the rest of his bus ride to work. Each blue to orange link brought him closer and closer to his own ecstasy. He gave out a little grunt and came in his pants when he directed a 19-year-old Japanese woman to a taboo fetish club that gave Japanese women sexual access to bound and gagged Chinese men—but only *after* the men had been flayed alive.

He looked back at the kind woman who had only seemed concerned for him. She still ignored him. Deciding she should pay for her current disgust and scorn, Marcus reached out with his mind. Accessing all the data on her phone felt as easy as a baby seeking out their mommy's nipple. He filtered through her data. Her entire life recorded on her phone was ripe for his taking. He sent her phone access code, biographical data, and the passwords to every single internet-based account she had to a Russian cartel that specialized in identity theft.

Good luck getting those Prime packages on time, cunt. That'll teach you to be rude.

The bus reached his stop. Marcus stood. He was not the slightest abashed from the sticky, squishy wetness between his legs that clung to his underwear as he walked off the bus. His headache was a thing of the past. He felt like he was on fire.

And he loved it.

Marcus threw his cell phone away in a trash can as he passed through the entrance to his high-rise office building. He wasn't going to need a cell phone, a tablet, or any connected device for the foreseeable future. He could feel all of that coursing through the hexagonal tattoos and into his now-diseased soul. The Dark Web granted him access to both the shadowy internet and its tamer tech cousin, the regular internet, as well as normal telecommunications. He now knew the Dark Web would allow him to call his parents, speaking to them and hearing their voices telepathically, as much as putting a hen-pecked husband in touch with a murderer for hire. He could mentally text his friends if he desired. The entire information superhighway and all the world's telecommunications networks now served him at his beck and call.

He doubted, however, that he'd have much further use for such basic relationships as parents or friends. Thanks to Diana, the whole world had opened up to him. The whole world *needed* him. The people populating it would worship him and the infectious gift he had to offer.

In return, Marcus would relieve humanity's suffering by hearing their dark, electronic prayers and rewarding his worshipers by satisfying whatever forbidden or profane needs they held deep in their hearts.

He would go to work, then work at his new calling.

Day Eight

Marcus sat cross-legged at his dining room table, his hands resting on his lap. His apartment was packed up. He would be moving later today. Fuck the landlord and their 30-day notice. He'd live. Or perhaps he wouldn't. His mind's eye scanning the Dark Web found more than a few people who had a beef with the man who ran the building. Perhaps some eager beaver wishing to learn how to hack and embezzle would receive anonymous instructions and passwords to the landlord's business accounts. He cared not. He already worked with a Chinese triad to launder money. His hefty cut of that service gave him enough to buy, outright and in cash, a nice top-floor condo overlooking Point Defiance.

And speaking of fucking, Marcus had sorted out one other element of it but had to yet sort the rest. He abruptly quit his job. Like his cell phone, he discovered two days ago he had no use for a normal job when the Dark Web could satisfy his financial needs. *More* than satisfy them. Collecting finder's fees for criminal enterprises of all sorts, untraceable to him thanks to the Dark Web, had proven very lucrative. Within a few days, he'd become a multi-millionaire, and he wasn't about to stop accruing wealth.

That just left the fun kind of fucking. Once he moved into his new pad later that day, he would want some female company. He'd searched the bowels of the Dark Web to find a local specialist who catered to just about any type of sexual desire. Marcus knew half the organization's men, women, and children on offer were trafficked for the sole purpose of becoming sex workers.

He cared not.

He was in a sampler type of mood. So, he ordered a woman from all six of the main populated continents for sexual services that night. He selected the most exotic and freaky ones available. He did make sure each of the six were older than eighteen.

He may be sick from the Dark Web, but he wasn't a sicko.

Plus, he wouldn't be fucking them, kissing them, or even touching them. Touching and kissing was how he became infected with the Dark Web in the first place. Part of him hated it, but the rest wasn't about to give up its power just yet. Which meant he couldn't chance any sort of physical contact with any of the six women. He would simply watch as they serviced one another. Now that the Dark Web coursed through him and he'd seen countless people live-streaming sex sessions and orgies, Marcus understood the appeal of voyeurism. He'd get off later that way tonight instead.

Plus... he developed other ways of fomenting carnal desires.

The Dark Web tattoos covered his entire body. He would come in his pants—again—when the darkish-brown ink wended its way under the tender skin of his penis and testicles. It was a delicious sort of pain that left him swooning and heady with ecstatic excitement.

There was so much more he wanted to do with the Dark Web coursing through him.

And that brought him to another subject.

Diana.

She was still out there. Still knew what she'd done with the Dark Web. Still aware of what she did to him. Still knew what the Dark Web was.

That made her a threat, and one he could not abide. Something would need to be done about her. It only took Marcus a few moments to plan a deserving end. Though he enjoyed having this dark gift, he hadn't asked for it. She infected him with the Dark Web without his knowledge or consent.

That was unforgivable, even if he now could not imagine his life without the disease.

The Dark Web gave him control over the Extreme All Goes Fight League. It was, after all, a creation of that disease. Diana had only been its custodian while the Dark Web infected her.

Now it was his. He scanned the world's information superhighway and its shadowy cousin until he found a ruthless, bloodthirsty candidate. Maurice LeBreaux. A man standing six-foot-six, bulging with muscle and overflowing with hateful rage along with the pathological need to vent it upon other human beings. He received an official invitation to fight for the Extreme All Goes Championship, all expenses paid from Montreal to Tacoma. Within moments, he accepted the invitation and the travel vouchers.

The Dark Web gave Diana power deriving from access to information on fighting styles and techniques to enhance her own abilities and gauge all possible opponents, including their strengths, weaknesses, prior injuries, and fighting style. Without access to the darker motivations and skillsets accessible through the Dark Web, Diana the Champion was likely in for a rough fight. He suspected, based on footage the Dark Web retrieved for him of her future opponent, she would not survive. He felt that was an acceptable outcome. Not for revenge, though that would likely prove a satisfying side-benefit. Instead, the Dark Web might be safer if there wasn't a past victim of its infection that could talk about their experience or existence. Even if it might sound utterly nuts to anyone hearing how humanity's darkness had melded with technology to make a transmittable disease.

He looked forward to seeing Diana fight one more time.

Day Twelve

As he predicted, Diana suffered a horrible loss in her title defense two days prior. What he hadn't predicted, much to his consternation, was that she hadn't died in her fight. She'd suffered a crushing blow to her C-3 vertebrae and a concussion that left her quadriplegic and comatose—but still, technically alive. And as long as she was alive, she posed a conceivable threat.

Marcus considered the best way to manage this situation as his new personal assistant placed a fresh cappuccino on the desk next to him. He didn't bother to thank her. It was her job to serve. He'd served others for years and rarely received any acknowledgement for his efforts, much less a proper thank you. And in a way he still provided a service to others. Only now he had found a way to make it more profitable and in turn it granted him such power. Nevertheless, it was someone else's turn to provide the menial services important people like him needed.

He felt her momentary stare. The henna-like hexagonal lattice tattoo covered his neck and face. He could no longer hide it unless he wanted to walk about under a sheet like a child playing in a ghost costume. Marcus would not do that. A pause and heavy sigh served the dual function of his consternation and dismissal from his presence.

Solitude allowed him to return to the problem at hand.

Diana.

His Dark Web tattoos burned as he considered how to seal her fate. He hated her. She'd used him. Infected him with this technological disease. Driven him to do things. The fact that he didn't mind hosting the Dark Web and all its powers within him was beside the point. She'd robbed him of his choice. He would not forgive her for that.

She would die for it.

Marcus examined the myriad of the Dark Web's HUD windows floating about his mind's eye, waiting for his attention and his willingness to make connections between dark needs and dark desires to help. He wasn't looking to make a connection between people seeking the dark web's help. *He* needed that help. *He* had his own dark need.

Marcus feared no repercussions to himself. He was too well insulated for that. The dark web's anonymity shielded his real life. Still, that didn't mean he wanted extra attention focused upon her situation. He made substantial passive income from the Extreme All

Goes tournaments. Plus, there was always the possibility she would wake up and rat out the fight league he now owned. Time was of the essence to find someone to do his bidding and discreetly do away with her, but he was also patient and careful.

Someone praying to his Dark Web would come along and help.

Day Sixteen

Marcus scratched at his arms. He should be happy. He was happy. Just not as happy as he felt like he should be.

Diana was dead.

Marcus located a man with radicalized political views who fell for his cleverly contrived electronic plethora of inflammatory social media posts. Posts supposedly created over the last five years with Diana's picture and location. A deposit—characterized as a "donation" to a "charity" for dispatching Diana— was sent with a promise of another million upon proof of death. The deal had been struck.

Within a day, the man delivered. He sent a photograph of Diana's pallid face set above a vicious cut across her throat. Marcus reciprocated, transferring the rest of the funds promised. It felt cold and clinical. In his short time having the Dark Web infection, he'd accumulated enormous wealth. His secret crypto-currency accounts barely registered the payments as a blip on their balance.

It had been an emotionally trying day, making sure the progenitor host could never tell her tale. It left him spent and physically exhausted.

Marcus writhed in his bed, unable to sleep. The Dark Web tattoos etched their way painfully through the soles of his feet—and the inside of his mouth.

Day Thirty

Marcus fought the urge to wretch after taking another difficult spoonful of broth. He hadn't kept down solid food in three days.

The Dark Web tattoos started to work through his insides. Though he could not see it, the net-like ink felt like it worked its way into his stomach lining. But unlike the hexagonal tattoos embedded into his skin, the Dark Web tattoos implanted into his stomach seemed unwilling to simply exist and stay put. They slid and writhed through his stomach, forcing it to contort and churn even when there was nothing in it. When he managed to have something in his belly, the net of tattoos reacted like a gangster protecting its turf. It made eating anything but the smallest doses of liquid a paralyzing agony.

Even moving the spoon to his mouth produced discomfort. The Dark Web tattoos, having covered every inch of his skin with its mesh, broke each individual hexagon into new, smaller hexagons. It created a tighter mesh covering his hands and feet that was spreading up his arms and legs. It created a pressure on his joints that made walking difficult and fine manipulation of any instrument—such as a spoon—quite uncomfortable.

The pain only abated when he used the Dark Web to facilitate the connection between a warlord in Myanmar and an arms dealer looking to unload some old weapons tech without attracting the attention of a UN peacekeeping force. The warlord didn't mind receiving weapons that were not technologically state of the art. They shot bullets and those bullets killed every man, woman, and child who dared to stand up to the warlord before the UN could react or figure out who was responsible for the slaughter of 300 innocent souls.

But now the pains wracking Marcus's body were back with a vengeance. He finished three more spoonfuls of broth, then doubled over.

Why hadn't Diana gone through this? He could not figure that out, try as he might, turning the problem over in his mind for an hour before pain made him pass out.

Day Fifty

Marcus discovered the reason why Diana hadn't seemed crippled by the Dark Web when he met her. There were stages. When the Dark Web grew within him, sapping his strength, it changed him in preparation for increasingly greater things. Diana had gone through the same thing, her fishnet bodysuit covered more of her body, making it more alluring as it made her more powerful. His tattoos were expanding in the same way, making him more terrible and fearsome in a way befitting his innate desires and talents.

It was growing pains. Nothing more.

He'd grown and it hurt, but he could do so much more now. Now he felt fantastic. Marcus leapt out of bed and made twenty connections in less than two seconds. Everything from more spouses looking for illicit hookups to helping a drug cartel map out routes to ferry drugs into the hands (and veins) of eagerly awaiting addicts. The Dark Web tattoos warmed his skin and his insides tickled with the pleasant heat that a chili-head experiences after a tongue-searing meal. He panted as the connections took place. Blue and orange HUD windows swarmed together to create chaos through humanity's base desires. It was like an exercise high, mushroom trip, massage, meal, and blowjob all in one.

He wanted nothing more than to keep that momentum. If that meant more drugs delivered to the streets of Tacoma, Kansas City, Biloxi, wherever... so be it. If broken homes kept up the sensations he craved, Marcus would wreck every last family he could. If ruined childhoods kept up this orgasmic intoxication touching every cell in his body, well... parents would just have to replace lost and broken progeny with new children.

Marcus would not feel one bit of remorse. He didn't *invent* drugs, or illicit relationships, political assassinations, or child abuse. All of those things existed long before his birth and would persist long after the worms consumed his dead flesh and his bones crumbled to dust. He was only doing what people wanted. Providing for needs they were afraid to ask for in a 'civilized' society.

No remorse. None whatsoever.

Marcus settled into his favorite armchair. He started with a senator poking around the internet at the edges of his Dark Web looking for a contract-killer to stop one of her staffers from revealing illicit campaign funds to the press. He introduced an eighty-year-old man who ran a film studio to twin call girls offering escort services, but who secretly had gold-digger aspirations and goals of fucking their way into fame.

Marcus kept these matches going on and on for the rest of the day, until it left him so spent and sweaty, he fell into a fitful sleep.

Day Seventy-One

Marcus awoke to a net of fire burning him inside and out.

He could concentrate on nothing else. He writhed in his bed. The Dark Web HUD windows came to him in a dark fuzzy mass, indistinguishable from each other as little dots swirled and shook in his mind. Knowing before he even tried to get up that he would not be able to stand, Marcus slithered out of his bed and crawled on his hands and knees to his bathroom. Fiery pains lanced up his arms and legs as elbows and knees propelled him forward. He screamed, knowing that no one could hear him in his giant condo, empty of any life but him. He'd fired the personal assistant for fear of discovery of his technological infection.

He plunged himself into an ice-cold bath. That granted a bit of relief, but the head perched upon his shoulders ached terribly. The one between his legs throbbed with agonizing pressure. He stared at his engorged cock. The skin and veins strained against the Dark Web tattoos constricting it. He found he was holding his breath and gasped. It hurt... so bad.

Unable to think of anything further to do, Marcus grasped his penis with a firm, tattooed grip of his right hand and yanked back and forth, hard. The masturbation continued for almost thirty minutes without any progress, though the sensations vacillated between pleasure and pain. His body wanted the pleasure, but the Dark Web tattoos pushed to control it with constricting pain. His cock reddened with bulging veins as though they would burst.

He kept at it, but for the first time he held a secret spark of hope his body would not prevail against his Dark Web infection. Though desperate, Marcus also felt sure he'd pull his damn cock off if that would help relieve whatever was going on in there.

His body quivered and shook from the combined yanking and shivering of the cold water. The Dark Web tattoos tightened their grip upon him.

And then it happened. Marcus ejaculated. A creamy, stringy, whitish-brown jet erupted from his tip and splatted against the tap end wall of his bathtub shower. He groaned and sank deeper into the frigid tub. There was relief with just the hint of an ache in his groin. It left him invigorated to see that he retained at least some control over his body.

He started to sit up. Dark brown strands coming from the urethra floated on the surface of the bath's water, flaring out and wriggling like little worms. They stretched to the end of the tub where he had ejaculated.

Marcus cried out, horrified, disgusted, surprised, and angry all at once. He dipped his hand into the water under the dark brown strands, gathered them up in a clutching grasp, and began to pull. At first the strands fought against him. Realizing it was part of the Dark Web's infectious tattoo, Marcus looped them around his hand and continued to pull, ignoring the sensation that he was pulling his penis inside out.

He enlisted his other hand and, alternating between left and right, he pulled at the strands, drawing more of them out from the tip of his penis as he went along. He yelled again as he yanked, scrunching his eyes closed as he sensed the Dark Web tattoo stretching to its breaking point. The collected strands eventually snapped, trailed by a squirt of blood that dissipated in the water from crimson to the slightest translucent of pinks.

"Ah... aaah... *AAAHH!*" Marcus cried out as he tried to fling away the strands.

It didn't work. The strands, with a mind of their own, wrapped around his wrist. The ends burrowed into the skin of his hands, making a tighter lattice of hexagons up and down his arms. He began to cough and sputter, prompting him to bring his hands to his mouth and rub at his eyes.

A mistake he realized a moment too late. His eyes burned from the strands stretching from his palms to scrabble into the tissues of his eyes. Heedless of the bathwater he spilled upon his floor, Marcus rushed out of the tub and staggered to the bathroom counter. He opened his eyes wide, knowing what he would see yet horrified all the same.

The milky white sclera of his eyeballs had tiny trails of brown wending their way into a hexagonal pattern. Marcus swooned. He fluttered his eyelids, hoping the rapid-fire blinking would rid his eyes of the invading Dark Web strands. He knew full well they would not. He needed to brace himself against the counter as he inspected his eyes, rolling them about. Sure enough, the whites of his eyes were covered in minute lines of brown, forming an interlocking hexagonal lattice.

He wasn't up for sowing any Dark Web chaos that day. He collapsed to the bathroom floor, a cheek pressing against the cold tile. His body shook.

He eventually passed out.

Day Seventy-Two

Relief. Blessed relief. Simply more growing pains. And worth it. He celebrated his greater powers by granting surges of funding for ten separate terrorist organizations of wildly divergent ideologies and based in different nations, each one eager to advance their goals.

Over 666,798 souls spread across twenty separate countries would lose their lives within the ensuing two months from targeted assassinations, bombings, suicide killers, dirty bombs left in shopping malls, packed concerts, capacity crowd sporting events, poisoned water supplies, and cyber-attacks that ignited contrived wars between nations with already simmering tensions.

Marcus wasn't sad. He was the Dark Web's host body. He *was* the Dark Web.

Day One-Hundred and Three

Marcus hadn't left his condo in over a month. Ten days ago, he'd emerged from another agonizing spate of growing pains. The Dark Web tattoo had interwoven into tight threads that resembled a window screen. He'd been busy for those ten days. So busy he hadn't paid attention to the basics. His food ran out. He could afford huge grocery bills, daily deliveries of ubiquitous to-go food, his own pizza chain, or even elegant meals personally delivered. He could afford a personal, in-house chef to cook for him privately within his residence. He could afford ten such chefs. Money was no object. He was among the richest people on the planet—secretly of course. Wealth held little interest for its own sake.

The Dark Web was all that mattered.

The Dark Web became his obsession. He had to protect it and protect his possession of it. He knew full well his appearance would prove alarming to the most casual of onlooker glances. He assumed that Diana had "relinquished" her position as the Dark Web's carrier far sooner than 103 days in. Otherwise, her bodysuit would have looked darker and would have formed a more tightly packed netting. But his own appearance would have looked bizarre, even in the liberal Pacific Northwest. Hence, not wanting to leave and be seen.

He was reticent to have someone deliver the necessities of life. That, again, risked being seen. He did not want that.

He could no longer ignore the gnaw of hunger deep in the pit of his guts and the consequent sapping of his bodily energy.

He knew before scouring his cupboards that they contained nothing. There was nothing edible anywhere in his condo. Not even the secret stashes where he would typically keep snacks of candy within ready access in his desk or his bedside table. There was nothing. Not one speck of food.

Except...

Marcus dropped to his knees in front of his kitchen sink and opened up the cabinet under the sink.

There it was. Right where he'd left it.

Marcus had been irritated when he discovered that his very expensive condo, despite all the owner's disclosures of the property's condition, the price tag, and the relatively clean neighborhood, had a bit of a cockroach problem. He'd found some in the kitchen, no doubt looking for food. He laid disposable traps that were supposed to attract, immobilize, and kill the hardy pests. He purchased ten times the number the packaging had recommended for his square footage.

Marcus had scattered them about in places he assumed would be appealing to a cockroach. Mostly in the kitchen but elsewhere too.

Then, he'd forgotten about them. The roaches disappeared. But the traps were still there. Marcus picked one up, tentatively at first, unsure what to expect. He'd been dealing with the disgusting, depraved, and dirtiest elements of the human soul, but he wasn't disgusting, depraved, or dirty himself. Hunger had other ideas and asserted itself. The trap rattled slightly as he brought it up to his eyes. He peered inside the cardboard box the size of a large matchbox. The Dark Web strands crisscrossing his eyes made it a bit hard to see, but even with inhibited vision he discerned several dead cockroaches stuck inside. They were old, desiccated carcasses. Marcus could now see that the rattling was portions of bodies, wing covers, legs, and several dried out cadaverous insect corpses.

Protein, dude. It's just protein.

Marcus realized he could not allow himself to go without food for so long again. If he wanted to continue doing the Dark Web's work, he had to live. He'd make sure he'd have the place stocked up somehow in the future. But for now...

He maneuvered the trap to his mouth and shook it. Prickly legs and random insectile bits tumbled into his mouth. He tried to swallow them whole but they were too big and too sharp to comfortably pass through his throat, forcing him to chew. He feared a repulsive taste would force him to gag, but it didn't. They had an acidic taste, almost like a preserved lemon. He found himself welcoming it. The Dark Web's advanced infection into his mouth covered his tongue forming a sheath that muted his taste which was part of the reason he lost interest in tasty food.

Up until now, everything tasted like soapy, slimy cottage cheese. And Marcus *hated* cottage cheese, so the cockroach bits seemed a pleasant, welcome surprise.

Marcus reached in and pulled three more cockroaches free of the dried-up glue. He crunched away at them while he gathered four more traps. They, too, were full of dead cockroaches. He carried his unconventional bounty to his sofa.

It occurred to Marcus the roaches he chemically murdered might now prove mildly toxic, having perished in the traps. He wouldn't make a habit of this. He would eat only enough to sustain him for the day and make arrangements for proper food deliveries. If he opened his unit and hid in the bathroom while the delivery was made, he wouldn't expose his freakish appearance to anyone.

The experience inspired him, too. He searched for blue HUD window importers looking for endangered species. There was everything for rich CEOs wanting a one-of-a-kind pet for their spoiled children to a dinner club looking to have the rarest of the rare game meats.

Damn it, Marcus thought. Now I'm hungry.

Marcus enlisted his Dark Web powers to access the standard internet and arranged for a delivery of a large number of provisions. Then, he focused his attention back to the dark web's seedier, taboo elements. He smiled when he came across an offering. Something to satisfy his ever-increasing depravity.

The Cannibal Cuisine Dining Club. Interesting. Well, I think I will give that a shot. I do like ribs...

Day Three-Hundred and Sixty-One

Marcus perspired heavily, a thick, greasy sheen coating his skin as he sat in an armchair. To amuse himself, he used the Dark Web to hack into a Chinese defense network and forced one hundred of their satellites to crash to the earth.

It created an orgasmic itch that shuddered his whole-body.

A moment after that, his heart seized up. His left arm writhed under the pressure of an invisible vice. His head swam and he nearly fell over. His right hand spasmodically thumped on his sternum, hard the first time, but the three successive blows trying to coax his heart back to pumping felt weaker each time.

Just when he felt an eternal darkness start to close in, his heart resumed its function, though seemingly grudgingly, leaving him weakened and immobile.

"I... I... I... can't anymore," Marcus muttered to himself.

No, I want this... I need this, his deep seated, darkened psyche responded as though his mind's voice was a separate entity. It sort of was. The Dark Web infection had nearly taken over his body. It was hard to breathe. Every movement produced agony. The interwoven inky threads tattooing his eyes had become so dense, it nearly blinded him. His hearing had devolved to a maddening combination of ringing and sounds of crashing waves filling his ears. Scratch and pick as he might, he could not rid his ears or nostrils from the clumps of Dark Web packed within them.

The Dark Web seemingly spared his brain from the infectious threads penetrating all other parts of his body and tattooing every millimeter of his skin with a mesh so dense now, he could find no trace of his original, untouched skin. Marcus felt fragile and degraded in body but enlightened as to humanity's true nature.

The Dark Web somehow managed to create a dichotomy within him where he realized the infection was killing him, bringing him rapidly closer to death with each passing day. Yet he still craved the power it granted him over humanity and the satisfaction of providing a dark and depraved outlet for millions.

Something had to give. In that moment, Marcus realized he needed to pass the Dark Web along to someone else. If he didn't, there might not *be* a Dark Web. Certainly, he would cease to exist today and perhaps tomorrow at the latest if the infection stayed within him.

Marcus had the vaguest sense the Dark Web had its own manner of intelligence. Whether it was primitive or something more advanced than a human's, or possibly just a symbiont driven by instinct, Marcus didn't know. There was something about the Dark Web and his connection to it he believed—hoped—he might reason with.

I want you. You know that I do. I want you more than I've ever wanted anything... Marcus thought. *Unsure whether the Dark Web could understand him, yet certain he could think of no other means of potential communication, he continued, but this is killing me. It may kill my soul to lose you, but I have to believe if I die, we both die. Neither of us wants that. I have to pass this to another. Think kindly of what I've helped us accomplish, but I have reached the end of what I can do.*

The pressure on all of his organs abated ever so slightly.

Please, Marcus implored, I will give you a good host.

The Dark Web strands tickled as they loosened their control over him. Marcus took in a breath deeper than he'd managed for the last three weeks.

His Dark Web mind's eye cleared itself of all distractions except two HUD windows. One was blue, bearing his avatar, and the other orange with what looked like a Hollywood headshot of a beautiful blond woman perhaps a few years younger than he. Marcus examined her HUD a bit closer. The Dark Web provided him all the information he needed. Lyudmyla Jangula, born in Kyiv, Ukraine. 28 years old. She started as a brilliant university student studying engineering before a Russia-based trafficking organization shipped her against her will to America to serve as a prostitute in Tacoma.

Yes. Yes, she will do. She will do quite nicely.

The Dark Web acted of its own accord and merged Marus's blue window to Lyudmyla's orange window. His powers allowed him to access Lyudmyla's laptop camera. Her handler, a rough looking man with tattoos, looked over her shoulder. He appeared to be directing her to open a text chat with him. He stood nearby as they made their connection. Marcus created a profile image of his pre-infection self sitting in front of a panoramic window overlooking Puget Sound instead of slumped in his own armchair covered in solid brown tattoos. If he was going to entice this young woman and her piece of crap pimp to allow Lyudmyla to come to his home and interact, he had to look respectable and not sickly.

A notification pinged and a text balloon popped up into Marcus's mind's eye.

Hello. My name is Lyudmyla. What's yours?

Marcus Moxley. Wow you are beautiful.

LOL. Nice to meet you Marcus Moxley. You are VERY handsome. Are you looking for a new friend?

Oh yes. Well... I actually hope I've just made one?

;) Maybe. Want to chat here or want to meet up? I would be fine with either. My friend can handle the details. Sound good?

Absolutely.

Want me to wear anything in particular?

Something dark. I'll leave it to your discretion. My address is...

Marcus leaned back. Lyudmyla would be perfect. She would soon be the custodian of the world's most powerful force, and one that no one else would understand. He'd gone almost a year without any physical contact with another person, much less intimacy. But this young Ukrainian woman would be perfect. Marcus suspected she would formulate big plans to help both herself and her people. She would undoubtedly take her revenge on her Russian captors and then perhaps that whole nation. Or maybe she would be out only for herself. He couldn't know for sure. All he knew was he needed to pass the Dark Web to her. The fact that he was in for a fun evening while doing so would be a very pleasant perk.

But enough of that. He had to get ready.

Soon it would be his turn to pay it darkward.

Through Rustling Willows The Spider Man Comes

A Spin-Off Of The Dark Web By Chad Singleton

July, 1955. 4 P.M.

Kofi sped madly down the old Sylvester dirt road, kicking up red clay in his wake. All he could see were miles of cotton and weeping willows, wafting in the warm southern wind. Even in his panicked state, he thought it was funny how perceptions of things could change depending on the context. As a child, he enjoyed the whistle of the warm winds rustling through the trees. He imagined the plants of the fields gleefully waving at him as he rode by on the back of his grandfather's tractor.

Now it felt different. The seemingly never-ending stretch of greenery appeared sinister through his adult eyes. His surroundings contorted, seeming to jeer and scowl at him as a sickening feeling of shame rose from beneath the surface. The once warm blood that soaked Kofi's overalls grew unbearably cold, sending chills throughout his body.

As much as he desired to continue his journey, the panicked young man pulled over to catch his breath. He tried to inhale, but air refused to penetrate his lungs. Next to him sat an old satchel full of money and a kitchen knife. Even though it was covered in dried blood, the knife shone as bright as the Georgia sun. He held the crimson weapon in his trembling hands as he pondered what he had done, just catching his reflection as he held it up to his face. After years of avoiding the truth, he finally saw the ghoul that had taken the place of where a human used to be.

October, 1935

In Sylvester, Georgia, the fall seasons felt just as frigid as the summers were blazing. The old wood in Tess Adabayo's cabin barely fended off the harsh, unforgiving October winds. That's why, whenever possible, she fired up that flat-top coal burner and cooked one of her many famous stews. Tess's oxtail stew and the roaring fire from the kindling-adorned fireplace mixed together to create a warm barrier, reminiscent of a hug from an old friend.

Since her husband passed, funds weren't plentiful, but she got by just fine for a medicine woman. Though it was no easy task, she did all she could to keep her two troublemakers warm and full, especially on nights like these.

Right before she was about to call for dinner, Kofi and Kimmie had already seemed to teleport to the kitchen table. Kofi was just about to put the first hearty spoonful into his mouth when his mother popped him on the shoulder.

"Why must I tell you this every night? Before we eat, we always give thanks!"

"Thanks to who?" Kofi sarcastically remarked as he rolled his eyes.

"Oh, not again," whispered Kimmie as she slowly sank her head into her folded arms.

"To God. He is the reason for the food on the table, for the roof over our heads, and for the air in your lungs. He's also our protection. Remember, through rustling willows—"

"The Spider Man comes," interjected the twins in unison, unenthusiastically.

"Here you go with that old wives' tale, Mama," shouted Kofi.

Before he could finish his sly remarks, he felt a swift but strong pop to the back of the head.

"One more smart remark from either of you, and I will make you go get a switch from outside. Do I make myself clear?"

"Yes, Mama," answered the twins in unison.

After eating enough food to feed an army, everyone's bellies were full to bursting. After the dishes were done, the twins shuffled their way back to their beds. Tess called for her son to come to her room. As he entered, he saw her crushing something with a mortar and pestle. She then took that mixture and poured it into a small glass vial.

"What is that, Mama?"

"These are a mixture of various herbs and neem leaves. Though often unseen, many evils haunt this world. Faith in God protects us from those evils. I can't understand for the life of me, but you're lacking in faith, my beautiful boy. I'm your mother and it's still my duty to protect you, whether ya like it or not."

He watched in disbelief as his mother took some string and fashioned the vial into a necklace.

"As long as you keep this vial of neem around your neck, you'll remain safe. Remember that, Kofi."

"Mama! Why are you so worried? You talk of Gods and spirits, but I see nothing. Let me guess, you don't want me to end up like Baba."

"You watch your tongue!"

"Baba was not right in the head, Mama. He was sick, and you want me to believe some spider spirit was the cause?"

Tess slowly sat down on her bed with her eyes closed, rubbing her temples.

"Ya know, you are more like your father than you know. Very smart, but bull-headed and prideful. He lost his faith too, and Anansi made confusion of his mind. I just don't want the same fate for you, my beautiful boy.

July, 1955. 3 P.M.

Kimmie stood in her kitchen prepping vegetables for a hearty stew that would surely satisfy her husband after a long, arduous day of tenant farming the tobacco fields. She felt tears run down her face as she shaved the carrots and potatoes for dinner.

Kimmie's mother had been gone for a while now. Cooking and seeing the joy on her family's face while eating her food made her feel a strong, tangible connection to her mother. She could almost feel her warmth, as if she were right beside her—just out of her line of sight.

She was surprised to hear a sudden knock at the door since it was too early for her kids or husband to be home. She swung her door open, only to see a face she was sure she'd never see again.

"K-Kofi?"

What stood in front of her was a husk of her brother. He was gaunt and unkempt. He wore slightly tattered overalls and reeked of alcohol. Tears ran down his glazed-over eyes as he stared at his sister. After giving him a quick once-over, she angrily started to shut the door, which he blocked with his foot.

"Move your foot!"

"C'mon, Kay, I just wanna—"

"Enough!" shouted Kimmie as she pushed on the door. "I'm done enabling you! You're not gonna wear me down like you did Mama. Who do you owe now, huh? How much is it this time?"

"They threatenin' to kill me, Kay, please."

Kimmie felt herself starting to give in, like she always had. For years he found himself in and out of troubles with gambling and the law. The last time he came around was the last straw for his sister. She swore she'd never help him again after he stole from their mother. Tess would pass away shortly after that, which Kimmie would never forgive him for. In her eyes, her mother died from a broken heart. She summoned every fiber of her being to utter her next words.

"Get the fuck off my porch!"

There was a brief, deafening silence in the air as the twins stared at each other. In a sudden fit of anger and desperation, Kofi rammed into the door, knocking his sister onto the floor. He slammed the door behind him and frantically scoured her home as she crawled away with terror in her eyes.

"Where's the money, Kay! I know Mama left us sumthin'!" howled her brother inconsolably as he ravaged her home like a tornado.

Kofi turned around to see his sister still on the ground, but slowly inching toward the kitchen. He locked eyes with her and then darted his eyes to her kitchen counter, where he spotted a large vegetable knife.

In a split second, both siblings dashed to the kitchen in a frenzy. Kofi reached the counter first, grabbing the knife. As he turned around, Kimmie simultaneously crashed into him, accidentally impaling herself with the knife her brother nervously held in his hand.

The air was still as her drunken brother realized what he had done.

"Oh my God, Kay! I—I'm so sorry."

Kimmie felt herself start to lose consciousness. With the last bit of energy her small frame could muster, she grabbed onto Kofi's necklace, pulling him close, and whispered in his ear, "M-my, beautiful boy."

She immediately collapsed to the ground, snapping her brother's necklace in the process. The vial lay shattered on the ground in a pool of blood next to his sister. Kofi was as still as a corpse. The only thing he could think to do was carefully back away from her body.

Suddenly, something caught the corner of his eye. One particular floorboard was raised slightly higher than the others. Upon lifting it, he found a dirty brown satchel half-full of green bills. A slight clatter at the front door startled him. He quickly grabbed the satchel and climbed out the kitchen window as the front door creaked open.

July, 1955. Four P.M.

After a moment to catch his breath, Kofi set the crimson knife next to the old satchel and headed back down the road. Time seemed to move slowly, but he attributed it to the suffocating guilt he felt for what happened to Kimmie. Her static body wasting away in a pool of her own blood was all he could think about.

Visions of his sister teased and ridiculed him. The more he thought about her face, the more he could almost swear he saw a slightly sinister grin painted across her burgundy lips. He banged on the side of his head with his fist as the same phrase passed through his lips over and over again.

"I didn't mean it!"

"I didn't mean it!"

"I didn't mean it!"

After a while he got a sneaking suspicion that something was amiss. After all, he grew up on these dirt roads. He distinctly remembered that from his mama's house to the train station was only a fifteen-minute ride. As he drove, he noticed fifteen minutes pass by, then thirty, then sixty.

It was impossible to get lost in this town. There was one road in and one road out.

He still continued on his trek, making sure to take note of all his surroundings. A chill ran up his spine when he realized that the same landmarks kept passing him by: Old Man Haggardy's cotton farm, the little white church house, and the rustling willow trees.

He felt as if he were on a carousel at the fair, going around and around in an endless loop. Suddenly there was a glimmer of hope. Just ahead he spotted a man walking down the road.

He was an older, gray-haired man with rich russet skin, but Kofi couldn't help but notice how sharply he was dressed. His jet-black fedora and suit fit him as if tailored by the gods. Though short in stature, his aura was that of a giant.

As Kofi approached the old man, he noticed that he wore a kindly, innocent expression across his face, but for some reason it didn't quite feel genuine.

"Hey! Excuse me, sir. I don't mean to bother you."

"Oh, no trouble at all, young man! How can I assist ya?" exclaimed the stranger cheerfully as he tipped his hat to Kofi.

"Welp, I'm a lil' lost. I was wonderin' if you could point me to the direction of the train station. I'm tryin' to get to Ashbury, Georgia. I would greatly appreciate your help!"

The old man's cheerful demeanor slowly started to fade.

"Hmmm. Now what would you need to be gettin' all the way to Ashburry for, Kofi? Especially with all that blood on them overalls?"

"Oh, these? Just from my slaughterhouse is all," said Kofi as he giggled nervously, trying to muster a believable smile. "But I'm headed there on account of a business opportunity and—" he paused for a moment. "Wait. How did you know my name, sir? I don't remember tellin' ya."

"Well, I just so happen to know a lot of things," the old man chuckled.

"I know all 'bout that bag of money in that automobile of yours, that you stole from yo' sister. I also know 'bout that knife that you stabbed her with when you took it. Such a shame, really. Now why would you go and do a thing like that?"

Kofi's heart dropped as he backed away from the man in disbelief.

"What the fuck is goin' on?"

"Let me enlighten you. No matter which way you go, you always end up on this same road—nowhere. The same road yo' daddy traveled, matter of fact! The same road every poor lost soul travels down! Boy, you ain't lost!"

The old man walked slowly toward Kofi, transforming with each step. His clothes ripped and tore as he grew, his disguise no longer able to contain his true form.

Kofi fell to the ground, gripping his chest in pure terror as he witnessed the skin on the old man's face begin to rot. Pieces of brown flesh and blood melted from his face and coated the ground, revealing a monster with eight bulbous eyes, long jagged teeth, and eight hairy spider-like limbs bursting from his back.

"You're trapped in my web," screeched the creature as it lurched forward at Kofi with a speed so fast he didn't have time to react.

A Few Months Later

Some time had passed since Kimmie's incident. Even though her wounds were healing well, her injuries still made it hard for her to get around.

"Ok now! Lucas, leave your uncle alone! Let 'im get his rest! Now close his door and help me down the hall to my room."

"Hey, Mom, Uncle Kofi never talks or moves. He just kinda stares into space. Was he always like that?"

"Not at all. You are actually a lot like he was. Energetic, charming, but bull-headed as all get out. Unfortunately, he wouldn't heed your grandmama's teachings about the evils in this world. The same evils I warn you about.

He actually wore the same kinda necklace that you do now. He wasn't a bad person, but he hurt Grandmama and me. That caused him to lose his necklace. Anansi immediately made confusion of his mind. He's been like this ever since."

Lucas showed more interest in his roots than her brother ever did growing up. He reminded her of herself in that way. Growing up, Kimmie always felt a strong tether, not only to her mother, but also to her Togolese roots.

Even with all that in his favor, kids would be kids. She just hoped her children wouldn't suffer the same fate as her father and brother.

As her son passed at the threshold of her door, he stumbled backward as if struck by a strong gust of wind.

"Baby! Are you ok?" yelled Kimmie in a state of distress.

"I'm actually okay. I just heard a voice. Kind of a whispery voice. It said..."My beautiful boy, always remember. Through rustling willows... the Spider Man comes."

Thank you!

You've reached the end of our stories...for now. We appreciate so much that you've read this volume, that we will refrain ourselves from casting hexes and spells on you–No, really, thank you. If you enjoyed reading, consider leaving a review on Amazon or Goodreads or wherever your heart desires.

Find Us!

Find us on Facebook:

https://www.facebook.com/share/
1B8PCJk2uG/?mibextid=wwXIfr

Instagram: Terror_Monthly

TikTok: @the_butchered_writers

Also be sure to visit our website to view our shop, find out about upcoming projects, listen to some creepy quickies, explore free stories and subscribe to our newsletters at Thebutcheredwriters.com

Did you love *The Butchered Writers Present: Caught In The Web*? Then you should read *The Butchered Writers Present Nightmares*[1] by The Butchered Writers!

[2]

The Butchered Writers Present: NIGHTMARES

Do you dare step into the dark? Nightmares is not just a book—it's a descent into fear itself.

Within these pages lurk eighteen chilling tales, each more terrifying than the last. A whisper in the dark that turns into a scream. Shadows that move when no one is watching. Doors that lead to places you were never meant to find. The Butchered Writers have stitched together a collection of horror so vivid, so unrelenting, it will seep into your mind and fester long after the final page.

---

1. https://books2read.com/u/bODeZN

2. https://books2read.com/u/bODeZN

These stories will haunt your dreams, but only if you're lucky. Because some nightmares don't end when you wake up... they just begin.

Sleep tight.

Also by The Butchered Writers

Terror Monthly
Terror Monthly Volume 12 What Lurks In The Deep
The Best Of Terror Monthly

The Butchered Writers Present
The Butchered Writers Present Nightmares
The Butchered Writers Present: 80s Death Mixtape: A Horror
Anthology
The Butchered Writers Present: Caught In The Web

www.ingramcontent.com/pod-product-compliance
Lightning Source LLC
Chambersburg PA
CBHW031226020726
47499CB00002B/660